5/12

LUCKY BASTARD

ALSO BY S.G. BROWNE:

Breathers

Fated

LUCKY
BASTARD

S. G. BROWNE

GALLERY BOOKS

NEW YORK   LONDON   TORONTO   SYDNEY   NEW DELHI

G

Gallery Books
A Division of Simon & Schuster, Inc.
1230 Avenue of the Americas
New York, NY 10020

First Gallery Books hardcover edition April 2012

GALLERY BOOKS and colophon are registered trademarks of Simon & Schuster, Inc.

For information about special discounts for bulk purchases, please contact Simon & Schuster Special Sales at 1-866-506-1949 or business@simonandschuster.com.

The Simon & Schuster Speakers Bureau can bring authors to your live event. For more information or to book an event contact the Simon & Schuster Speakers Bureau at 1-866-248-3049 or visit our website at www.simonspeakers.com.

Designed by Jaime Putorti

Manufactured in the United States of America

10 9 8 7 6 5 4 3 2 1

Library of Congress Cataloging-in-Publication Data

Browne, S. G.
  Lucky bastard / S. G. Browne. — First Gallery Books hardcover edition.
      pages   cm
1. Private investigators—Fiction. 2. Fortune—Fiction. I. Title.
PS3602.R7369L83 2012
  813'.6—dc23   2011050997

ISBN 978-1-4516-5719-7
ISBN 978-1-4516-5720-3 (ebook)

For Perry, Joe, Keith, Brad, Dave, Matt, Kristie, Steve,
Michelle, Andrea, Kim, and Doug.
I'm one lucky bastard.

LUCKY BASTARD

1

It's my understanding that naked women don't generally tend to carry knives.

But considering all that's happened since I woke up this morning, I wouldn't have been surprised if she'd pulled out a meat cleaver. Or a chain saw.

"Why don't you put that thing away," I say, before I realize that was probably a bad choice of words.

From the glint in her eye I can see she's considering obliging me, so I take a couple of steps back, which is about all of the wiggle room I have, since it's less than three feet before my luck runs out.

Where I am is the roof of the Sir Francis Drake Hotel in San Francisco after ten o'clock on a late-August night with an angry, naked woman holding me at knifepoint. Which doesn't completely explain my current predicament, but at least it gives you an idea of what my day's been like.

A helicopter approaches, the propeller *thwup thwup thwup*ping, the lights cutting through the darkness and fog. At first I think it's the cops until I see the CBS logo painted across the side.

Great. I'm making the evening news. This is all I need.

Maybe I could have prevented all of this from happening had I paid more attention to my better judgment.

Or found a four-leaf clover.

Or eaten another bowl of Lucky Charms.

I'm not superstitious, but sometimes it doesn't hurt to take precautions.

"This is all your fault!" she says, holding on to the eight-inch carving knife with both hands. "All of it. Your fault!"

It's at times like this that I wish I'd taken some classes in situational diplomacy.

Even though I grew up in a somewhat lax home environment and had the opportunity to embrace a lot of personal freedom at an early age, I still know how to behave in a civilized manner. Like saying *please* and *thank you.* Or turning off my phone in a movie theater. But tact and finesse have never been my strong suits. Not that I have an inflammatory personality. I've just never been particularly adept at managing interpersonal relationships. And if any situation called for a little skill and tact in dealing with someone, this is it. But I don't know if this type of scenario calls for humor or reason. Plus it's a little awkward considering she's naked, so I try to keep my eyes above the horizon.

Still, I have to do something to let her know I'm not

the enemy, so I give her a smile, one that's meant to be reassuring. Something to ease the tension and lighten the mood. Not that I'm thrilled to be here. I can think of other things I'd rather be doing. Like sleeping or playing naked Twister. Instead, I'm on the roof of a hotel trying to defuse a tense situation before anyone else gets hurt. But like any naked woman holding a knife, she completely misreads my intention.

"Do you think this is funny?" she says, pointing the knife at me, stabbing at the air. Not in a menacing way, but more like Rachael Ray making a point about how to properly slice eggplant. Only this isn't the Food Network. And I'm not a big fan of ratatouille.

"No," I say, shaking my head. "It's not funny at all."

A crowd has gathered on Sutter Street, twenty-two stories below, their faces upturned and indistinct in the hollow glow of the streetlights, but even from this height I can make out the media circus pitching its tent. News vans, reporters, floodlights. A dozen cameras trained at the top of the hotel. The CBS helicopter circles us, the cameraman hanging out the open door with a video camera, his lens pointed my way.

I smile and wave.

I feel like I'm in a Hollywood movie, a dark action-comedy, with a little bit of intrigue and personal drama thrown in for fun. Characters die, illusions are shattered, and things get messy. I just wish I knew how this ended. How things wrapped up. My personal denouement. But

I forgot to read my copy of the script. So I just wait and hope that someone gives me a cue.

The helicopter circles, the videotape rolls, the people on the street below wait for the scene to play out, and I'm an actor trying to remember my lines.

2

The name's Monday. Nick Monday.

I'm a private investigator.

At least that's what I tell people when they ask what I do for a living.

I have my own little office in downtown San Francisco. And when I say *little,* I don't mean in a quaint or a charming kind of way. Like a little cottage or a little eccentric.

It's more like a little hungover. Or a little anorexic.

Barely more than a hundred square feet, my office sits on the third floor at the corner of Sutter and Kearny, a few blocks from Union Square. In spite of my limited accommodations, I do have an official private investigator's license, issued by the State of California, authenticating my job title.

But let's get one thing straight. I'm no Sherlock Holmes. Intellectual prowess and astute observation were never my strong points. Plus I don't have a constant companion to document my exploits. And I'm not the type of private investigator you'd read about in a Raymond Chandler or a Dashiell Hammett novel. I'm not the pessimistic and cynical type. I'm not encumbered with a tarnished idealism that comes from dealing with a corrupt society.

I'm more over easy than hard-boiled.

Ever since I was a kid, I've approached life with a certain level of cheerful irresponsibility. A carefree opportunism. I never really made any plans or thought about the consequences, but just did what seemed to help me get what I wanted. A search for the path of least resistance. A means of attaining an end.

My father, who worked nine to five all his life and came from stock that did the same, used to tell me I had all the ambition of a fart and that I'd probably amount to not much more than just that. A reflex of convenience. A by-product of societal indigestion. Something that would make people wrinkle their noses and say, *What's that smell?* or *Oh my God!*

We never did see eye to eye.

I know my father wouldn't approve of how I turned out and what I do to make a living. But then, he never really had much say in the matter. I'm the way I am because of my mom, and he could never accept that. He always thought people should have to work for what they got in life. I guess my father figured he could instill that same philosophy in me. But his blue-collar morals didn't stand a chance against Mom's genetic expedience.

Still, when you're in my line of work, it doesn't hurt to

stick to a process. Something that creates at least the illusion of a sense of order. I don't believe in heaven and hell, but I do believe the devil is in the details.

I also believe in routine.

I wake up every morning at seven thirty.

I eat Lucky Charms for breakfast.

I drink cappuccinos from Starbucks and mochas from Peet's.

The coffee is more habitual than routine, but everyone has his vices. And I have more vices than your average detective.

So this morning—before the Sir Francis Drake; before the naked woman with the butcher knife; before the helicopter and the crowds—I'm sitting in my office in my T-shirt and jeans and Chuck Taylors, drinking my cappuccino and eating Lucky Charms while researching my current case, which involves a lot of web surfing and coffee drinking and time spent looking out my single window in my cramped closet of an office.

A common literary misconception about private investigators is that we lead these glamorous lives, filled with mystery and intrigue and seductive femmes fatales. Filled with murder and extortion and corruption. Filled with missing persons and stolen artifacts and cases of mistaken identity.

No one wants to read about what really happens, about what private investigators *really* do. Process serving and insurance fraud and corporate investigation. Tracing debtors and investigating copyright infringement and working computer forensics. Spending most of your time in your shabby little office doing research on the Internet.

Yawn.

But that's the reality. That's what most of today's private investigators do to earn their keep. Some of them specialize in one particular field, while others might dabble in two or three areas of investigation, but no one's getting shot at. No one's meeting clients in dark alleys. No one's having sex with Lauren Bacall.

At least not me.

Most of my cases involve suspicious insurance claims, antifraud, calls from frustrated creditors, and investigations of adultery. Even with no-fault divorce, infidelity is still one of the most lucrative activities for PIs, since marital indiscretions can be used by spouses as leverage for child custody, alimony, and property disputes.

Apparently, when it comes to *for better or for worse,* most couples are opting to pursue the latter.

Lately, however, I've been getting calls from people asking me to help them retrieve their stolen luck.

HALF A DOZEN times over the past several months I've been contacted by would-be clients who wanted to hire me to find their good luck. I'm not talking about crank phone calls from teenagers. These aren't homeless people or mental patients off their meds. These are normal, everyday people who had been living nice lives filled with good fortune and happy moments and circumstances that more often than not fell their way.

Until one day, something went wrong.

They lost a big client. Got in a car accident. Discovered they had termites. Maybe one of them had to go to the dentist for a root canal. Another took a beating in the stock market. Someone else is sick for the first time in years.

Most of these people who call are just overreacting to the normal ebbs and flows of life. Normal things that happen to normal people. Even if you're born lucky, there's no guarantee everything will always fall your way. Sometimes, things just go wrong.

But these people who call me believe they're entitled to the life they were living and that the only possible explanation for these tragedies that have befallen them is that their luck has been stolen. They believe this because of the news reports about luck poachers. About people who have the ability to actually steal another person's luck.

These aren't stories that have appeared in reputable newspapers, national magazines, or on twenty-four-hour news channels. You won't hear about them from the *Wall Street Journal* or *Newsweek* or CNN. These are more like urban legends and pop-culture myths you'd find in supermarket tabloids and on celebrity news programs and tabloid talk shows.

A story in the *Weekly World News*. A report on *Inside Edition*. An episode of *Jerry Springer*.

"My Ex-Husband Slept with a Luck Poacher!"

These more unsavory media outlets discuss how the thieves steal luck from normal people and then sell it on the black market for tens of thousands of dollars, creating an entire unregulated commerce and culture of luck-dealing.

Some people think luck poachers are extraterrestrials. Others think they're genetic mutants. Other, more paranoid types think they're government science projects created to steal all of the good fortune in the world and give it to corporations and politicians. That the government hasn't done anything and denies the existence of luck poachers only adds fuel to that particular fire.

At least once a week I read something in the tabloids or see something on trash television about luck thieves preying on people who survive lightning strikes or who win the lottery or who bowl a perfect game. And most of those who call me asking to help them find their stolen luck are just incapable of taking responsibility for their own problems or dealing with their bad decisions.

They haven't had their luck stolen. If they had, I would have known about it.

Because I would have been the one who'd stolen it.

3

On January 26, 1972, JAT Yugoslav Airlines Flight 367 was en route from Stockholm to Belgrade when it exploded and broke into two pieces, spun out of control, and crashed in what is now the Czech Republic. Twenty-seven of the twenty-eight people aboard the plane were killed, most of them on impact.

At the time of the explosion, Vesna Vulovic, a crew member, was at the rear of the plane, which tore away from the main fuselage and fell thirty-three thousand feet before hitting the ground. A food cart pinned Vesna to the back of the plane, acting as a seat belt and preventing her from being sucked out. Although she suffered a fractured skull, three broken vertebrae, two broken legs, and was temporarily paralyzed from the waist down, Vesna Vulovic survived the explosion and the fall. She holds the official world record for the highest survived fall without a parachute.

Most would say Vesna Vulovic was lucky. Others might say she was born lucky. And they'd all be right. But the chances that Vesna Vulovic held on to her luck for any length of time after her record-breaking fall are about as likely as finding a human-rights activist on an 1860 Georgia slave plantation.

You don't publicize that quality of luck without attracting attention. I'm not talking about people who want to tell your life story or sign you to a contract or put you on talk shows. I'm talking about people who want to literally take what you were born with and turn it into personal profit by selling it to others.

Luck thieves. Poachers.

Like me.

Not long after Vesna's story hit the papers and she was out of her coma and meeting her curious and loving public, someone walked up to her, someone nondescript and armed with nothing but his or her unique physiology, shook Vesna's hand, and stole her luck.

Ta-dah. Just like that.

I wasn't there. I didn't poach Vesna Vulovic's luck. I wasn't even alive in 1972. But I guarantee that whoever did poach it was able to sell it on the black market for fifty grand. Even back in the 1970s, celebrity good luck like Vesna's came at a premium.

Not just anyone can steal luck. It's not a skill you can pick up by reading a how-to book or learn in a weekend seminar. You can't clone the ability in a lab or re-create it in a chemical reaction. It's something you're born with. Great-grandma passed it on to Grandpa, who passed it on to Mom, who passed it on to me—though Mom refused to use it. Said it wasn't right, stealing someone's luck.

Had Mom used her gift once in a while, she probably wouldn't have pulled out of the parking lot an instant before that bus ran a red light.

I can still see her sometimes, broken and bleeding in the driver's seat, safety glass in her hair, her head twisted to one side. Nothing happened to me. Not a scratch. Even at the age of nine, I'd already learned the fine art of poaching.

Physically, my skin looks and feels like anyone else's. I sweat, I get sunburned, and I've had my share of paper cuts, road rashes, and rug burns. But my skin heals faster than most others'. Maybe I have more keratin. Or collagen. Or a greater abundance of cells that are involved in immune defenses. But whatever helps my skin heal also allows it to absorb another person's luck simply by grasping his or her hand.

You can't just touch someone on an arm or a leg or any exposed flesh and steal their good luck. But shaking hands, at least in the United States, is common courtesy. A display of friendship and goodwill. Most people will shake a stranger's hand without giving it a second thought, so you don't even have to think twice about what you're doing and poof! Your good luck is gone.

And you won't feel a thing.

Of course, good luck isn't something your average person knows how to measure or define, so no one can prove that anyone is actually *stealing* someone else's good fortune. A lot of people don't even believe good luck exists. That it's just a concept made up as an excuse for why some people live charmed lives while others stumble from one disaster to another. It's not because they did anything right or wrong. It's not karma or fate or some ancient curse.

It's just because they were born that way.

Those who aren't genetically endowed with good luck or who want to acquire more can purchase some on the black market. But even though people pay good money to acquire it, for those who aren't born with it, good luck can be unpredictable. Fickle. Which I suppose is why it's frequently personified as a lady. And like the song says, sometimes it has a way of running out.

For those fortunate enough to be born with it, good luck will never run out. Unless, of course, someone like me comes along and takes it.

People are born unlucky, too, though it's not a good idea to poach bad luck. It's like inviting an unwanted guest into your home and discovering that he's planning to spend the rest of his life with you.

Of course, just because it's a bad idea doesn't mean someone hasn't tried it. Look at the Edsel. Or *Battlefield Earth*. History is full of bad decisions.

Trust me. I know.

I'm not a private investigator because I want to be. But after I left Tucson I had to figure out a way to pay my bills. And being a PI seemed like a good fit, considering I had twenty-five years of experience watching people. I just didn't realize how boring it would be.

My current case deals with a suspicious claim against an insurance company, which is about as exciting as oatmeal, so instead of doing Internet research on my case, I find myself surfing websites looking for stories about people cheating death or coming into money or winning a contest.

Looking for marks, in other words.

Twenty years ago, finding marks was more research-intensive. You went to the library to read the national papers. You waited for the local news to come on at six o'clock. You listened to the radio. You had to work at it and spend a lot of time on the road and hope another poacher didn't beat you to the score.

Now, with the Internet and twenty-four-hour news channels and an almost endless supply of information, you don't even have to leave your apartment to find a recent lottery winner or a surfer who survived a shark attack or a nineteen handicap golfer who got a hole in one. And today, instead of racing from one location to another to poach a potential mark, we have territories that are off-limits to other poachers. It's an unwritten code that most of us live by. But considering we're modern-day pirates, it's really more of a guideline than a code.

Like the saying goes, there's not a lot of honor among thieves.

Unfortunately, I'm not finding much of anything on the Internet within my territory, which is the San Francisco Bay Area, so I have to resort to traditional means to find potential marks.

Today's *San Francisco Examiner* is filled with articles about local politics, the state budget problems, and the threat of a Muni strike. The only story of interest is about a local man named James Saltzman, who apparently caught the final home runs hit by both Ken Griffey Jr. and Sammy Sosa. It's not exactly Vesna Vulovic, but at least it's something.

Other than James Saltzman, there's nothing useful, so I file his name away in my head and throw the paper aside. I'm thinking I may have to start digging through the celebrity rags, maybe even see if I can find something in the *Weekly World News,* when one of my smartphones rings.

I have two phones. One for my personal use and detective business, and the other under an alias that's used strictly for poaching.

The other is the one that's ringing.

It hasn't rung much in the past three years. Hence the need to earn my living as a PI. If you can't move product, you have to find some other way to earn a living, and the last thing I want is a desk job in a cubicle and some socially defective, middle-management douche bag hovering over me and telling me what to do.

I never was good at following directions.

I answer: "Lucky Dragon Restaurant."

Silence on the other end of the line, though I can hear breathing and the sound of traffic and a fire engine off in the distance. I hear the same thing out my office window. Minus the breathing.

I wait another thirty seconds, listening to whoever is on the other end continue to breathe, then the connection is lost.

They probably have AT&T.

I set my phone aside and return to my pursuit of finding a mark, glancing occasionally at the phone, waiting to see if it rings again, hoping it was just a customer who had second thoughts. But the phone remains silent on my desk.

A few seconds later, there's a knock at my door.

I'm not expecting company. Or a client. Or the Spanish Inquisition. But before I can choose between inviting my company in or climbing out my window onto the fire escape, the door opens and in walk two well-groomed Asian thugs in matching designer suits.

How do I know they're thugs? It's just a look they have. Either that or they're constipated.

They close the door behind them and approach my desk.

"Nick Monday?" says the one on my left.

I nod. "Last I checked. Who wants to know?"

"Tommy Wong would like to speak with you."

Tommy Wong is a local figure in San Francisco. I've never met the man, but he's apparently the head of the Chinese Mafia. The so-called Lord of Chinatown, Tommy takes a cut on just about everything from bars to dim-sum restaurants to massage parlors.

Why Tommy Wong would want to speak with me, I have no idea.

"What does he want to talk about?" I ask.

"A business proposition," says Thug One.

I wait for more information, but apparently I'm not getting it.

"What kind of a business proposition?"

"One that involves your unique abilities," says Thug One.

"Juggling? Cat whispering? Or the fact that I can tie a cherry stem in a knot with my tongue?"

Thug Two just stares at me, unimpressed.

"Let's not play games," says Thug One, the chattier of the two. "There's only one man in San Francisco who can steal luck."

It's true that there aren't a lot of us around. There's a mother and daughter in Seattle, a family of four in Los Angeles, and two brothers and a grandfather in the San Joaquin Valley. Those are just the ones I know of on the West Coast. I've also heard about poachers in Chicago, Miami, Las Vegas, Phoenix, St. Louis, Denver, Memphis, Boston, and New York, as well as up in Canada and scattered throughout Europe. While we're not taking over the world anytime soon, there are more of us than you'd think.

And Tommy's thug is wrong. I'm not the only one in San Francisco who can poach luck.

"I don't know what you're talking about," I say. "I'm just a private investigator."

"I understand your desire to maintain this facade," says Thug One. "But the fact remains Mr. Wong would like to acquire your services on a regular basis."

"You mean like an independent contractor?"

"More like an employee," he says, as Thug Two opens my office door and waits expectantly. "But you can discuss the details of the arrangement with Mr. Wong."

That the Chinese Mafia knows who I am isn't surprising, though it's a bit disconcerting. Not quite like Clark Kent getting outed, but the last thing I need is to have my cover blown. Still, the idea of working for anyone is about as appealing as a used diaper.

"Thanks for the offer, but I'm going to have to pass."

"You don't understand," says Thug One. "This isn't an offer you refuse."

"I do understand. But I like things the way they are."

Which isn't exactly the truth. I'd like to be making more money and living in Kauai with a view of Hanalei Bay and a private masseuse. But just because someone makes you an offer that you shouldn't refuse doesn't mean it's a good idea to take it.

"Last chance to change your mind," says Thug One.

"Thanks," I say, hoping he doesn't pull out a gun and shoot me. Which would really put a damper on my day. "But my mind's made up."

Instead of shooting me, he gives me one final menacing look, then turns and walks out of the office. Thug Two follows suit, minus the glower, and smiles at me as he leaves.

"See you around, Mr. Monday," he says, then closes the door behind him.

4

The last thing I want is to see the Chinese Mafia Welcome Wagon again. Not that I'm worried they'll actually shoot me, but I'm guessing the next time I run into them it might not be so pleasant.

So much for my boring life as a private investigator.

It's moments like this that make you appreciate that you don't have anything tying you down and you can just pack up and go at a moment's notice. Even though we're able to settle down more than we used to, the nature of luck poaching still requires a nomadic lifestyle. After all, you can't steal from your neighbors and expect to develop a real sense of community. That's why most poachers rent instead of own. And why we embrace a solitary existence.

When everyone you meet is just potential income, making friends becomes a problem.

While luck poachers don't generally form long-lasting relationships, we do marry and reproduce with non-poachers. Otherwise, I wouldn't be here. But people who aren't born with this ability can't understand what makes us tick. They don't know how to deal with our genetic anomaly. It's the ultimate in irreconcilable differences.

Even though my mother refused to poach, my father couldn't accept that she passed her abilities along to his progeny. My grandmother cut out on my grandfather when my mom was just a little girl. And my great-grandfather abandoned my great-grandmother before Grandpa was even born.

You can see the pattern here. When you can't relate to your partner, chances are things won't work out.

Poaching luck isn't for the sentimental. You need a strong sense of resolve and the ability to sever any relationship without a second thought. Or better yet, avoid developing relationships altogether. They just get in the way.

No one ever mistook me for a hopeless romantic.

While Tony Bennett may have left his heart in San Francisco, I'm thinking it might be time for me to find a new place to call home. Three years in one place is like ten in poacher years, especially after a not-so-social call from the Chinese Mafia. So I'm considering my options, running through potential territories, wondering if I could get enough work in Kauai to make setting up shop feasible, when my office door opens and in walks a woman who looks like she just stepped off a 1950s Hollywood film set.

My office is suddenly the popular place to be.

With long, dark hair, dark eyes, and ruby-red lips, the woman has a face that could make a happily married man forget all about his wife and kids at home. Since I'm not married and I don't have any kids, I'm already two steps ahead. Although I can't see all of her curves inside her red circle skirt and her clinging, black, V-neck wool sweater, I can see enough to make me wonder if she's the type to wear French-cut underwear or a thong.

And suddenly Kauai is on the back burner.

"Can I help you?" I say, wishing I'd worn a green T-shirt. I look good in green.

She doesn't answer right away but looks around my office, which isn't much to look at. I'm a bit of a minimalist when it comes to interior decorating. It's just a desk, two chairs, a lamp, a filing cabinet, a small refrigerator, my laptop computer, and me.

"I'm looking for Nick Monday," she says, saying my name with such disdain that I'm wondering if we've met.

"It's your lucky day," I say, flashing my most charming smile. "Because you've found him."

She gives me a forced smile that lets me know she's not charmed.

I have that kind of effect on women. Unless they're corporate-coffeehouse baristas. It's complicated.

"Have a seat," I say, pointing to the chair across from my desk.

She walks toward me, not smiling, her shoes clicking loud and hollow on the hardwood floor. When she reaches the chair, she checks to make sure it's clean, then sits down, smoothing out her red skirt. I catch a glimpse of one white, creamy thigh as she crosses her legs, and she catches me glimpsing.

I look back up and smile. She doesn't seem impressed.

"So how can I help you, Miss . . ."

"Knight," she says. "Tuesday Knight."

"Really?" I say, with a smile.

"Do you find something amusing, Mr. Monday?"

I lean back in my chair. "Have you been following me?"

She gets this offended look on her face like I just flashed her. "I don't know what you're talking about."

"Sorry, I was only . . . the whole day of the week thing? Tuesday follows Monday?"

She just stares at me like I'm an idiot.

"Never mind," I say. "Why don't we start over?"

"I hadn't realized we'd started at all."

There's no trace of humor in her voice or on her face. Either she's bluffing, or she needs to do more recreational drugs.

"Then why don't we start with why you wandered into my office."

The majority of my potential cases are messages left on my voice mail. I don't get a lot of walk-ins. Especially good-looking ones with ample amounts of cleavage.

"I didn't wander in," she says. "I knew where I was going."

"And how, may I ask, did you hear about my services?"

"A friend of a friend."

"Would this friend of a friend have a name?"

She just looks at me, not saying a word. For a few seconds I think she's trying to remember, until I realize she has no intention of sharing a name with me.

I've got a name. A good one. It starts with a *b* and rhymes with *itch*.

But that still doesn't mean I'm not interested in seeing what she looks like under her cool, humorless veneer. I am, after all, a man. A woman's personality has nothing to do with whether I'd actually sleep with her.

"So what did this friend of a friend tell you I could do for you?" I ask.

"Help me find something that's been misplaced," she says, blinking once, slow and deliberate. It's almost like she's taking a miniature nap.

I notice that her eyebrows are lighter than her hair. Almost blond. I wonder if she dyes her hair. And if the carpet matches the drapes.

"And what, exactly, have you misplaced?" I ask.

Your virginity? Your warmth? Your sense of humor?

She continues to just sit there, staring at me, as if she read my thoughts and is not amused.

Finally she says, "I need you to help me find some luck."

I'm not sure if she's asking me to help her find some stolen luck or if she's looking to hire me because of my unique talents. If it's the former, then I'm wondering how I could have forgotten stealing luck from this woman. If it's the latter, then I'm thinking it's *definitely* time for me to pack up and find a new place to live, because as of today, it's become pretty obvious that my cover is completely blown.

She must take my hesitation in answering as incredulity rather than uncertainty because before I can find my voice and stammer out a reply, she says, "It's not *my* luck," as if to admit otherwise would be an embarrassment. "It's for someone else."

"Someone else?"

"My father," she says. "Someone stole his luck and I would like you to help me get it back."

It's always kind of awkward when I'm put in this situation. After all, if her father's luck was stolen, then chances are I'm the one responsible. And the last thing I want to do is attempt to retrieve something that either never existed in the first place or is impossible to reclaim.

I lean forward. "Tuesday . . ."

"Miss Knight."

Did it get frosty in here, or is it just me?

"Miss Knight, whatever it is that has caused your father to fall on difficult times, I'm sure that luck has nothing . . ."

And perception finally dawns on me like the proverbial sunlight on a distant shore. "Wait a minute. Are we talking about Gordon Knight?"

Gordon Knight is the mayor of San Francisco, the latest golden boy of local politics, whose popularity shot up the charts like a happy song with a catchy chorus. Everyone has been singing his praises, with his name being tossed around by political pundits for offices ranging from senator to the governor of California.

Or should I say, it was.

I poached Gordon Knight's luck a couple of months ago and sold it on the black market for fifteen grand.

Since then, he's managed to lose public support for several of his programs and to get caught up in a sex scandal with a local stripper. In the last eight weeks, his popularity has taken more hits than a joint at a reggae concert.

People who are in the public eye are the easiest targets for luck poachers.

Moguls and movie stars. CEOs and celebrities. Politicians and professional athletes.

While they're not always easily accessible, they're good for a solid payday. And they've been the target of poachers for decades. My grandfather used to tell me stories about all sorts of famous people who had their luck stolen.

Amelia Earhart. Harry Houdini. James Dean.

Buddy Holly. John Belushi. Marilyn Monroe.

Just to name a few.

And today's headlines are filled with examples of celebrities melting down, politicians falling from grace, and professional athletes losing the luster of their previously untarnished fame.

Charlie Sheen. Arnold Schwarzenegger. Tiger Woods.

They didn't implode all on their own, you know.

"I'd like you to find the person responsible for stealing my father's luck and return the luck to me," says Tuesday.

Finding the person isn't the issue. But returning the luck?

"Miss Knight, as much as I'd like—"

"I'm willing to pay you one hundred thousand dollars."

I've suddenly forgotten what I was going to say. And the idea of skipping town just got buried beneath a bunch of zeros.

The problem is, even if I could find the person who purchased Gordon Knight's luck, at this point it's most likely been used. And even if it hasn't, the luck's been removed from Gordon Knight's DNA. He can't put it back. Not permanently. It's been extracted from his genetic structure and is now a commodity. A consumer good. It can't be owned. It can only be borrowed. Even by him.

But I don't have to tell that to Tuesday Knight. If she's willing to pay me a hundred grand to get her father's luck back, the least I can do is try to accommodate her. Providing that the buyer hasn't used it all up yet. Which is possible. You don't have to consume all of the luck at once for it to be effective. Depending on the quality, just half an ounce a day can keep a steady flow of luck in your system until it runs out. And it's healthier, too. Gorging yourself on good luck can wreak havoc on your system. Better to be sensible about your consumption. Kind of like eating a pint of Ben & Jerry's over several nights rather than all in one sitting.

So I'm thinking if I am *really* lucky, maybe there's a chance I can make this work.

"I'd also like the identity of the person who did this to my father," says Tuesday.

Or maybe not.

"That might be a problem."

"Isn't finding people what you do?" she asks.

Well, not exactly. But I don't want to tell her that my last case dealt with serving a summons to a deadbeat dad.

"It's not as simple as that."

"I don't care about simple." Tuesday stands up and reaches into her purse and sets an envelope on my desk. "I just care about getting my father's luck restored."

"What's that?" I say, indicating the envelope.

"Consider it a retainer."

I open the envelope, which contains in the neighborhood of ten thousand dollars. Which is a pretty nice neighborhood.

"I haven't said I'd take the case."

"Find my father's luck." Tuesday drops a business card on my desk and leans forward, providing me with a purposeful glimpse of her soft, creamy breasts pressing against her sweater, obeying Newton's law of gravity, half spilling out of the neckline.

I love gravity.

"And if you find the person responsible," says Tuesday from somewhere above her breasts, "I'll make sure to make it worth your while."

With that, she stands up, puts on a pair of red sunglasses, then turns around and glides out of my office, taking her breasts with her.

5

I give Tuesday a head start, waiting until I'm sure she's not coming back, then I toss the ten grand in my backpack, lock up my office, and head down the back stairs and out past the garbage chute to Sutter Street. At first I don't see Tuesday and figure she grabbed a cab right out the front door. Then I catch a glimpse of her red skirt moving away down Kearny, so I cross the street to the opposite side, keeping myself shielded by tourists who have no idea where they're going and who are speaking in some language that requires a lot of phlegm, until Tuesday turns the corner.

I race down Sutter in the same direction, stopping behind a light post at the corner of Grant in front of Banana Republic. I wait in front of the politically unstable clothing store for less than sixty seconds before Tuesday appears a block down, crossing the street and continuing toward Union Square. I watch her disappear behind the

Shreve and Company building, then I cross Grant and race ahead of her toward Stockton.

Halfway there, my poaching phone rings again, playing "Luck Be a Lady." I answer, hoping it's a job but figuring it's just a wrong number. Or the same crank caller from before.

"Lucky Dragon."

"Do you have any specials today?" asks a male voice on the other end.

An actual customer. Imagine that. The last time I had one of those was more than two months ago. And considering my phone has only rung a dozen times in the past three years, then this must be my lucky day.

"No specials today," I say. "Just the regular menu. But we're out of the seafood delight."

That's code for high-grade good luck.

Most people think luck is just luck. That would be like saying ice cream is just ice cream or that a steak is just a steak. But you can't compare gelato to soft serve or a filet mignon to brisket. It's a question of quality.

Good luck comes in grades.

People with high-grade good luck win the lottery, get discovered by a talent agent, and always escape serious injury.

Medium-grade good luck helps people win progressive jackpots, marry the right person, and frequently be in the right place at the right time.

Those who possess low-grade good luck win money

and prizes on game shows, become friends with a celebrity, and get an occasional hole in one.

Bad luck comes in grades, too. But there aren't as many options with bad luck. Just bad and worse.

I reach Stockton, where I do a quick check before running across the street and staking out a spot in front of the Grand Hyatt, waiting for Tuesday to show.

"Hello?" I say, thinking I've lost a potential sale, which wouldn't be the first time. "Anyone there?"

There's silence on the other end of the line, followed by the clearing of a throat. "What do you have that's good today?"

"I'd recommend going with the mandarin beef," I say.

Medium-grade good luck. That can often fetch an asking price of twenty grand or more, depending on supply and demand, but in the current economic climate, your run-of-the-mill medium-grade has been going for ten grand, tops. The market price right now for high-grade good luck is twenty-five thousand.

While prices aren't as low as those Grandpa complained about during the stock market crash of 1987, it's almost like giving it away, though you do have to adjust for inflation. Conversely, during the boom time leading up to the dot-com crash, it wasn't uncommon to find buyers willing to shell out forty grand for medium-grade luck poached from someone who won the progressive jackpot at Harrah's.

"Do you have any egg foo young?" he asks.

I can't get more than two to three grand for the egg foo young, but it's better than nothing.

"Yes. We have egg foo young. Would you like to place an order?"

More silence on the other end of the line. He's either a first-time customer or trying to figure out how much he can afford. After all, this is a cash-only transaction. We don't accept credit cards or personal checks. And you can't make a payment plan.

Buying luck isn't any different from buying any other drug. And make no mistake about it—luck is a drug. And like any narcotic, it has its drawbacks. It's illegal and addictive and it can drain your savings account dry. But luck also provides a rush that rivals the high of an eight-ball or the euphoria of an ecstasy tablet. Usually without the hangover, though I've known my share of addicts who got the lucky shakes. And although the current market prices make it more accessible, luck has become the drug of choice for the wealthy and the privileged.

You'd think those who were already rich wouldn't need to add to their good fortune, but the market dictates that only those with excess disposable income can afford to buy good luck. Especially the medium- and high-grade stuff. So the rich get richer while the rest of us fall behind. Or settle for the egg foo young.

I've only had a handful of customers since I moved to San Francisco, and most of them are luck junkies. Addicts who are strung out on luck and who jones for the rush and who can only afford the lowest quality available. I haven't sold any mandarin beef in a couple of months. And I've been out of seafood delight ever since I moved here.

"I'll take an order of mandarin beef," says the buyer. "How soon can you deliver?"

After the social call from Tommy Wong's men, I can't help but wonder if this is some kind of a setup. But that's why I pick public places for drop-offs. It cuts down on the surprise factor. And right now, turning down ten thousand dollars isn't something I have the luxury of doing.

Besides, after the visit from Tuesday Knight and the envelope full of money she dropped on my desk, I'm feeling lucky.

I arrange for delivery of the medium-grade good luck at ten o'clock, which gives me just under an hour to pick up the product from my apartment and meet my customer at the designated drop location. That should leave plenty of time to see if I can find out where Tuesday's going. And I'd like to find out who this friend of a friend of hers is who originally sent her to me.

Call it a hunch, but my poacher's intuition tells me she's hiding something.

6

I end the phone call and continue to look down the street, waiting for Tuesday. A Starbucks sits across from me, calling to me like the sirens to Odysseus, and I'm wondering if I have time for a quick cappuccino without dashing myself on the rocks, when Tuesday appears, crosses Stockton, and starts up the steps into Union Square. I walk past the Levi Strauss flagship store, cross against the light, and follow Tuesday, making sure to keep myself concealed behind some palm trees and a group of French tourists before I settle in behind a shrub-lined wall.

I watch as Tuesday walks over to one of the tables at Café Rulli, sits down, and places her order. When the server walks away, Tuesday pulls out her cell phone and presses a single button and starts talking to someone.

From my vantage point, I can watch her without being seen. Unfortunately, I can't hear any part of her conversation and I'm not a lip-reader. I didn't bother to wear a disguise. I don't even have a camera to take any photos. I'm thinking I make a piss-poor private investigator.

You'd think that someone who poaches luck for a living would lead a more glamorous life than this. Hiding behind tourists. Working as a part-time PI to pay the bills. Eating Lucky Charms for breakfast. I can almost hear my father laughing and telling me he knew this would happen to me.

I'm the first to admit that this isn't exactly the life I envisioned. Though not all poachers are like me. Some are better off, some are worse. Some don't even make it this far. A lot of poachers succumb to the solitary nature of the lifestyle and end up taking their own lives. Although there's not any official data, the life span of your average luck poacher is around forty years. Which means I've got seven more to go before I exceed expectations.

Maybe that's why Mom never poached luck. Because she knew the consequences of going down this path. Though things didn't exactly come up roses for her, either. Not unless you include the ones next to her headstone.

That's one of the reasons I sell the luck I poach instead of keeping it and using it for myself. Out of respect for Mom. If I truly wanted to respect her ideals, I wouldn't use my gift at all. But I can't ignore what I am. It's in my blood.

But if I'm going to be honest, the main reason I sell the luck I steal is because using it to try to improve your own good fortune can create problems. The addictive properties of good luck aside, you win the lottery or become a celebrity or make the national news and suddenly you're drawing attention to yourself, doing interviews and having to report your income on a tax return. The last thing I want is to have the IRS or the general public involved in my life. Poachers have to live under the radar to avoid complications. But just because you take precautions doesn't mean you can avoid the consequences.

Every decision you make has risks and repercussions. Some more so than others. It just so happens, most of my decisions tend to be of the more-so variety. That's the reality of being born the way I am. Even though I wouldn't trade the thrill of poaching for anything, I still understand the risks. And while stealing luck from others isn't the most honorable way to make a living, you do what you have to do to pretend that your actions are justified.

The problem with poaching luck is that sooner or later, karma is bound to catch up with you. After all, you can't take something from someone without paying a price.

While Tuesday continues her phone conversation and her drink arrives, something clear and cold in a tall glass, I notice a big, bald white guy reading the newspaper and watching her from two tables away. His head is shaved, he's wearing sunglasses, and he's dressed in a black, short-sleeve shirt and jeans. Whoever he is, he's watching Tuesday with as much interest as I am.

I watch Tuesday and Baldy for about ten minutes, hiding behind my camouflage of shrubs and palm trees and tourists. Whatever the topic of Tuesday's conversation, it seems to end abruptly. With a single push back in her chair and a final tip of her glass, Tuesday stands up and walks off, leaving half her drink behind, and starts walking right toward where I'm hiding.

Before I can manage to duck behind my shrubs or hide behind a family of four from Holland, Tuesday walks past and crosses the street, then heads toward the Stockton Tunnel, apparently oblivious to my presence. I watch her from the corner of my eye and let her get halfway to Starbucks before I start after her, staying on the opposite side of the street. I'm almost to the Grand Hyatt when I notice Baldy directly across from me, following Tuesday.

And now I'm wondering if I'm the only private investigator with an interest in Tuesday Knight.

She crosses Sutter to the parking garage, then stops and turns around, looking back down the street, so I blend in with a group of Chinese tourists, which isn't easy to do when you're taller than most of them and about as Chinese as bacon. When I look up, Tuesday is flagging down a cab near the bus stop and climbing inside.

I pull out the business card she gave me, which just has her name and a local phone number on it. No address. I can find out where she lives by doing an Internet search, but that won't tell me where she's going. Or what she plans to do when she gets there.

I watch the cab take off through the Stockton Tunnel toward Chinatown, then I see Baldy cross the street up ahead of me and disappear around the corner of the Hyatt. I pocket Tuesday's card and follow him down Sutter to Powell, where he turns the corner and walks into the Sir Francis Drake Hotel. I continue past the entrance and a couple of doormen in Beefeater costumes who are jawing with each other and opening doors, then I double back on the other side of the street.

Baldy doesn't reappear. I think about waiting him out or going inside, but it's pushing half past time-to-go and I can't risk missing my ten o'clock appointment and losing a sale. So I grab a cab and ask the driver to take me to my crappy little apartment in the Marina.

"I didn't know they had crappy apartments in the Marina," he says.

"I'm lucky," I say. "I got the last one."

"What's the address?"

I live in a studio on the third floor of a four-story building on Lombard Street, next to a dry cleaner's, across from a transient motel, and just this side of dilapidated. Not my first choice for living accommodations, but sometimes you take what you can get. Or go where your mistakes take you.

I remind myself that it's only temporary. That someday I'll get back into a top-floor apartment or a flat in a well-maintained building with quiet neighbors and double-paned windows and an entryway that doesn't smell like urine. Until then, I'll just have to deal with the consequences of my hubris.

The cab drops me off in front of my apartment building, where a homeless guy sits camped out in front with a mostly empty donation cup and a black cat.

Black cats were historically associated with witches and thus imbued with the evil of the underworld, which is why today you have people who think it's bad luck to have a black cat cross your path. Nothing creates luck, good or bad. It just exists. Yet most people go around believing they can somehow manipulate it to their advantage.

Even poachers can't manipulate luck. We're more like conduits or brokers, transferring luck from owners to buyers. However, we don't just capitalize on situations to suit our needs, but often create the circumstances that compel others to seek us out.

The stock market crashes of 1929 and 1987 didn't happen all on their own. Neither did the dot-com crash, the Enron scandal, or the mortgage-lending crisis. Not that we orchestrated these events, but we helped to precipitate them. When you poach luck from enough people and sell it to others, sometimes things like this are bound to happen.

Grandpa even told me stories about how luck poachers were responsible for some of the most famous downfalls and deaths in history.

Marie Antoinette. Adolf Hitler. Richard II.

Abraham Lincoln. Al Capone. George Armstrong Custer.

Just to name a few.

And who's to say there weren't luck poachers two thousand years ago in Jerusalem? Maybe Jesus ended up dying for our sins because he shook the wrong hand.

I run upstairs, past the peeling hallway walls and the stained carpeting and the tenant who plays his music so loud it thumps through my floor, and I open my refrigerator, which contains eggs, bacon, juice, bread, condiments, and more than half a dozen Odwalla bottles—five of them of the lemonade variety, three Super Protein, and all of them on the plus side of half-full. All of my Vanilla Protein Monster bottles are clean and empty, sitting on a shelf in my cabinet, waiting for product.

They've been empty for three years.

While good luck doesn't go bad if not ingested right away and doesn't have a shelf life, it tends to keep better when refrigerated or stored in a cool, dry place.

I use the Super Protein bottles to store medium-grade good luck, which has the consistency of 2 percent milk, while the Lemonade bottles hold the low-grade stuff, which, conveniently, looks like lemonade. There's not as much demand for low-grade good luck, though you can usually sell it to a junkie, who'll overpay for a fix.

The empty Protein Monster bottles in my cabinet would hold top-grade good luck if I could ever get my hands on some.

Not every poacher uses Odwalla bottles to store and sell his or her product, but it's less expensive than buying sport water bottles and the word association helps me to keep the grades straight. Plus it makes for easy drop-offs. You leave the bottle on the table after you get your payment and the buyer walks out with a bottle of Odwalla. No one notices a thing.

While good luck can be injected into the bloodstream, which has a much more immediate effect, it can also be combined with mixers to make lucky cocktails, or substituted for milk to make lucky brownies. The preferred choice of ingestion, however, is drinking it in its pure form. Though if most people knew where their luck actually came from, they might choose another form of consumption.

He pissed it all away isn't just an anecdotal expression. If you haven't processed poached luck out of your system before you have to take a leak, then all of that potential income is going to end up in a toilet bowl or on a bush or running down your leg. Though technically, you can't piss it *all* away. The human body is nearly 70 percent water, so some residual luck stays behind. And those who are born with luck never lose it through urination or perspiration or any other kind of ay-tion. It stays in the system until a poacher like me comes along.

Those of us who aren't born with it have to settle for the shadows of other people's good fortunes.

While poaching luck is almost as easy as catching a cold, processing it into a consumable form is a little more involved. For my customers to use the luck I've poached, it has to be extracted and processed from my bladder using a catheter connected to a series of tubes that run through a portable centrifuge, where the luck is separated from the urine and deposited through one of the tubes into a plastic container.

It's kind of like donating blood platelets, only without the movie or the free cookies or the American Red Cross T-shirt.

Not the most pleasant or sanitary way to extract luck, but it cuts down on the volume loss that can occur when using other, less-efficient processes. Up until the 1960s, poachers collected urine in a glass flask with a rubber stopper and condensation tube, then placed the flask over a Bunsen burner and let the urine and water boil off, leaving the luck residue behind. Trouble was, some of the luck always got lost in the evaporation. Then there were the adverse effects from the heat or flame. Burned luck doesn't hold its market value. And it tastes horrible.

Might as well just drink the urine straight.

I grab a bottle of Odwalla Super Protein, a little more than half full of a white liquid that can pass for the real thing, and I put the bottle in my leather backpack. I'm almost out the door when I stop and go back to the refrigerator and grab a bottle of lemonade, which I give to the homeless guy on my way out.

While admittedly not an altruistic gesture, that doesn't make it any less sincere.

"What's this?" he says with a complete lack of gratitude.

"It's good luck."

"Good luck?" He holds it up and turns it back and forth. "It's not even full."

Some people just don't know how to show their appreciation.

"Here." I throw him a five-dollar bill. "Put a shot of tequila in it. It'll taste like a margarita."

Then I make my way up Lombard to the Starbucks on Union and Laguna for my ten o'clock delivery.

7

$\int$tarbucks is an ideal place for making drop-offs. It's out in the open where no one expects it. No one's looking around to see what anyone else is doing. People are too busy reading the paper or surfing the Internet or playing with their iPhones to care. Sometimes I think you could be masturbating while waiting in line and no one would notice.

The cute brunette with a Celtic-knot tattoo on the inside of her left wrist who takes my order looks like she just passed legal when she got out of bed this morning. I'm a sucker for brunettes. So despite that I know nothing good is likely to come of it, I chat her up to feed my ego.

"I like your tattoo," I say.

"Thanks," she says, without a smile.

"No beginnings or endings. Timeless nature of the spirit. Infinite cycles of birth and rebirth. Or is it just for good luck?"

She glances at her wrist and looks up at me with a little more interest than before. "Most guys don't know about all that stuff."

I just smile and thank her for taking my order, then I claim a chair and wait for my cappuccino, catching the barista glancing over at me every so often.

In addition to my morning routine, I've developed some repetitive consumptive behaviors that, while not destructive, are a definite by-product of my lifestyle.

Cappuccinos. Apple fritters. Lucky Charms.

Mochas. Mentos. Corporate-coffeehouse baristas.

Just to name a few.

Some might look at my behaviors and call them addictions. Fixations. Arrested development.

I prefer to think of them as endearing eccentricities.

I look around Starbucks, checking to see if my ten o'clock is here, looking for furtive glances or a knowing nod or an index finger brushing across the nose à la Paul Newman and Robert Redford in *The Sting*. But no one looks my way other than the cute barista and an attractive Asian woman in a red coat talking on her cell phone as she walks out the front door. I'm hoping my buyer actually shows. If things don't pick up soon, I might have to start poaching door-to-door and selling my product at a discount.

"Grande cappuccino!"

When I walk up to the counter, the barista who took my order hands me my drink. "It's for no beginnings or endings," she says, displaying her wrist like an offering. "The timeless nature of the spirit, like you said. I don't believe in good luck."

"That's too bad," I say, taking my cappuccino. "Because I was kind of looking forward to testing out mine."

I give her a smile, then I walk back to my table and sit down and wait for my appointment, trying not to look desperate.

My life used to be a lot easier. Poaching luck provided an ultimate lifestyle of freedom and wealth and endless opportunities. I had everything I ever wanted and more. But that's the problem with feeling like you're on top of the world. Eventually, you begin to think you own it.

Three years ago in Tucson, I was contacted by a woman for a contract job. Not for a particular mark, but for a specific type of luck. Something I'd never poached before. A job I shouldn't have taken. But the amount of money she was offering was too good to pass up.

For people who are born with it, bad luck isn't toxic. It's just something they live with, something their systems have acclimated to. But for poachers and people who aren't born with it, bad luck is like a virus that grows exponentially the longer it stays in your system. Though Grandpa used to tell me stories about poachers who only trafficked in bad luck. Specters, he called them. I can't imagine what it would be like to steal bad luck for a living. Once was bad enough.

I'd poached long enough to have a constant dose of

low-grade good luck running through me for most of my first thirty years, but when you steal bad luck, it stays in your system, too. And bad luck, whatever the quality, pretty much cancels out anything but pure, soft, high-grade good luck. Which isn't easy to find when you really need it.

I learned that lesson the hard way.

But when someone hands you a bag full of money that amounts to more than you made poaching the previous two years combined, you figure you're young and strong enough to handle it. Of course, it doesn't enter your mind that all that money might get lost or stolen or fall into a black hole. I still don't know what happened to it. The next day, the money just wasn't there.

Bad luck has a way of making you realize your full potential for stupidity.

By the time I finish my grande cappuccino, my ten o'clock still hasn't shown up. I check my voice mail and my text messages but there's nothing. As far as I can tell, no one other than the cute brunette barista has been checking me out and I haven't noticed anyone suspicious hanging around outside. If this was a setup then somebody didn't get the memo. Which means I'm dealing with another customer who got cold feet. Just my luck. At least I've got the ten grand from Tuesday, which should help to cover my expenses for a few months.

Before I leave, the barista with the Celtic-knot tattoo comes over to my table and gives me her phone number on a napkin.

"I'm free for dinner," she says, then bites her lower lip in that seductive way only women can get away with. Kind of like grooving to music at a bar. When a woman does it, it's alluring. Appealing. Acceptable. When a guy does it, it's like watching the end of *cool* as we know it.

When the barista turns and walks away, she glances back over her shoulder and gives me a seductive smile. An unspoken promise of secret treasures to be found. But at the moment, I'm not channeling my inner pirate.

For some reason, the bad luck I poached three years ago has left me with some sort of vibe or pheromone that attracts female baristas from corporate-coffeehouse chains. Which you wouldn't think is a bad thing. Not only do I have all of these young, cute, sexy baristas coming on to me every time I go into a Starbucks or a Peet's, but I have a world of free cappuccinos and mochas at my veritable fingertips. Free sex and all-you-can-drink espresso beverages. And with more than seven dozen Starbucks and Peet's combined in San Francisco and several baristas at each location offering up their phone numbers and their sexual charms, who could ask for more?

Except every barista I've slept with, from the Peet's in West Portal to the Starbucks at Ghirardelli Square, wants something serious while I just want to have some fun.

I prefer short-term relationships. Ideally, relationships that last one night. That way, you never have to worry about developing feelings for the woman or seeing her go to the bathroom while you brush your teeth.

Even nearly halfway through my thirties, I still avoid emotional intimacy.

Call it an occupational hazard.

To be honest, the main reason I avoid relationships is because no normal woman would understand what I do. Who I am. She'd try to change me. Or else end up leaving me. So I just save them the trouble by leaving first.

I never was good at making commitments.

More than once, things have started to get complicated and I've had to make a list of Starbucks and Peet's that I can't patronize anymore. I even swore off baristas after the fiasco at the Peet's on Fillmore, but some habits are harder to break than others.

I watch the brunette with the Celtic-knot tattoo return to her post behind the counter, where she continues to glance my way, then I pocket the napkin she gave me without any intention of calling the number on it. But when it comes to baristas, my intentions are about as dependable as an incontinent bladder.

On my way out the door, I bump into Mandy.

"Hey," I say.

"Hey," she says back.

We stand there, me half leaving and her half coming, the two of us half blocking the entrance to Starbucks, half staring at each other, neither of us saying anything.

I never was good with awkward moments.

I watch her face, waiting for her to say something, to give me a cue to play off of. But she just looks at me with that expression of disapproval, as if I'm perpetually disappointing her.

"How are the girls?" I finally ask.

"They have names, you know."

"Right." I never was good with names. "So how are they?"

"Fine. You missed their birthdays again."

I never was good with birthdays, either. Or anniversaries. Or holidays. I even forgot it was Christmas one year.

We stand and stare some more without making eye contact. It's not easy to do, but we've had lots of time to practice.

"And your husband," I say. "What's his name?"

"Ted. His name is Ted. And he's fine. We're all fine."

I just nod, trying to ignore the rising color in Mandy's cheeks, wondering if she's going to ask how I'm doing. If I'm still poaching. Though it's more likely she'd rather not know.

"You still up to your old tricks?" she asks.

"A little here and there."

Mandy nods, her lips pursed. I can tell by her expression that she wants to ask me if I'm ever going to grow up, but she won't. Not here. Not in public.

Mandy never did like to make a scene.

Several customers come and go, squeezing past us as we continue to half block the entrance.

"I should be going," she says.

"Sure. It was good to see you."

She doesn't reciprocate and we don't hug. Instead, I just step to the side and let her walk past me into Starbucks. Unlike the barista, she doesn't look back as the door closes shut behind her.

8

With a container of medium-grade good luck and ten thousand dollars in my backpack, I figure it's a good idea for me to leave the money someplace safe before I head back downtown to my office. While my apartment isn't necessarily the safest place, considering I live across from a motel for ex-cons and drug addicts, it's closer than my office and more practical than the bank.

Before heading straight to my place, I walk up Laguna to the Green Street Market to pick up a roll of Mentos. There are other markets and corner stores that I could hit up on my way home, but I've been going to the Green Street Market ever since I happened upon it more than two years ago. And like my Lucky Charms and my Starbucks cappuccinos, I'm a creature of habit.

When I walk into the store, an older guy in a suit is down at the end of the counter, talking on his cell phone. Sam, the proprietor, is standing behind the counter wearing a black, short-sleeve silk shirt and an unfamiliar expression.

His smile seems strained, his eyes unnaturally fixed on me, like he's trying not to look anywhere else. Even though the weather is typical San Francisco summer foggy, Sam's suntanned chrome dome is shiny with perspiration.

"'Morning, Sam," I say.

At first Sam doesn't say anything. Just keeps staring at me with that odd expression, like he knows me but he's pretending not to. Then he says, with too much formality, "Good morning."

Behind me, the same attractive Asian woman in a red coat from Starbucks steps through the front door, talking on her cell, saying that she just walked into the store.

I'm the first to admit I'm not much of a detective. It's more of a day job than a calling. But I don't have to channel my inner Columbo to know that something's up.

I glance around, thinking maybe I walked into the middle of a robbery, but other than the guy in the suit, who walks past me and out the door past the Asian woman, who is now picking out a jar of Kalamata olives, no one else is in the store. I don't know what's up and part of me doesn't want to know. I'm beginning to think I made a mistake coming in here, but I'm out of Mentos.

As I throw a couple of rolls on the counter and pull a five spot from my wallet, a black sedan with tinted windows pulls up in front of the store. Before I can get my change, the Asian woman walks up and puts a gun in my ribs.

"Hello, Mr. Monday," she purrs in my ear like a promise. "Care to go for a ride?"

"Do I have a choice?"

"Not really," she says, nudging me toward the door. "After you."

I'm guessing this is the setup that I thought didn't happen. Silly me.

"Sorry, Nick," says Sam.

"No worries," I say as I'm escorted out the door and into the sedan. It's the luxurious type, with the two back bench seats facing each other. I'm facing backward, sitting next to the Asian woman. I'm expecting Tommy Wong but instead, sitting across from me with a laptop next to him is a white man in a Brooks Brothers suit with swooping light-brown hair and a nose the size of the Transamerica Pyramid.

"This is nice," I say, as the sedan pulls away from the curb. "Are we going to prom? Or is this a bachelorette party?"

"Nick Monday?" says the suit, looking up from the laptop. "Is that your real name?"

"Who wants to know?" I ask.

"Does it matter?"

"Does it matter that you're a dead ringer for Barry Manilow?"

He laughs. It's not a friendly laugh. More condescending, with a hint of malice. I never really liked Barry Manilow.

I glance over at the Asian woman, who gives me a pro-

fessional smile, no teeth, and I wonder if she had a collagen injection or if her lips are natural.

We're two blocks away when I realize I left my Mentos
sitting on the counter.

"What's in the bag?" Barry asks, indicating my leather
backpack.

"Schoolbooks," I say. "I'm going to night school."

Barry glances at his watch. "At half past ten in the
morning?"

"I like to make sure I get a seat in the front row."

"Open the bag."

He knows what's in it. And I know he knows. So I open
up my backpack and remove the bottle of Odwalla Super
Protein, which the Asian woman takes from me and hands
to Barry.

"What's the grade?" asks Barry, holding up the bottle.

"Medium," I say.

Even without the tinted windows and the black
sedan, I figure the two of them work for the government.
Considering the sedan is nicer than my apartment, I'm
wondering if I should look into getting a job in the public
sector.

"So what do you want?" I ask.

Barry looks at me with half-lidded eyes. I almost expect
him to break into the opening lines of "Weekend in New
England."

"We could have you arrested," he says.

I don't know which branch of the government they work for: the IRS, seeking its cut of unreported income; the FBI, attempting to regulate luck poachers; or the FTC, looking to make luck a tradable commodity. Just because the government denies any knowledge of luck poachers doesn't mean they aren't aware of our existence. Whoever they are, I'm guessing they didn't go through all of this trouble to audit my taxes.

"What. Do. You. Want?" I repeat.

He smiles. "Your assistance."

"What kind of assistance?"

"Are you familiar with a man by the name of Tommy Wong?"

"I've heard of him," I say, playing nonchalant. "Old Chinese guy. Well connected. Some kind of Lord of Chinatown."

"That's one way to put it," says Barry.

"According to our sources," says the Asian woman, "Tommy's been buying up as much good luck as he can and using it for himself, which has made it virtually impossible for us to catch him doing anything illegal or come up with any evidence to convict him of racketeering or extortion."

"Or murder," says Barry. "And since we can't seem to manipulate any of Tommy's employees, we decided our best chance to get to him was to find a luck poacher. So we got ourselves a luck junkie and made him an offer he couldn't refuse."

"My ten o'clock Starbucks appointment."

"Bingo," says Barry. "Though we've been looking for you for the past couple of months, ever since Gordon Knight's fortunes took a dive."

I don't give him the satisfaction of a reaction, though I'm suddenly wondering if Tuesday Knight knows more about the circumstances of her father's luck poaching than she's letting on.

"We figured there was a good chance of finding a poacher in San Francisco when the mayor's popularity plummeted," says Barry, who spreads his arms out like a game show host. "And now, here you are."

"Lucky me."

"That depends," says Barry.

"On what?"

"The way we figure it," he says, "the only way to catch Tommy is to counteract the good luck he's accumulated. And the only way to do that is to give him a healthy dose of bad luck."

When it comes to bad luck, everything that can go wrong, will—sickness, bankruptcy, divorce, hair loss, impotency, sterility, car accidents, shark attacks, canceled flights, termites, flood damage, herpes.

And that's just your garden-variety bad luck. When it comes to low-grade hard, imagine the worst thing that can happen to you short of death, then dip it in oil and set it on fire. Just a trace amount of the stuff can stick around like a bad infection—making you sick for two months, sending your business into the tank, and elevating Lucky Charms to a gourmet breakfast.

"So why do you need me?"

"To deliver the bad luck to Tommy Wong," says Barry.

I shake my head. "I won't poach bad luck. That's not my game."

"The game has changed, Mr. Monday. You're playing by our rules now."

"Maybe so. But there's nothing you can do to me that would convince me to poach bad luck."

"No," says Barry, turning the laptop screen toward me so I can see it. "But we can do something to *her*."

On the laptop screen is a photo of a woman walking out of the Starbucks on Union, the only other person living in San Francisco who can poach luck.

Amanda Hennings. Mandy. My sister.

Fuck.

"Fortunately for you," says Barry, "the dirty work has already been done."

Next to me, the Asian woman produces a metal case the size of a mass-market paperback. Something by Elmore Leonard or Sue Grafton rather than James Michener. She opens it to display a stainless steel vial encased in foam.

"Two ounces of low-grade hard," she says, then closes the case and hands it to me.

I take it and hold it out in front of me like a used diaper filled to capacity. "What am I supposed to do? Just walk up to him and say, 'Happy birthday'?"

"Tommy's recently started contracting luck poachers from out of state to expand his search for good luck," says Barry. "Paying top dollar for luck poached and delivered to him. We figure it's only a matter of time before he contacts you."

Barry needs to learn how to tell time better.

"When he does," says Barry, "that's when you deliver the package."

"Deliver how?" I say, as the Asian woman pulls out her phone. "You can't disguise bad luck as good luck. It's not possible."

Good luck, no matter the grade, comes in varying degrees of white. The highest grade is the color of alabaster, while the lowest grade looks like diluted lemonade. Bad luck, conversely, is as black as the shadows in the barrel of a gun. Low-grade hard absorbs light like a black hole.

The sedan comes to a stop in front of Grace Cathedral.

"How you deliver it is your problem," says Barry. "My problem is Tommy Wong. If you don't take care of my problem, then *you* become my problem. Do we have an understanding?"

I look at the Asian woman, who is either texting or playing Angry Birds, I can't tell. All I know is that it's bad form to use your cell phone when you're in the company of others. Some people have no manners.

"Can I have my luck back?" I ask.

Barry picks up the Odwalla bottle. "I think I'll hold on to this for good luck."

"You're a funny guy." I get out of the sedan and thank Barry and his partner for the lovely time. "We should get together for lunch. I know this really great Thai restaurant."

Barry gives me a condescending smile and says, "I'll be in touch, Mr. Monday."

Then the door closes and I watch as the sedan turns right and vanishes around the corner.

9

The first thought that comes into my head is that it's definitely time for me to cut and run. Grab a cab back to my apartment, pack up what I need, gather up the cash and fake IDs I have stashed away in my apartment and in my office, and head north to Canada or south to Mexico. I hear Vancouver's nice, but I don't really care for the snow. And now that I think about it, I hate Mexican food.

The destination isn't important. All that matters is the getting out of town.

I've called San Francisco home for the past three years, and in spite of the problems I've encountered up until now, I figured I could manage to stick around for a while longer. But once you've been kidnapped and blackmailed by some unknown government agency that wants you to deliver thermonuclear bad luck to a Chinese Mafia overlord who has built up an impenetrable barrier of good luck and already sent a couple of his thugs to threaten you, it's time to think about a change of scenery.

I'm even thinking it might be a good idea to give up the lifestyle altogether. Go legit. Maybe become a full-time private investigator. Sure, it would take some getting used to, but nearly half of my income since I moved here has been of the taxable kind, anyway. So I figure I'm halfway there. Besides, if Mandy could quit the lifestyle and live the so-called American dream, I don't see why it would be such a hard adjustment for me to make.

I'm already starting to look for a garbage can to deposit the bad luck so I can pack up and get the hell out of here when I stop.

I see Mandy's face on Barry Manilow's laptop screen, and I hear his voice telling me that they can do something to her, and I know I can't leave. I can't allow anything to happen to Mandy. Not if there's anything I can do to prevent her from getting caught up in this. I have to stick around until I deliver this bad luck to Tommy Wong and get the government out of the picture.

I sit down on the steps of Grace Cathedral and try to plan my next move. Which isn't my strong point. It's bad enough to have to deal with choices like buying a car or choosing a college or picking an entrée on the menu. But when you've been blackmailed by the Feds, threatened by the Chinese Mafia, and hired to find the mayor's stolen luck, which you poached, figuring out what to do next can be kind of overwhelming.

I never was good at decision-making.

What I need is an adviser. Someone to help me come up with a plan. I'd even settle for a list of Things to Do:

- Buy groceries.
- Pay rent.
- Deliver bad luck to Chinese Mafia kingpin.

Even as a kid I had trouble picking which flavor of ice cream I wanted. I always felt that no matter what choice I made, it would always be the wrong one.

My father used to tell me he wondered how I managed to get dressed when I couldn't choose between putting on my pants right leg or left leg first. Using the same rationale, he told me he never worried about catching me masturbating because I wouldn't know which hand to use.

Which, by the way, constituted our entire conversation about the birds and the bees.

Thanks for the talk, Dad.

The first thing I have to do is figure out how to find Tommy Wong. And what to do with this stash of bad luck in the meantime.

The cable car comes rolling along California, headed toward Van Ness. I consider running over to catch it, but decide that jogging across traffic to catch a cable car at an unauthorized stop while packing extremely volatile bad luck isn't the smartest idea I've ever had. Even catching a cab or the bus suddenly seems about as prudent as French-kissing an electrical outlet, so I put the case in my back-pack and walk over to Huntington Park to find a bench and consider my options. When you've spent twenty-five years poaching luck, you understand the risks. When you're suddenly walking around with two ounces of low-grade hard, the risks tend to increase exponentially.

Bad luck isn't literally hard, like granite or Homer Simpson's skull. It's curdled and heavy, with the odor of sour milk and the consistency and color of hot asphalt. Except bad luck isn't warm. It's cold, like death. Poachers call it hard because of what it does to you.

Imagine paper cuts the size of the Grand Canyon or ingrown toenails with fangs. Phrases like *industrial accident* and *burned beyond recognition* come to mind.

Not exactly my idea of a good time.

Good luck, conversely, is soft. The higher the grade, the softer the luck.

Silk gloves against velvet pajamas. Goose-down pillows on a bed at the Ritz.

But even those analogies don't come close to its texture. Top-grade soft is indescribable. I don't even think the gods of Olympus had anything to rival it. Except maybe Aphrodite. I bet she felt like top-grade soft.

As I sit down on a bench in Huntington Park at the top of Nob Hill, a woman walks past wearing a white tank top, her long blond hair cascading over her bare shoulders. While she's no Aphrodite, and while no one would ever confuse Nob Hill with Mount Olympus, it's high enough above the fog that the August sun has actually made a cameo.

Several women in bikinis are camped out on the grass with laptops and iPods, while two shirtless gay men, one tall and black and the other short and white, compare six-packs. On the other bench to my right sits a middle-aged woman reading a paperback, one of those *Dragon Tattoo* novels, while a young mother chases her toddler around the water fountain.

I watch the young mother and think about Mandy— about what I can do to keep her out of this, about whether I should warn her, about how she's going to be pissed off that she got dragged into my business.

We didn't used to be like this.

After Mom died, Mandy and I got pretty close. She was eleven at the time, but even though she was two years older than me, I was already a more experienced luck poacher. Mandy tended to take after Mom. She didn't think it was right taking something that belonged to others unless they deserved it. Which usually meant some bully at school or some stuck-up little princess who needed an attitude adjustment.

But with Mom gone and Dad emotionally unavailable, Mandy and I started hanging out together, watching out for each other, keeping each other safe. I didn't have a lot of friends. None, actually. When you can steal luck, it makes it tough to develop any kind of camaraderie. Plus when you have that level of power at nine years old, you tend to acquire an overdeveloped sense of omnipotence. My mouth didn't help matters.

Over the next few years, I helped Mandy develop her poaching skills. We didn't use the luck we stole, but just discarded it or used it to water the garden or gave it to Grandpa.

Once Grandpa died, Mandy was all I had.

In high school, during my freshman year and when Mandy was a junior, we started full-on collaborating, stealing luck from the jocks and the rah-rahs and the social elite and giving it to the kids who didn't fit in and who got stuffed into gym lockers. Nobody knew what we were doing. Not even the nerds and social misfits we gave it to. We'd just process the luck and spike their sodas or milk shakes with it. Or bake it into cookies and give them out at band practice.

We were like social equalizers, smoothing out the disparity of the high school dynamic. Robin Hood and Maid Marian, robbing luck from the asshole popular kids and giving it to the geeks.

It was one of the happiest times of my life.

But once I started to poach for money as a sophomore, Mandy and I started to drift apart. She didn't believe in stealing luck for personal profit, and I was starting to embrace the inevitability of my calling. The summer after she graduated high school, we hung out a couple of times and pilfered some luck from a bunch of yuppies for old times' sake, but it wasn't the same. When she met Ted a year later in college, she gave up the lifestyle entirely. We didn't see each other much after that.

Once Mandy left, that's when I realized I couldn't count on anyone but myself, and that relationships would only end up causing me grief and disappointment. Grandpa tried to teach me that lesson years earlier, but at the time I didn't understand what he was talking about.

A few years later, when Mandy and Ted got married and I missed the wedding because I was poaching luck from a lottery winner in Iowa, Mandy called to ream me out.

"Where were you?"

No "Hey" or "How's it going?" Just right into attack mode.

"Where was I when?"

"Last weekend, asshole."

"I was in Iowa. Why? What are you so upset about?"

"Oh, I don't know. Maybe I'm upset because *you missed my wedding*!"

That's one of those *ohhh* moments, when you realize no matter what you say it's not going to make things better.

"Ohhh. I'm sorry. I totally forgot."

But you can definitely make them worse.

"You forgot?"

"Yeah. I was poaching from a Powerball winner who won three hundred and eighteen million dollars in the lottery."

It seemed like a reasonable excuse in my head but when the words came out of my mouth, I suddenly realized how petty it sounded.

"Mandy?"

"I can't believe that poaching luck is more important to you than your own sister's wedding."

I tried to explain my actions, but the best I could come up with on short notice was, "It was top-grade soft, though." *Click*. "Hello?"

We've barely spoken since.

The little boy running around the park's water fountain races past me and continues his circular journey past an elderly Asian man in sunglasses and a San Francisco Giants baseball cap who has now joined the party and is doing some kind of martial arts exercises. He stands near the bench to my right, swinging his arms back and forth like a monkey. I watch him for a few minutes as the boy runs around the fountain and past the gay, shirtless men and the middle-aged woman reading her paperback.

Now the old man's rotating his hips.

Now he's thrusting his pelvis.

Now he's making gestures that look like simulated masturbation.

It doesn't seem to faze anyone else in the park, not even the mother of the little boy. Maybe the old man comes here every day and does the same thing, so now he's just part of the experience. Still, it's kind of creepy. In a tai chi sort of way.

On my left, a young Chinese woman in a blue bikini top and a pair of denim cutoff shorts walks up and spreads out a towel on the grass, bending over in such a way that I can tell she's not wearing matching bikini bottoms. I consider going over to introduce myself, but that's not exactly going to help me figure out what to do about the delivery I'm supposed to make to Tommy Wong. Still, it wouldn't hurt to offer to rub a little sunscreen on her back.

When I turn to grab my backpack, the old Asian guy is sitting on the bench next to me.

"Nice day," he says.

I nod. I don't know how he got over here so fast and sat down without my noticing, but it's a little weird. Plus he's sitting right next to me. No buffer. No man space.

"Do I know you?" I ask.

Anyone sitting this close to me, I figure I've met them. Or pissed them off. Or attracted them with the bad luck Barry Manilow gave me.

He puts his hand on my shoulder and says, "Not officially."

Other than a slight tingling sensation in my shoulder, I don't notice anything's wrong until I try to respond and I realize my lips are numb and weigh about a thousand pounds.

"Blllbb," I say.

The old Asian guy is on his phone, calling someone for help, saying he has an emergency. At the edges of my fading vision, people are looking at me, coming my way, offering help. I'm surrounded by naked abs and bikini-clad breasts.

"Blllbb," I say again.

I hear a siren as an ambulance pulls into view and I feel like I'm floating up into the cosmos.

The Earth spins on its axis, the planets revolve around the sun, the universe continues to expand, and I'm getting sucked into a black hole.

10

When I wake up, I'm on the floor in a room the size of a leprechaun's walk-in closet, with no windows and no furniture, just a liter of bottled water on the hardwood floor and a rack of fluorescent lights buzzing into my eyes and frying my brain. My head is pounding and my mouth feels like a used box of cat litter.

The clumping kind.

I close my eyes and roll onto my hands and knees, groping for the water bottle. Once I find it, I unscrew the cap and drink more than half of the contents before I realize I should probably have stopped to think if it was poisoned.

Oh, well. Too late now.

By the time I drain the last of the bottle, my headache is beginning to fade and my mouth no longer feels like it's filled with Fresh Step. I look around the room and wonder where I am, if I'm still in San Francisco, and how I'm going to get out of here. The door seems like the logical choice, from the other side of which I hear male voices, though they're not speaking English. Sounds more like Cantonese.

A light switch is on the wall next to the door, which I presume is locked. The door, not the wall. Though I wouldn't be surprised either way. But when I turn the knob, the door opens and I step into a mostly empty room with hardwood floors, wall-to-wall dust, a single window, a curtain covering another doorway, and a table surrounded by four old Chinese men playing mah-jongg.

"Mei," says one of the old men without looking up. "Get our friend a chair."

The old man is the same one who drugged me in Huntington Park. Apparently, he and I have different ideas about friendship.

I still don't know where I am, but it looks like I'm in the city, somewhere in Chinatown. It also looks like the curtained doorway is the only way out, unless I want to try the window. Which I don't.

A young Chinese woman in a white shirt and black pants appears through the curtained doorway carrying a chair, which she sets near the four men who continue to play mah-jongg. She bows to the old man, then vanishes through the same doorway.

Maybe it's the hangover from the drugs, but she looks familiar.

"Feeling better?" the old man says, still not looking up from the game.

"I could use something to drink," I say, taking a seat.

"Mei!"

Seconds later, Mei returns with a tray and a pot of tea with five cups.

I was thinking more along the lines of whiskey. Or maybe a shot of tequila with a lime and some salt. I'd ask for a margarita, but that would probably just be pushing my luck.

"Oolong tea," says my host as Mei sets the cups on a nearby table and fills them. She never glances up or makes eye contact, but something about her still makes me think we've met. I'm pretty sure it wasn't at Starbucks or Peet's; otherwise she'd probably throw the cup of tea in my face.

She finishes pouring the tea and exits the room in silence. Before she leaves, I catch a glimpse of a blue bikini top beneath her white shirt, and I realize she's the same hot young woman from Huntington Park.

I grab a cup of tea and inhale, then I take a sip of the steaming brew, half expecting to go numb and pass out again. But I can still feel my extremities, so I've got that going for me.

I glance around the room, which is decorated in early hovel. The walls are yellowed and peeling, the hardwood floors scuffed and water stained. Battered venetian blinds cover the only window, and the single rack of fluorescent lights buzzes uncovered next to a crack in the ceiling. The only decoration is a ceramic lucky-cat sculpture, its left paw raised, sitting on a small, solitary shelf by the curtained doorway.

"You know," I say, after taking another sip of tea, "for someone who's supposed to have bought up as much luck as you, I was expecting accommodations that were a little less, I don't know, crack-addict-prostitute."

"You should have accepted my earlier invitation from my men," says the old man. "We would have had dim sum at Yank Sing."

Tommy Wong finally looks at me and smiles, and I realize he's not as old as I thought he was. I also realize my backpack is missing. Along with the case of bad luck Barry Manilow gave me.

"What happened to my case?"

"It's in a safe place," he says. "At least until I use it."

"And when will that be?"

"What does it matter? You're no Samaritan. You have your own troubles to worry about."

One of the other three Chinese men picks up a discarded mah-jongg tile, eliciting an angry reaction from the man on his left.

"*D'iu ne ma la!*"

Somehow, I don't think he's complimenting his partner's playing skills.

"So how did you know who I am?" I ask. "Or that I'd be in Huntington Park?"

"When you're in my line of business, it pays to know

who people are." Tommy sips his tea. "And as I'm sure you've come to realize, you and I share a common interest."

"Philanthropy?"

Tommy laughs, then throws down a tile that elicits an *"Aayah!"* from the old man across from him. "As for where you'd be, it's easy to find someone when you know where they're going."

Tommy pours the rest of the tea for his playing partners, then calls out for a refill. This time, instead of Mei, an attractive Asian woman walks through the curtained doorway wearing a red dress and red pumps and carrying a fresh pot of tea. The same Asian woman who was in the limo with Barry Manilow.

"I believe you've met S'iu Lei," says Tommy.

She walks over and sets the teapot on the table. "Pleasure to see you again, Mr. Monday."

"Nice dress," I say. "Where do you hide your gun?"

She smiles and pours Tommy a fresh cup of tea as he throws down the rest of his tiles in triumph, winning the game and sending the other three men out of the room with their wallets carrying a whole lot less than when they came in.

I need to learn how to play this game.

"I keep track of what goes on in my city," says Tommy. "So when the mayor of San Francisco lost the shine on his armor, it was only a matter of time before I found the man responsible. A man whose talents I could use."

I'm beginning to think poaching Gordon Knight's luck wasn't such a good idea.

"But I was disappointed when my associates told me you refused my offer of employment," says Tommy.

"*Refused* is a strong word." I finish my tea and hand my empty cup to S'iu Lei. "I prefer to think of it as exercising my right of independence."

"Does your independence allow you to take vacations to Europe and Tahiti? Or to live in a penthouse flat in Pacific Heights?"

"It's part of my five-year plan."

"I can make that happen right now," says Tommy, running his hand along S'iu Lei's backside as she refills my cup. "No five-year plan. How does that sound?"

"I don't look good in red."

Tommy laughs.

"Besides," I say, "from what I hear, you've already got some other poachers on your payroll."

"Rumors," says Tommy, waving a dismissive hand in the air.

S'iu Lei sets the pot down next to my cup, then leans in and whispers something to Tommy, who nods.

"Until next time," she says to me with a wink and a smile before she turns and saunters away, her red curves outlined with sex.

"I'll pay you twenty-five percent above what you get on the open market," says Tommy, nodding toward S'iu Lei as she exits the room. "Plus . . . benefits."

It's tempting. But like I said, I don't look good in red. Plus I swore I'd never go corporate.

"No thanks," I say. "I prefer the entrepreneurial path. Cuts down on the chain of command."

Though I'm wondering if I'd have a better chance of delivering the bad luck to Tommy if I took his offer. Problem is, I don't know what to make of S'iu Lei's role in all of this. Whose side she's on. Plus I don't have the bad luck anymore, which is another kind of problem.

"I respect a man who stays true to his nature," says Tommy, handing me my fresh cup of tea. "Of course, that doesn't mean I can let you just walk out of here."

Crap. I hadn't considered that. I never did plan well for the future. So the thought of actually dying here in this dilapidated room didn't occur to me. Until now.

I can almost hear my father's voice, telling me that one way or another, I'd end up paying for my lifestyle in the end.

Tommy seems to read my mind. "No need to worry," he says, picking up his cup of tea but not taking a drink. "I have no plans to dispose of you. It's not good business to kill a luck poacher. Besides, I have a feeling you'll end up changing your mind."

"Don't hold your breath. But thanks for not killing me."

Tommy just smiles at me over the top of his teacup.

"I suppose you're going to have to blindfold me," I say, then take a sip of my tea. "Or put a bag over my head."

"Not exactly," says Tommy, setting his cup down.

I open my mouth to respond, but all that comes out is "Blllbb."

I slide off the chair and onto the floor, turning into a puddle of Nick Monday. Tommy steps up to the puddle and leans over.

"Don't take too long changing your mind, Mr. Monday," he says, his voice growing muddled and distant. "Otherwise next time, I won't be such a good host."

11

In September 1960, during a speed trial at Bonneville Salt Flats in Utah, Donald Campbell crashed his car while traveling at 360 miles per hour. The vehicle tumbled multiple times and was destroyed, yet Donald Campbell survived with only a fractured skull. Seven years later, he wasn't so fortunate, dying while attempting to set the water speed record.

When I wake up, I feel like Donald Campbell. The 1960 version. Not because I feel lucky to be alive, but because I feel like my skull is in several pieces.

I'm in an alley. I don't know where. Next to me is a guy who smells like desperation and hopelessness and who is passed out in his own urine, so I'm guessing I'm in the Tenderloin. On the wall across from me is written:

TEMPTATION WEIGHTS

Someone needs a spelling lesson. I need some coffee.

Actually what I need is to poach some good luck, any grade, even if it's diluted. Something to help me get rid of this headache and figure out how I'm going to get out of this mess with Barry Manilow and Tommy Wong. Though I have no idea how I'm supposed to retrieve the stolen bad luck from Tommy so I can make Barry happy, not unless I accept Tommy's offer to work for him. Which was really more of a threat than an offer.

You say potato . . .

Semantics aside, whatever I'm going to do I better do it soon. But first I need some caffeine and some good luck.

I could grab one of the bottles of medium-grade from my apartment, provided neither the Feds nor Tommy Wong's thugs have ransacked it and taken my stash. Which wouldn't surprise me considering the way this day is turning out. But consuming good luck and poaching it are two different experiences. It's like the difference between drinking a beer and dropping acid. Or masturbating and having tantric sex. One just gives you some personal satisfaction while the other is transcendent.

And I'm realizing that giving up this lifestyle might be more of a challenge than I thought.

I walk out of the alley onto Polk Street and hoof it a couple of blocks to Peet's by Max's Opera Café, where I order a large mocha and get another phone number from a blond barista with a pageboy haircut and a nose ring who tells me she loves guys who have that rumpled look. I don't have the heart to tell her that I woke up drugged in an alley, so I pocket her digits and head back to Polk Street to grab an apple fritter from Bob's Doughnuts.

It's not so much out of hunger, but the combination of sugar and caffeine helps with the processing of good luck into a marketable form. For others, sugar and alcohol does the trick. I don't know why, since I never got better than a C in chemistry, but it's what's worked for generations. My great-grandma washed down rock candy with straight vodka, while Grandpa swore by powdered doughnuts and Budweiser. For me, it's cappuccinos or mochas and apple fritters. Beer just makes me sleepy.

And I wouldn't be caught dead drinking a Budweiser.

Drinking my mocha, I walk up Polk Street, looking for potential marks, but all I see are homeless people trying to sell copies of the *Street Sheet* and minimum-wage employees standing outside taking a smoke break.

Not exactly the best options for good luck.

Trolling for luck out in the open like this isn't the smartest idea. First of all, you have to deal with the problem of personal hygiene. Second, without research, you never know what you're getting.

But sometimes you're forced to take your chances.

If you're going to poach luck off the streets or door-to-door in San Francisco, your best bets are Nob Hill, Pacific Heights, and the Marina District. With multimillion-dollar homes and their central location to tourist attractions and shops, they offer the best combination of wealth and accessibility. No one looks twice at you walking around those neighborhoods. Your chances of walking away with some medium-grade good luck are decent enough to make it worth considering.

Instead of mansions and manicured gardens and beauty salons, I'm walking past the Red Coach Motor Lodge and graffiti-covered awnings and the Shine Day Spa Massage Parlor. I don't know if Tommy's getting a cut of their business, but when I look around at the people in this neighborhood, I'm guessing most of them aren't getting any happy endings.

Why some people are born with good luck and others aren't, I don't have an answer. Maybe it has something to do with karma, if you believe in that sort of thing. A reward for making the right decisions or doing the right thing in a past life. Or maybe it's the reverse. People who had a hard life last time around get a spiritual hall pass to help balance things out.

Or maybe it's just random chance.

As for luck poachers, I don't know why we can do what we do. How we were chosen. Why we were born this way. Maybe we *are* mutants or aliens.

Outside of my family, I've never met another luck poacher. Because of our limited numbers, we don't tend to cross paths all that often. It's not like we have our own version of Hogwarts to teach us the art and rules and etiquette of stealing luck. And we don't exactly have support groups to help us understand who we are and what we do. Everything I know about luck poaching I learned from Grandpa. And other than Grandpa, Mom, and Mandy, I've never known anyone else I could count on. Anyone who would understand me. Which is another reason why it's a bad idea to develop relationships: You never know whom you can trust.

So for the most part, it's just been me, myself, and I.

When I was a kid, I had to learn how to make my own fun. I played in my room, made up games, and poached from other kids. Sometimes I'd hang out with Grandpa or Mandy, but otherwise I spent a lot of time by myself.

In the past two decades, not much has changed.

12

Once I get my apple fritter from Bob's, I continue along Polk Street into Russian Hill, keeping my eyes open for potential marks. It's not easy spotting them and there aren't any guarantees, but you find someone wearing an expensive suit and a Rolex or stopping just in time to avoid getting hit by a bus and at least you've got someplace to start.

What I really need is a residential street with some homeowners out in their gardens or washing their cars. At least that way I'd know where they live. I'm much more likely to poach from someone who owns a three-story Victorian in Pacific Heights than I am from someone who rents a one-bedroom apartment in Russian Hill. But wealth is only one part of the package. When you're cold-calling, ideally you want someone who not only has some financial security but who also looks like they went to college.

Right now, all I see are renters and bag ladies and a bunch of people who look like they took remedial classes.

I walk past a rack of newspaper vending machines for *USA Today,* the *San Francisco Chronicle,* and *SF Weekly* and stop when I see a blurb on the front page of the *Chronicle* about the Giants game last night. That's when I remember the article I read this morning about James Saltzman.

I finish off the rest of my apple fritter and mocha, then I take out my smartphone and open my white-pages app and type in the last name Saltzman in San Francisco. The list comes up and I scroll down. There's a Barry Saltzman who lives on Jersey Street, a Charles Saltzman on Sixteenth, a Gloria Saltzman on Twenty-Second, and a James and Sheila Saltzman at 1331 Greenwich.

Bingo.

I touch the screen above his address and Google Maps comes up. A few seconds later I've got the location of James Saltzman's home, located at the corner of Polk and Greenwich, right down the street.

I love modern technology.

Ten years ago, I would have had to find a phone book and some store or business that could look up the address for me. Or gone into a Kinko's and rented one of their computers. But now I have all of the tools a modern luck poacher needs right at my fingertips.

1331 Greenwich Street is less than eight blocks away, which prevents me from having to grab a cab or jump on the bus, but it gives me enough time to formulate a plan of attack. With my T-shirt and jeans and Chuck Taylors,

I don't exactly have that running-for-political-office look or that dressed-for-success appearance that puts most people at ease. For some reason, your average person tends to respect someone wearing a coat and a tie more than someone who's dressed like the drummer of a garage band, even if you're not interviewing for a job. Though in effect, when you're poaching luck, that's exactly what you're doing.

I could go home to clean up and change into something more respectable, but with the way my day's been going, I'll get kidnapped and drugged yet again before I can get there, so I decide to play this one as the friendly neighbor and hope that James Saltzman doesn't know all of his.

Except that he caught the final home runs of two of baseball's most prolific sluggers, I don't know anything about James Saltzman. His age. His politics. His favorite sports team. If he has kids. What he does for a living. Who his friends are. Where he likes to eat. How often he hits the strip clubs in North Beach.

I would normally research those details before approaching a mark, especially at home. You never know when some bit of information can make the difference between a successful poaching and an aborted one. But this is kind of an emergency. And in an emergency, I tend to let things flow. Though my father used to tell me I wouldn't know an emergency from a hangnail.

When I reach Greenwich, I walk down the street to scope out the address, then I walk back up the other side before I take several deep breaths to find my center. Poaching luck requires focus and concentration. It's almost a spiritual process. Minus that I'm stealing from someone.

I admit I feel bad sometimes about what I'm doing, about the impact I'm having on the lives of the people I poach from, but when you have this kind of power it's difficult to keep from wielding it. The lifestyle has a way of sucking you in and before you know it, you're just another societal leech freeloading off the good fortunes of others.

Which is another reason why poachers end up committing suicide. And why I've always tried to avoid too much self-reflection.

Once I'm settled, I walk up the steps and knock on the front door.

No one answers, so I ring the doorbell. Still nothing. I knock once more, hoping James Saltzman is home on a Tuesday morning in August and not on vacation or, more likely, at work.

Ten seconds later, a young boy, maybe ten years old, opens the door and stands back several feet from the doorway. Normally I'd abort any planned poaching when kids are part of the equation, but I'm desperate for a score. Even if it is just questionable medium-grade luck.

"Good morning," I say, flashing a smile.

"It's afternoon," he says.

I look at my watch and see that it's almost one o'clock. Fuck. Where has the day gone? You get drugged twice by a Chinese Mafia overlord and you lose all track of time.

"Right you are," I say with a smile. "My mistake."

He just stands there and stares at me, his arms folded, unimpressed.

I'm getting a lot of that today.

"What do you want?" he asks.

It's not surprising that he doesn't have any manners. Most kids today don't. But if you ask me, it's a direct reflection of bad parenting. I can say this with complete certainty because I've never parented a day in my life and I enjoy making sweeping generalizations about how other people do a piss-poor job at something about which I have absolutely no experience.

"May I speak with James Saltzman, please?"

"Junior or Senior?"

"Senior," I say. "Is he home?"

"Who wants to know?" asks the kid, who I'm presuming is Junior.

"Paul Jefferson."

Names are important when poaching. You don't want to make up a name on the spot and end up with something like John Smith or Fabio Delucci. You want a name that's benign and forgettable but that makes your marks comfortable and gets them to relax.

Paul was the primary public-relations mouthpiece for Christianity, and I've found that even those who aren't religious respond to the name favorably. And Jefferson still commands admiration and a sense of patriotism for the third president of the United States nearly two hundred years after his death. Even if he did grow pot and have sex with his slaves.

I figure a ten-year-old kid has heard the names enough that his subconscious will be put at ease.

"Paul Jefferson? That sounds like a made-up name."

Or maybe not.

I can feel my face growing warm and my T-shirt beginning to stick to my back, which is unsettling because I never sweat during a poaching. Sweating is a sign of nervousness. And being nervous is bad for business.

I look at him and smile without meaning it.

"Is your father home?" I ask.

"That depends."

"On what?"

"On what you want him for."

In addition to feeling unusually warm, I'm beginning to get a little light-headed and I'm suddenly beginning to wonder if this was such a good idea.

"I was hoping to talk to him about some important neighborhood issues."

"What kind of issues?"

This is why I refuse to deal with kids. With an adult, it's just a quick introduction and a handshake and the rest is gravy. With kids, it's a series of whats and whys and hows. Especially, it seems, with this one.

I never was good with being patient.

"It's regarding planned development in Russian Hill." I don't know what I'm saying. Or where I'm going with this.

"What kind of development?"

"Anyone ever tell you that you ask a lot of questions?"

"Anyone ever tell you that you smell like cat pee?"

"Look," I say, barely editing out the accompanying phrase *you little shit,* "I'd just like to speak with your father."

"Do you have an appointment?"

"What? No. I don't have an appointment."

"Then come back next week." He closes the door.

I stand there a few moments, staring at the door, wanting to give it a good kick or ring the doorbell a hundred times, but instead I just stick out my tongue and walk away.

Well, that was productive.

Feeling deflated, not to mention a little humiliated, I walk up Lombard Street to Hyde to take in the view of the Coit Tower and the Bay Bridge and to try to clear my head, cool off, and figure out my next move. Maybe see if I can find some random tourist brimming with good luck to cheer me up. But I'm not counting on it.

At the top of the hill where Lombard crosses Hyde, it becomes paved with bricks and descends down a steep grade through eight terraced switchbacks past residential homes. Crowds of summer tourists have gathered at the top of Lombard to take pictures of the view and to watch the cars wind their way down the alleged crookedest street in the world. I stand with the tourists, listening to the symphony of foreign languages and laughter, wondering if any of them are worth taking the risk of a quick hit-and-run poaching.

While I'm perusing the tourists, a Hispanic couple comes over and asks me to take their picture. I don't have anything better to do, and I figure I might at least be able to bum a low-grade high from them, so I have them line up to one side of the stairs with Coit Tower and Telegraph Hill and the Bay Bridge in the background.

Just as they have their canned smiles ready and I press down on the shutter release, a sixteen-year-old kid on a skateboard races past between us on the sidewalk, does a ninety-degree turn at the entrance to Lombard Street, then takes off down the twisting road, maneuvering between cars and eliciting honks and shouts from the drivers.

Still holding the camera while the Hispanic couple asks me if I could please take another picture, I watch the kid on the skateboard glide between fenders and curbs, past bumpers and hedges, oozing teenage bravado and confidence. Halfway down the hill, the kid gets clipped by a Volvo, rolls over the hood of the car, and lands in some bushes blooming with pink flowers. Then he pops up and gets back on his skateboard unscathed and continues down the street with a smile on his face and a triumphant middle finger raised in salute for the driver of the Volvo.

And behold, I think I've just found my mark.

13

I'm racing down the stairs along the side of Lombard Street, dodging tourists and trying to act like this is all perfectly normal, hoping I can somehow manage to beat the kid on the skateboard to the bottom, when I realize I'm still holding the Hispanic couple's camera.

I turn around and see the husband chasing after me, about two flights back, while his wife is at the top of the street yelling and pointing my way.

Sometimes I really hate that my father might be watching me and nodding and saying, *I told you so.*

Just because I figure it'll add to their memories, I take a quick picture of the husband racing toward me with his wife screaming in the background, shout out, "Sorry," then toss the camera safely in a flower bed and continue down the stairs.

The kid on the skateboard has almost reached the bottom of Lombard and I still have half a dozen flights of tourist-encumbered stairs to negotiate, when I notice a woman on a scooter maneuvering down the crooked, brick-paved street, weaving through and past a couple of cars, until she reaches the bottom of the street, pulls to one side, and looks back my way. At first I think she's just savoring the moment, enjoying the view. But as I make my way past a family of four from Germany and a young couple arguing about their lunch plans, I realize the woman is watching me . . . almost as if she knows me. I have no idea who she is.

From this distance she looks like she could be attractive. Young. Slender. Short brown hair poking out of her helmet. I'm thinking maybe she's one of the baristas I've slept with and I'm trying to remember her name and whether she works at Starbucks or Peet's. I suppose it doesn't really matter. Eventually, they all end up hating me, so this one could just be a stalker out for vengeance. Or an admirer. I've had both.

Then she glances at the kid on the skateboard, who has finished his slalom course and is high-fiving his skate-rat friends across the street, and she looks back up at me.

That's when she smiles.

I don't know who she is or where she came from, but I realize she was watching me not because of *who* I am, but because of *what* I am. I'm also pretty sure from her triumphant smile that she plans on taking what I thought was mine.

Another luck poacher. In my city.

And I'm wondering if this has anything to do with Tommy Wong.

How she knows I'm a poacher, I don't know. Maybe it's my obvious intent. Or the Hispanic couple chasing me down the stairs. It doesn't matter. What matters is that she's here, in San Francisco, and she shouldn't be.

I race down the stairs, taking two at a time as the woman rides her scooter over to the teenage kid and immediately starts up a conversation with him. Whatever she says does the trick. Even from my vantage point, I can see from the look on his face that he's flattered by her words. And I know I don't have much time.

I'm one flight from the bottom, hoping I can get to them in time, to intrude, to maybe work my own charms on the kid before it's too late. But then I see her extend her soft, feminine hand out to him, an invitation of intimacy, the possibility of sexual delights, and I know I never stood a chance.

The kid takes her hand with a smile just as I hit the sidewalk.

"Hey!" I shout out.

I don't know what I expect to accomplish by yelling at her. The damage is already done. She's stolen his luck and it's not like she's going to share. But I'm pissed off. This is my city. These are my people. No one else is entitled to steal from them except me.

The cute brunette glances back over her shoulder, still holding on to the kid's hand, then she says something to him before she lets go and takes off on her scooter down Leavenworth, turns the corner, and disappears from view.

I chase after her for half a block, shouting at her to stop, then I give up because I realize it's pointless. When I turn around, the teenage Evel Knievel is blocking my way, his skate-rat friends spread out on either side of him.

"What's your problem, dude?" says the kid, a high school punk with long hair and his baseball hat turned around backward.

"Take your pick," I say, moving to walk around them. I don't have the time to deal with them, whatever it is they want.

They counter to keep me in check, spreading out to block my way.

I'm not sure what's going on here, but I feel like I'm in a bad 1980s movie starring Corey Haim. Or maybe Corey Feldman. I never could keep those two straight.

Their leader steps up to me, a shadow of a mustache on his upper lip. "Why don't you leave that chick alone?"

Now I understand. Nothing engenders male bravado like coming to the rescue of a cute damsel in distress.

It's bad enough that I lost my potential score to a woman poacher who encroached on my territory, but now I'm being challenged by a bunch of teenagers with baggy pants and peach fuzz who have delusions of grandeur.

"Why don't you mind your own business?" I say.

I never was good at diplomacy.

"How about if we mind it for you?" says one of the

other kids. I don't know which one. They all look the same to me.

On the Lombard Street stairs, the Hispanic husband whose camera I sort of accidentally stole hurries down the steps and points me out to some big steroid monkey who has apparently decided to play the role of the helpful ass kicker.

Great. This just keeps getting better.

"Look," I say, "I don't know what she told you . . ."

Before I can finish my sentence, a fist pops me in the face. I don't know who threw the punch. I never even saw it coming. But the next thing I know, I'm stumbling backward and reaching up to stop the blood from pouring out of my nose.

In front of me, Corey and the Skater Boys are moving in for the kill, either dropping their boards to free up their teenage fists or tightening their grips to use their boards as weapons. Behind them, the Hispanic husband and his bodyguard have reached the bottom of the stairs and are coming over to join the party.

Ever have one of those moments when you know you're completely fucked?

Like when your second parachute doesn't open?

Or when you get pulled over for speeding, holding ten kilos of cocaine?

Or when you wake up naked in bed with your mother-in-law?

I'm wondering if I can talk my way out of this or just

start grabbing hands and poaching, hoping to strike a vein of good luck, when the cute little bitch on the scooter pulls up next to me and says, "Get on!"

I'm not exactly in a position to play the indignant card or to enter into a discourse on the etiquette of luck poaching, so I climb on the back, wrap my arms around her waist, and hold on as she floors the scooter.

She turns right on Chestnut, and for a moment we're in the clear. Then I look behind me and see the pack of skate rats bearing down on us, taking the next right onto Jones faster than we can. We scoot across Lombard and Greenwich without stopping, our pursuers less than half a block behind us, when Scooter Girl makes use of San Francisco's legendary topography to prove that age-old wisdom:

You can't skateboard uphill.

She blows through the stop sign at Filbert, then starts climbing. Granted, we're not exactly flying up Jones, which is a good thirty-degree slope, but we've definitely put some distance between us and our pursuers. When I glance back, most of the Skater Boys have picked up their boards and have given up the chase. Only Corey is still trying, but eventually even he succumbs to the laws of physics.

I breathe a sigh of relief and hold on tight to Scooter Girl's waist to keep from sliding backward off the seat.

"That's not my waist," she says.

"What?"

"Where you're grabbing on to me. Try lower."

"Oh." I readjust my grip. "Sorry."

When we reach the corner of Jones and Union, we pull to a stop and glance back down the hill, just to make sure we're safe. Two blocks down, the skate rats are skateboarding away in the other direction.

"Sorry about that," she says.

"Which part?" I say, climbing off the scooter, wiping the blood from my nose. "The part where you stole my mark or the part where you incited him and his friends to want to kick my ass?"

"The second one," she says. "I just wanted to slow you down. I didn't think they'd get physical."

From halfway up Lombard, she looked potentially cute. Up close, there's no question now about her potential. Clear skin. Slightly upturned nose. Delicate jaw. Nice smile. Plus she has real breasts. Not that I felt them or anything.

"And I didn't steal anything. We both saw him at the same time. I just made it to the bottom of the hill faster than you did."

"That's not the point," I say, trying to remember what the point was. I think it had something to do with the rules of poaching, with her encroaching on my territory, but I'm suddenly wondering what she's doing for lunch. And if she has a boyfriend.

It's not just that she's cute. There's something else. An intangible essence I can't put my finger on. Then I realize it's because this is the first time I've ever met another woman, other than my mother and my sister, who could understand why I do what I do.

I wonder if she's ever met another poacher. And if she thinks I'm attractive. And what she's doing in San Francisco.

"What are you doing here?" I ask.

"Are you talking about my raison d'être? Or are you digging for something more banal?"

"What are you doing in San Francisco?"

My guess is she's working for Tommy Wong. I just want to hear her admit it.

"It's top secret," she says, with a smile and a wink. "I'd tell you, but then I'd have to fuck you."

"What?"

She just smiles at me and tilts her head. "But I don't have sex with men who poach bad luck."

Before I have a chance to respond, she pulls out onto Union Street and drops down the hill toward North Beach, disappearing from view. I wonder how she could tell I'd poached bad luck. I'm guessing she just made that up as a lame excuse to bail out before she had to explain herself, but I'm not going to let her get away that easily.

Maybe I'm just kidding myself, but I felt a spark. Something passed between us. And I intend to find out what that something is. And what she's doing in my town.

I walk to the Searchlight Market on Hyde Street and buy some Advil and a bottle of water, along with some Mentos and a pack of fragrance-free baby wipes that I use to clean off my face. There's nothing I can do about the blood on my T-shirt, which makes me look kind of intimidating. Either that or like I just got my ass kicked. So I leave it and head out of the market to plan my next move.

Who am I kidding? Like I have a plan. Or any moves. All I have is a headache and a bloody T-shirt. And a tiny little crush on a female poacher.

True, she's to blame for my failed poaching *and* my headache *and* my bloody T-shirt. But I'm willing to let all of that slide because she's attractive and because she threatened to have sex with me. There's also this little fact that in the few minutes I've known her, she's unlike any other woman I've ever met. At least any woman I could have sex with and not end up on *Jerry Springer*. My sister's animosity aside, poachers understand one another in a way that other people can't.

And I'm wondering if Scooter Girl might be able to help me with my Tommy Wong dilemma.

Despite that she's most likely working for Tommy, she's still a poacher, so I'm hoping I can use our common genetic mutation to get her to see my side of things. I just need to figure out how to find her. And how many other poachers Tommy's hired. So I grab the 45 bus downtown to see someone who might be able to help me find the answers to those questions.

14

On July 28, 1945, Lieutenant Colonel William F. Smith Jr. got lost in the fog over Manhattan on his way to LaGuardia Airport and crashed his B-25 Mitchell bomber into the seventy-ninth floor of the Empire State Building. The fuel tanks exploded, sending flames racing across the floor in all directions. Betty Lou Oliver, the elevator attendant on duty at the time on the eightieth floor, was thrown from her post and badly burned, though she survived the incident while more than a dozen others died.

When help arrived, rescue workers decided to use one of the elevators to transport casualties, unaware that the accident had weakened the cables. Once the elevator doors closed, the cables snapped, and the elevator, with Betty Lou Oliver inside, plummeted seventy-five stories to the basement. Oliver survived the fall but was taken to the hospital and treated for serious injuries. She still holds the record for the longest elevator fall ever survived.

At the moment I'm feeling a bit like Betty Lou Oliver. Bloodied and battered, moving from one catastrophe to the next.

I get off the 45 bus at Union Square, then I walk east along Geary past Macy's and the Westin St. Francis before winding my way toward Market Street, walking back and forth in a serpentine route that takes me past a homeless person tiptoeing over cracks, a woman standing in a doorway wishing another woman good luck, and several restaurants and shops with ceramic lucky cats in their windows, beckoning in good fortune.

Human beings are such a superstitious bunch. Lighting Reiki candles to attract wealth and abundance. Knocking on wood in the hopes that good fortune will continue. Carrying around charms, amulets, and talismans for protection ever since the first caveman was trampled by a woolly mammoth.

Most people have no idea why they do the things they do in their attempts to either attract good fortune or avoid bad luck. They're completely unaware of the historical context behind their irrational beliefs.

Knocking on wood comes from pagans who were summoning tree gods. Throwing spilled salt over your left shoulder blinded the devil who was sneaking up on you. And the number thirteen is allegedly unlucky because thirteen people were at the infamous Last Supper.

But even if people understood the origins of their superstitions, it wouldn't make a difference. Contrary to what a lot of people think and what these New Age quacks try to sell you, you can't create luck or draw it to you. You're either born with it or you're not. Everything else is just random circumstance. Sometimes things work out and sometimes they don't. Lighting candles and knocking on wood and rubbing good-luck charms isn't going to improve your fortunes any more than wishing to have sex with a porn star is going to get you laid.

But don't try to tell that to Doug.

Doug's a superstitious kid just north of twenty-one who fancies himself a gangsta rapper even though he's Irish-Italian and grew up in Danville, a suburb that's about as white as Wonder bread. He showed up in my office a couple of years ago out of the blue, looking for a job as an assistant private investigator. Said he always wanted to be a PI and that he could be my eyes and ears on the street, someone who knew what was going on and who could help me to keep on top of the news that doesn't make it into the news.

I told him I worked alone and couldn't afford an assistant even if I wanted one, but he went out and got himself an investigator's license to prove his dedication and kept showing up at my office until I finally relented, though I told him I couldn't pay him much and that I'd likely have to let him go after a month.

That was nearly two years ago. I've had Doug on my under-the-table payroll ever since.

For the most part, the information I get from Doug

doesn't help me in either my private investigations or in my poaching, but I like him, despite his being as ignorant about luck as the rest of the masses. He's kind of like a little brother or a loyal dog who wants to please me. I have to admit, when it comes to knowing what's going on in the city, Doug *is* the man.

I find Doug on Market Street at Powell, eating an apple and talking to a couple of street peddlers across from the Westfield shopping center, where a year ago some guy pretending to be God told everyone to eschew their consumer lifestyles before he allegedly vanished into thin air. It turned out to be a hoax, but some people around here still believe it happened.

Doug spends most of his time hanging out on the streets downtown, talking to people and being friendly. It's one of his most valuable traits. People tend to open up to others who offer a smile and a warm greeting and who come across as harmless and engaging. And although he often dresses like a cross between a circus clown and a ghetto drug lord, Doug is rather harmless.

Today, Doug's wearing an oversize, throwback New York Jets jersey tucked into his baggy, yellow Dickies, which are held up just below his ass with a belt that has a buckle the size of New Jersey. On his feet are red Nike Jordans. On his head is a royal-blue Los Angeles Dodgers cap. Around his neck hangs a half-inch-thick gold medallion with the letters *BW* emblazoned upon it.

"Holmes!" he says, taking a bite of his apple, his face exploding in a smile, then morphing into concern. "What's up with the hemoglobin on your threads?"

At first I don't understand what he's talking about, mostly because more often than not, I don't understand what Doug's saying. But then I look down and notice the blood covering my shirt.

"I cut myself shaving."

"You need to use a mirror, Holmes. You didn't break your mirror, did you?"

"No," I say. "I'm good."

"'Cause if you did, you can reverse the seven years of bad luck by turning seven times in a clockwise circle."

"I'll take that under advisement."

Doug smiles and nods and raises his fist to me for a knuckle tap.

I used to try to explain to Doug that superstitions are ridiculous and that luck is like energy: It can't be created or destroyed. But he argued that following his superstitions had kept him lucky all of his life, so he wasn't going to stop.

I couldn't tell him that the reason he's lucky is because he was born that way.

When I tap Doug's knuckles with my own, I get a slight burst of static energy. But Doug doesn't notice. People who are born with good luck aren't aware of the electric charge they give off.

I've known Doug was packing luck ever since I met him. Although I can only guess as to the quality of the grade, Doug's got some pretty healthy stuff running through him. It's what helps him to get the information he acquires and what keeps him from getting his ass kicked by the punks and the criminals who actually live on the street. And what's given him that good fortune he attributes to his superstitions.

But even though I could use an infusion of good luck right now, I'd never poach from Doug.

"How's it hanging, Holmes?" he says, taking a bite of his apple.

"Big and low."

Which is what I say every time he asks me this, but for some reason it always cracks Doug up, causing him to giggle and snort and slap his knee.

Just up the block at Powell, tourists wait in line for the cable car, while a street preacher shouts into a megaphone that Jesus wants them to repent of their sins. And it will cost them only one dollar.

"So what's the word, Dog?"

"It's Bow Wow, Holmes."

Doug used to go by Dog, a derivative of Doug, because he liked the expression *What up, dawg?* But then he realized people would say *What up, dawg?* even if they didn't know his name, so he changed it to Bow Wow.

"Sounds more like a forizzle gangsta," he says, pursing his lips and making a hand gesture that he apparently thinks is smooth and edgy and indicative of his gangster-rap appeal. I don't have the heart to tell him it's the official Hawaiian sign for *hang loose*. "Know what I mean, Holmes?"

He doesn't call anyone else Holmes. Just me. Because of the private investigator thing. I think it's kind of sweet.

"Sorry, Bow Wow."

"No worries, Holmes." He pulls another apple out of his pocket and offers it to me.

"No thanks."

"You sure? An apple a day keeps the doctor away."

"I'm good."

"Just trying to keep you healthy," he says, pocketing the apple.

"So what's the word on the street, Bow Wow?"

"You on a new case, Holmes?" he says, lowering his voice.

Although Doug tends to be about as subtle as a money shot in a bad porno, he knows when to play it cool.

I nod. "But this one's on the down-low. No one else can know about this."

Not that I'm worried about Doug sharing the details of my questions with anyone, and I don't need to remind him to keep things hush-hush, but he's always under the impression that I'm perpetually dealing with nefarious criminals and shady characters and seductive women. So I play it up every now and then because I know it makes him feel like he's involved in something exciting.

Of course, today's turning out to be more like Doug's imaginative musings than I'd like to admit.

Doug puts one hand over his heart. "I always got your back, Holmes." He likes to think of himself as my Dr. Watson. "So what info you lookin' to find?"

"You hear any word on the street about luck poachers?"

"Luck poachers?" His eyes grow wide. He looks left and right as if someone might be listening in on our conversation. "Snap! You looking to score some luck, Holmes?"

"No," I say, though I actually am. "I was just wondering if you might have heard anyone talking about the latest luck gossip. Something going down. New luck poachers in town. Anything out of the ordinary."

He looks left and right over his shoulders, then steps in a bit closer. "You hear of a guy named Tommy Wang?"

"Wong."

"What?"

"Wong," I say. "It's Tommy Wong."

"So you heard of him."

I just nod.

"Anyway," he says, "this Tommy Wong is apparently some sort of Chinese gangsta badass, and he's been buyin' up as much luck as he can get hold of. Hiring poachers from out of town and puttin' 'em on his payroll. No one knows who they are, but rumor has it a bunch of 'em have moved into town."

Which pretty much confirms my suspicions about Scooter Girl. Apparently, Tommy's not only contracting luck poachers but bringing them into my territory. I wonder how many more of them there are. And how the hell I'm going to get rid of them.

Just add it to my list of Things to Do.

"You ever seen a luck poacher, Holmes?"

I shake my head and do my best impersonation of someone who's telling the truth. "Not that I know of."

"I seen one."

"Is that so?"

"Word. Saw this dude cruisin' past the Orpheum the other night, checking out the scene. He was a tall, white dude. And when I say white, I don't mean Conan O'Brien white. We're talking creepy-dude white. Like he's allergic to the sun."

"You mean an albino?"

"Yeah, that's it. Dude was freaky."

"How did you know he was a poacher?"

"I just knew, Holmes. I just knew."

I don't know who this guy was, but no respect-able poacher would be caught hanging out by the Orpheum. You don't tend to find a lot of good luck in the Tenderloin. More likely you're going to find a lot of drug addiction and failure. And I'm not putting any stock in Doug's ability to identify poachers, considering he has one standing right in front of him. Still, if Tommy's hiring poachers and bringing them into the city, I suppose any-thing's possible.

"You know what, Holmes?" Doug leans in even closer.

"I hear that if a poacher takes your luck, it's like he's taking your soul."

So much for Doug's powers of perception.

"I had no idea," I say.

Doug gives a single nod, slow and solemn. Like a little kid silently admitting to something he's done. "I also heard that if you carry a rabbit's foot or some sort of lucky charm, it keeps poachers away."

"Kind of like garlic and vampires?"

"Word. You ever seen a vampire, Holmes?"

"No."

"Me neither," he says, sounding disappointed. "But I always carry this, just in case."

Doug reaches inside his shirt and pulls out something on a cord that's hanging around his neck. I think it's going to be a bulb of garlic or a silver cross or a vial of holy water, but when he opens his hand, there's a brass ring the size of a rolled-up condom in his palm.

"Had this since my dad gave it to me when I was ten," he says. "Just before he died. Got it from the carousel at the boardwalk in Santa Cruz. Told me I should always reach for the brass ring."

My father always told me I needed to develop brass balls.

"Anyway," he says, "I always keep it on me. Not for vampires, but just, you know, for good luck."

In the United States, people kiss crosses and carry around a rabbit's foot for good luck, which obviously wasn't very lucky for the rabbit, while in other countries, people attempt to control and enhance their good fortune through all sorts of ridiculous behaviors.

In Russia, carrying a fish scale in your purse or wallet is considered good luck.

In Germany, the spotting of a chimney sweep in traditional garb is regarded as fortuitous.

In Scandinavia, trolls are thought to be lucky.

Which I find kind of confusing. I always thought trolls lived in caves or mounds or under bridges and ate billy goats or little children. Not really sure what's so lucky about that. Unless you're a troll.

Others believe luck can be created by looking for opportunities, listening to their intuition, using the power of positive thinking, and adopting a resilient attitude. Which is more ridiculous than carrying around a fish scale in your wallet.

"You carry any good-luck charms?" asks Doug, putting the brass ring back inside his shirt.

"No." But with the way today is shaping up, I'm beginning to wonder if I should.

"Can't hurt, Holmes. You don't want some dude walking up to you and fleecing your mojo."

Yeah, well, too late for that.

"Thanks for the advice, Bow Wow," I say, giving him another knuckle tap.

He smiles and tells me to stay cool and flashes some kind of gangsta peace sign that looks more like he's got a rash he's trying not to scratch.

"Don't step on any cracks, Holmes."

I'm just about to turn away and find out what it's like to have my personal space back when Doug leans in again.

"Oh, one other thing. Word on the street is that this Tommy Wong has offered to pay half a million to any poacher who brings him something called Pure. You have any idea what that means?"

"No," I say, playing dumb. "I have no idea."

15

When I was little, my grandfather used to tell stories about famous poachers throughout history who stole luck from the likes of Napoleon, JFK, and the captain of the *Titanic*. Sometimes he'd make up stories just to entertain us and make us laugh. Other times he'd tell us cautionary tales about poachers who gave in to temptation and greed. Who took the wrong path and ended up addicted to good luck or infected with bad luck.

Guess I should have paid more attention to that one.

But the story I remember most was the one he told about something he liked to call the Holy Grail of poaching. The cleanest form of luck you could find. Untainted by the corruption of the soul. As white and soft as the clouds of heaven and more powerful than the highest-quality top-grade soft.

Pure.

He would speak of it with this look of absolute joy, as

if just by talking about it he could imagine how it would feel to have that kind of luck flowing through him. When I asked him once if he'd ever poached Pure, the spark went out of his eyes and he looked at me with an expression that was a combination of longing and disgust.

"No," he'd said. "It's just a fairy tale. It doesn't exist."

Not until I was older did I find out the truth.

I head up Powell Street, past the crowds lined up and waiting to ride the cable car to Ghirardelli Square, thinking about what Doug said, wanting to believe his information was wrong but knowing that Tommy Wong was offering half a million dollars for the poaching and delivery of 100 percent pure good luck.

The longer you live with the luck you're born with, the more that luck absorbs your life experiences and the impurities that go along with the condition of being human. With all of the neuroses and phobias and emotional baggage we collect, like jealousy and homophobia and abandonment issues. With all of the mistakes and bad decisions that encompass a lifetime.

Like lying to your parents or cheating on your wife or taking steroids.

Even the highest grade of good luck can become diluted. Infused with the emotions and experiences of those who carry it in their DNA. Kind of like an emotional thumbprint. So when you poach luck, you don't always know what you're getting with it.

A perfect marriage mixed with codependence. An all-expenses-paid vacation blended with paranoia. A dream job cut with a drug addiction.

People are walking sponges, absorbing praise and criticism, joy and pain, love and hate. All of these experiences make up who we are, what we think of ourselves, affecting us not just emotionally, but on a cellular level. And good luck is part of the cellular makeup for those who are born with it.

It doesn't matter if you're a vegetarian or a carnivore. It doesn't matter if you believe in God or Buddha. It doesn't matter if you're an atheist or a nihilist. Eventually, your luck is going to become polluted with the mileage you put on it. It's like engine oil, collecting the dirt and deposits of living. Only problem is, you don't get to change your luck every three thousand miles. It just keeps getting dirtier.

The only way to maintain the purity of the luck is to live a life filled with honesty and integrity and selflessness. To live without judgment or fear or desire. Even the smallest of temptations can pollute your luck, especially in the United States, where judging your neighbors is a God-given right, fear is propagated by the media, and desire is plastered on twenty-five-foot-tall billboards and advertised on commercial breaks.

Like any rule, there's always the exception. I'm sure any luck Gandhi or Joan of Arc or the Dalai Lama might have had was cleaner than that of your average lucky person. But since they're either dead, martyred, or living in exile, I'm guessing they're not the target of Tommy Wong's reward offer.

I walk up to Union Square and stop to look around at all of the tourists enjoying their vacations, unaware of the bounty that's been placed on their potential good fortune. Specifically, I'm noticing the families. The ones with young children eating ice cream and pointing at homeless people and throwing tantrums. Laughing and crying and staring in wonder. Reacting to a world that hasn't yet beaten them down and crushed their spirits.

The only way to get Pure is to poach it from those who aren't yet adults. Ideally from those who haven't reached puberty and had their innocence corrupted with hormones and sexual desire and the discovery of self-gratification. Who still believe in magic and heroes and the idea that anything is possible.

I've never poached Pure. Never even considered it. And I don't need the memory of the look of longing and disgust on my grandfather's face to keep me in line. Taking luck from children is taboo among poachers. Although not as perverse as child pornography or pedophilia, it definitely has a pervasive stigma attached to it. Like kicking a dog or hitting your wife or masturbating in public.

But five hundred thousand dollars is a lot of money.

Enough to live on comfortably for at least five years. Enough to help buy a way to protect Mandy. Enough to challenge the beliefs of any poacher. Especially someone who might be able to get rid of the bad luck in his system by poaching pure, untainted good luck.

I never was good with moral dilemmas.

But finding a kid with Pure isn't easy. Unless some ten-year-old boy or eight-year-old girl makes the news for cheating death or some other stroke of luck, it's virtually impossible to find such a child. It's not like poachers can hang around outside of schools or day-care centers without attracting unwanted attention from teachers and parents and the police. So to claim Tommy Wong's reward, someone would have to find an innovative way of drawing children to him. Or to her.

In Union Square, in front of the Dewey Monument in the center of the square, a woman is dressed like a clown. Not a circus clown or a killer clown from outer space but a friendly one, with bright clothes and blue hair and a big red Rudolph bulb of a nose.

She's making animal balloons and handing them out to the children gathered around her, their eyes watching her and their faces filled with expectant smiles. Chances are she's just a normal person who enjoys kids. A teacher or an aspiring actress who likes to make animal balloons for a few extra bucks.

Or she could be one of Tommy's hired thieves, a luck poacher, looking for an underage mark.

The same way I can tell that Doug was born with good luck, poachers can sense the energy of luck flowing through a person by making the slightest physical contact—the brush of a hand, the tap of knuckles, or an inadvertent touch. What you feel is a static buildup. A low-level charge. Nothing that would cause your hair to stand up or your hand to flinch back in surprise.

But in the case of top-grade soft, being within touching distance is enough to get a reading. And the electric charge given off by someone carrying Pure would cause a definite physical reaction.

Such as laughing. Or breaking out in a sweat. Or a full-body twitch. Maybe even an orgasm. Which is a lot easier to get away with if you're a woman.

Although the clown is being careful not to touch any of the children, she's still coming close enough to determine if any of them are carrying Pure. I watch her for another few minutes, but as far as I can tell, she's not laughing or twitching or sweating or showing any signs of experiencing a moment of sexual ecstasy.

That doesn't mean she's not a poacher. That just means if she is, she hasn't found what she's looking for. But from what I can tell, she's not acting like someone who's trolling for prepubescent luck. Still, knowing that Tommy Wong has a half-million-dollar bounty out for a delivery of Pure makes me give second looks to the guys working the ice cream carts.

I've always wondered about them anyway.

I walk past a kid arguing with his mom, an eight- or nine-year-old boy talking back, arms folded, petulant and defiant, showing no respect at all. He pouts and shouts, screams and whines, and throws a tantrum that would put Russell Crowe and Christian Bale to shame. He's a living advertisement for contraceptives.

And I'm suddenly thinking about James Saltzman.

Not James Sr., but little Jimmy Jr.

While the gene for poaching luck can be hereditary, for those who are born lucky the gene isn't always passed along from one generation to the next. Or if it is, it can mutate, turn into something less or more. Or it might not exist at all.

So just because James Saltzman Sr. was apparently born with some degree of good luck, that doesn't mean his son has the same quality of luck flowing through him. Just like red hair or green eyes or the ability to paint or write or play a musical instrument, the genetic blueprint doesn't always follow form. You never know what can happen when two sets of DNA are thrown together.

But in the case of Jimmy Saltzman, I can't help but wonder if he might be carrying more than just an unpleasant disposition.

I didn't experience a full-body twitch or start laughing inexplicably or have an orgasm. Which would have been disturbing on so many levels. But I'm thinking about how I suddenly started to sweat in Jimmy's presence, standing there on the front porch in the shade on an overcast August afternoon, wearing a T-shirt and jeans. At the time I thought it was just a reaction to a poaching gone wrong.

To having to exert more energy working on my pitch, combined with my desperation for the score.

But maybe it was a reaction to something that went beyond a palpable discomfort. Maybe there's a genetic connection. Maybe Jimmy Jr. is a chip off his old man.

The only way for me to find out for sure is to have another chat with little Jimmy Saltzman. I don't know if that's such a good idea, considering how things went the last time we met. But the half million dollars Tommy is offering, along with the knowledge that poaching Pure would eradicate all traces of the bad luck that's been lingering in my system for the past three years, is one hell of a motivator.

As a general rule, poachers tend to have some latitude when it comes to questions of morality and honor. It comes with the job description. But poaching Pure isn't something I should even be considering. Not if I have any self-respect. Which at the moment is questionable.

Let's just say my resistance to temptation is running on fumes.

16

I watch the clown make another animal balloon, then I make my way across Union Square, keeping an eye out for anyone else who looks like a poacher. But all I see are potential marks.

With my headache still hanging around like an unwanted pregnancy, I head into Café Rulli for a caffeine fix.

Walking into Rulli's reminds me of Baldy and Tuesday Knight, which then reminds me that the ten-thousand-dollar retainer Tuesday gave me was in my backpack when Tommy Wong took it from me. Including the luck Barry Manilow confiscated, that's a good twenty grand in income I've lost so far today in less than two hours.

If I didn't already have a headache, that would definitely do the trick.

I pop another couple of Advil, then I dry-swallow them as I try to figure out what I should do next.

I'm thinking I should try to track down the buyer of Gordon Knight's luck and collect on the hundred grand

Tuesday offered, use the money to buy myself some time. Or maybe even buy some more bad luck to deliver to Tommy, only this time in a way that makes things better instead of worse. I don't know if I can find the buyer of Gordon Knight's luck or how I'll get it back from him, but since I don't have a hundred thousand dollars lying around and I don't have any other ideas at the moment, then that's the plan I'm following.

Better yet, if I could find someone with top-grade soft, I could solve my problems in one shot. Except other than little Jimmy Saltzman, I haven't met any potential marks carrying high-grade good luck. But considering my lack of options, it couldn't hurt to look.

So while I'm standing in line, I focus on the customers in Rulli's, looking for a possible mark among the men and the women sitting at tables and waiting in line in front of me.

There's the Ralph Lauren poster boy sitting at a table and talking on his cell phone while his Laura Ashley girlfriend sits across from him, ignored. Or the buttoned-down brunette at the front of the line who answers her cell while she's placing her order. Or the Japanese tourist who accepts his cappuccino from the barista and walks away without saying *Thank you.*

I watch them, the behaviorally challenged and the etiquette inept, the cellular criminals and the courtesy thugs, my headache waxing and my patience waning as I step up to the counter to place my order.

Maybe it's because I'm desperate for a fix or because I'm surrounded by people who live in social ignorance or because I've had a rough day and it's not even time for my afternoon nap, but I decide to take my chances with a simple hit-and-run.

I'm not so much concerned with making a score and earning some money, but rather with getting a little good luck flowing through my system and turning around this debacle of a day. Something to help get rid of this headache and take my mind off the temptation of the five hundred grand Tommy is offering for Pure. And nothing is more distracting than having freshly poached luck pumping through your system. Okay, maybe the girl-on-girl shows at Mitchell Brothers are a little more distracting, but they wouldn't help with my headache.

I order a double cappuccino with a *please,* which gets me a smile from the cute cashier with dimples, then I do a quick scan of the customers before I decide. It's a toss-up between the Ralph Lauren poster boy and the buttoned-down brunette, who is now talking so loud into her cell phone that the passengers on the cable car going up Powell can hear her. But I decide to go with Ralph.

Number one, with his Polo shirt and Rolex watch and Hugo Boss shoes, he looks financially successful. Number two, he's arrogant, which means he's used to having things go his way. And number three, it's generally easier to get a man to shake your hand before he has a chance to think about it. Even if he's socially inept, a man will offer his hand almost as a reflex. Especially someone who looks like he shakes hands for a living. And Ralph Lauren looks like a professional flesh presser.

The origin of the handshake goes back more than four thousand years, both as a gesture of peace between warriors and between enemies demonstrating that their hands held no weapons. Which, in the case of someone like me, is an obvious deceit.

It makes you wonder if the first handshake was initiated by a luck poacher.

Once my order is up, I say, "Thank you," then I grab my cappuccino, take a couple of sips to calibrate my nerves, and walk up to the table where Ralph is still chatting away on his phone while his girlfriend sits bored and annoyed across from him.

She's prettier up close. Not in a pretentious kind of way but more natural, with just enough makeup to accent her eyes and lips. And she has a lot of patience. She's obviously too good for someone who chooses a phone conversation over the company of a flesh-and-blood woman. Which is another reason to poach whatever luck Ralph has running through his system.

He's an idiot.

"I just wanted to say that it's a pleasure to meet you," I say, reaching my hand out toward him.

Before Ralph can figure out how to react or tell me that I must have him mistaken for someone else, which he probably wouldn't do anyway because he's an arrogant bastard, I'm clasping his hand in mine, shaking it once, then walking out the front door with my double cappuccino.

A simple hit-and-run.

I step outside into the sunshine and I feel the warmth envelop me like a cocoon. I walk out of Union Square and I hear laughter and arguments, conversations from half a block away, buses and cable cars and all the noises of the city emanating from unseen speakers like a THX surround-sound system. I head up Stockton Street and I see faces and flowers, clouds and trees, everything crystal clear in high-definition, digital-quality reception.

And that's just three of my senses.

I take a sip of my double cappuccino, and the flavor and the warmth course through me, filling my mouth and my stomach with Colombian coffee fields. A woman walks past, a blonde in a sundress, the scent of her shampoo lingering in my nostrils, and I can see her in the shower, her head wet and lathered, suds and water cascading down her bare shoulders and breasts.

You can see why it's easy to get addicted to the lifestyle.

When poaching low-grade good luck, the experience isn't nearly as intense, but it's still better than sex. And top-grade soft has been compared to an out-of-body experience. Like taking mushrooms or LSD or mescaline.

Ralph was apparently born with some good-quality medium-grade. Of course, I don't know what he does for a living or if he has any emotional hang-ups or addictions, but I should be able to sell his luck for between ten and fifteen grand. Presuming I can get a buyer, which has been about as easy to find as an all-you-can-eat buffet in Ethiopia.

At least my headache is gone.

Plus with some good-quality luck pumping through me, all of those decisions I had to make don't seem as daunting. I feel lighter. More relaxed. Able to handle whatever challenges come my way. Even the temptation of poaching Pure has lost its grip on me.

Although good luck won't always solve your problems, it gives you the confidence things will work out.

Tourists and suits walk past, homeowners and homeless fill the sidewalks, mortal men and women surround me, and I stand on the corner, feeling invincible.

But I know this feeling won't last. Eventually the rush will subside and I'll need to process the luck into a consumable form. The sooner, the better. The last thing I want is to end up addicted to luck like one of the poachers in Grandpa's cautionary tales. And after the large mocha from Peet's and the two cappuccinos from Starbucks, my bladder is lobbying for some stage time. So I catch a cab home to transfer Ralph's luck out of my system and into an empty Odwalla bottle, which I put into my refrigerator with the two other bottles of Super Protein and the four remaining bottles of Lemonade.

At least my stash is still there.

The rush of poaching good luck is offset by the complete feeling of abandonment when you process it from your body. It's as if all of the hope and confidence and strength you obtained suddenly drains away, leaving you feeling empty and useless. Add to that the discomfort of having a catheter inserted into your urethra and you might understand why so many poachers end up committing suicide.

Transferring luck from your system isn't the most pleasant part of being a luck poacher, but it's part of the job. I could collect my urine in a jar and boil out the impurities, but you just can't compete in today's economy with outdated methods. No one wants to buy partially urinated good luck. Unless you live in Arkansas. I hear it's a delicacy there.

The homeless guy who was camped out in front of my building a few hours ago is gone, but on the corner is a woman who looks as if she hasn't seen a bar of soap in a few months. To balance out the karma for the luck I just stole, I give her one of the Lemonades and tell her it's spiked with vodka, then I grab a cab back to my office to do a little research on my Gordon Knight poaching, see if I can find the client who purchased his luck and get that ball rolling. I know it's a shot in the dark, but at least I have some direction and purpose, so that should count for something.

My dad would be so proud.

As I step out of the cab on the corner of Sutter and Kearny, I get a smile from a leggy redhead with abundant cleavage, who glances back at me over her shoulder, and I'm thinking maybe, in spite of all that's happened today, things will work themselves out.

I'm still thinking that when I walk into my office and find a dead body.

17

There aren't a whole lot of places to hide a dead body in a room that's barely a hundred square feet and decorated in Early American austere. Other than behind the door, under the desk, or camouflaged as white stucco walls or faded cherry hardwood floors, your options are pretty limited. But I'm guessing that whoever put the dead body in the corner behind my desk wasn't going for subtlety.

This isn't what I would exactly call things working themselves out.

I'm not used to dealing with a dead body. Let's try never. The only other time I saw a dead person was my mother, and that was twenty-four years ago. To be honest, I think I was more traumatized by my father blaming me for my mother's death than I was by the accident.

So when I see the body slumped against the wall, legs splayed out from the red dress, head tilted to one side, dark hair spilled across the face, mouth open and eyes staring vacantly at the floor, the first thing I do is scream.

At least it's an honest reaction.

It's not a long or loud scream. More like a yelp. I doubt anyone heard it, but it's still not one of my defining moments. Despite that no one else is in the office, I look around self-consciously and try to play it off, like I was walking down the street and tripped over my own feet and I'm hoping to pawn the blame off on the sidewalk.

Once I get over the initial shock, I walk over to the body and crouch down to get a closer look to make sure she's really dead. I don't touch her but I snap my fingers, clap my hands, and lean in close enough to whistle in her ear. Nothing. Not a peep or a flinch or a smile. She's just sitting there, eyes wide-open and not breathing, waiting for rigor mortis to set in. So she's not faking. Which would explain why she doesn't smell so much like sugar or spice or everything nice anymore.

I back up to give her some space, more for me than for her, and notice that her dress is riding up on her thighs. I wasn't lying to Tommy when I said I don't look good in red. Not my color. Put me in greens and blues and I'm good to go. But I look better in red than Tommy's dead eye candy.

I check around S'iu Lei for blood, marks on her throat, signs of a struggle, anything to let me know what might have happened. But there's nothing. It's as if she just dropped into the corner of my office and died.

I know this is a setup. My father's assessment notwithstanding, I'm not an idiot. The problem is, do I call this in? Do I wait for whoever killed her to report it? Or do I try to dispose of the evidence without getting caught?

I could stuff her in a garbage bag and dump her down the trash chute, except I don't have any garbage bags and we're not supposed to put oversize garbage in the chute that might clog it up. I could cut her up into smaller pieces so she'd fit, just like on *The Sopranos,* but that would make a mess, and besides, I got a B- in woodshop. And walking out the front door of my building with a dead woman over my shoulder and hailing a cab is bound to draw attention.

So disposing of her body is out.

If I wait around for whoever killed her to call it in, I'll look suspicious. The last thing I need is to have the police digging around in my life, doing a background check, and discovering that I'm not who I say I am.

Which doesn't leave me with many other options.

Before I realize what I'm doing, I'm taking out my phone to dial 911.

Because I poach luck for a living, I often find myself in compromising or awkward situations, but I'm not used to dealing with dead Asian double agents and rich femmes fatales and getting kidnapped and drugged by Chinese Mafia overlords. Things were a lot less complicated when I lived in the suburbs. So it takes a few seconds before my synapses start firing and I realize how much trouble I'll be in if a dead body is found in my office, no matter who calls it in.

I hang up the phone without dialing and look down at S'iu Lei, at her body growing cold and stiff on my floor, and I wonder who killed her and put her here and why. I wonder if Tommy killed her as some kind of warning. I wonder if Barry found out she was double-crossing him and wanted to use my office to store her for safekeeping.

But mostly, I wonder how the hell I'm going to get her dead body out of here without getting arrested.

I'm still wondering this when my phone rings.

"Nick Monday," I say, as if nothing is wrong. As if this is business as usual. As if I'm not trying to ignore the hot, dead Asian double agent slumped in the corner of my office.

"Did you find the surprise I left for you?" says Tommy.

"I'm not real big on surprises."

And from the expression on S'iu Lei's face, I'm guessing neither is she.

"Consider it a going-away present," says Tommy.

"I didn't know I was going anywhere."

"That depends on how smart you are."

I suddenly feel like I'm having another conversation with my father.

"You know, if you wanted to get me something, a bottle of wine would have been just fine," I say. "Or maybe a nice spinach dip."

"You joke a lot for a man who doesn't have too many options."

"Oh, I've got plenty of options. The fact that I don't like any of them is the problem."

There's laughter on the other end of the line. Soft. Chuckling. Kind of creepy. "I like you, Nick Monday."

"Yeah, well, you've got a strange way of showing it."

I glance over again at S'iu Lei, at her splayed legs and her half-hidden face and her slightly parted lips, and I wonder what she did to get here.

"So what happened?" I ask.

"Let's just say anyone who plays too many sides eventually ends up forgetting which one they're on."

"That's why I prefer circles. There's just an inside and an outside. Less confusing."

"Yes, but if you walk in circles, you never get anywhere."

Definitely like talking to my father.

"From where I'm standing, you seem to be on the outside," says Tommy. "And that's the wrong side."

I never was good at geometry. "Is that what this is all about? Choosing sides?"

"More like a friendly reminder," he says.

"Well, for future reference, you might want to try some positive reinforcement. Movie passes are always good. Or a box of chocolates. Nuts and chews. I'm not a big fan of liqueur-filled truffles."

"You want to continue being a smart-ass or you want to be smart?"

"Have you ever met my father?" I ask. "Tall, heavyset, prematurely balding? Lots of control issues?"

"I can make your problem go away. In return, all I ask is one favor."

"I told you. I don't look good in red."

Silence on the other end of the line. Apparently Tommy isn't in much of a joking mood.

"Okay. What's the favor?" I ask.

"Can I trust you?"

"Do I have a choice?"

"Not really. But you have to choose a side. Inside or outside?"

I consider saying something about triangles and parallelograms, but I decide that probably won't help matters.

"I'm on the inside."

"Good," says Tommy. "Now that's what I like to hear."

An awkward silence follows. I'm not sure if it's because of Tommy, me, or that I'm staring at a dead body.

"So about this gift you left me?" I ask, looking at S'iu Lei. "It doesn't really go with my office. Is there any way I can return it?"

"I'll send someone over to take you out to lunch."

"Lunch? Is that code for something?"

"It's code for someone taking you out to lunch," he says. "When you get back, your visitor will be gone. You're welcome."

"Great. Can we get Italian?"

"I don't care. Just make sure you don't ask any stupid questions. And don't disappoint me. Or else the next time you get dumped in an alley, you won't wake up."

"Good to know," I say. "By the way, you didn't happen to find ten thousand dollars in the backpack that you took from me, did you?"

"No."

I didn't think so.

Then he's gone, leaving me with a dead connection in my hand and a dead body in my office.

Just because I'm curious, I walk over to S'iu Lei, bend down, then reach out a single index finger and poke her in the calf.

Less than a minute later, there's a knock on my office door.

I have to hand it to Tommy. He's drugged me. Kidnapped me. Drugged me again. Threatened me. And extorted me into working for him. But I have to give him props for following through and getting someone over here so quickly to remove the dead body from my office. It's hard to find good customer service these days.

When I open the door, I expect to find a couple of Mafia thugs with a laundry bag or a crate, maybe a skill saw and wall-to-wall disposable plastic tarps. I know it's just my imagination running away with me, and not in a Rolling Stones kind of way, but right now, my imagination, not time, is the only thing on my side.

Instead of one of Tommy's men standing in the hallway, I find Scooter Girl.

"Hey," she says.

She stands there, wearing her precocious smile framed by her soft lips, staring at me with her big, innocent eyes beneath her cute little bangs. She's like an anime cartoon. My heart's suddenly pounding and my palms are sweating.

Either she's carrying Pure or I'm falling in love.

"Are you here to take me out to lunch?"

"Yes." She nods once as if I've asked the right question. "That's why I'm here."

I stand there for a moment, just looking at her, which she responds to by smiling and cocking her head in a way that makes me wish I had a breath mint.

The longer I look at her, the more I realize that she reminds me of Tuesday a little around the eyes and mouth. But as opposed to Tuesday's adorned, movie-star voluptuousness, Scooter Girl is attractive in a girl-next-door kind of way. Cute, pleasant face. No makeup. The kind of woman I could definitely fall for rather than lust after, even if she did encroach on my poaching territory and get me beat up by a bunch of skater dudes and is apparently working for Tommy Wong. But then, I guess I'm technically working for him now, too. So I can't exactly throw any stones without shattering my own house. Or hitting an adulteress. Whatever.

I never was good with proverbs and metaphors.

"Just a second," I say, stepping into my office and closing the door and removing my bloodstained shirt, then grabbing my navy-blue Gap sweatshirt off the coatrack. I look once more at S'iu Lei collapsed in the corner like an abandoned erotic marionette, then I step back out into the hallway and lock the door behind me.

"So," I say, "what's for lunch?"

18

We're sitting at a window table at Scala's Bistro, an upscale Italian restaurant next to the Sir Francis Drake Hotel on Powell Street. Scooter Girl is having the spinach-and-goat-cheese tortellini while I chow down on the linguine and clams. It's the most expensive pasta item on the menu. Throw in half a dozen oysters for an appetizer and a couple of Bellinis and this is the priciest meal I've had in months. I figure if Tommy's picking up the tab, I might as well make the most of it.

"How's your tortellini?" I ask.

"It's good. How's the linguine?"

"Great."

This is what our conversation has been like. Me asking banal questions and Scooter Girl responding in kind. It's like I've forgotten how to talk to a woman. And most of my attempts at humor have either fallen flat or elicited a cold stare. I'd talk about Tommy and our common genetics, but when you're luck poachers, you can't really discuss business in public.

Of course, there's the whole dead-body-in-my-office thing, which could have something to do with the stilted conversation.

We eat in silence for a few minutes. No meaningful glances. No awkward smiles. Any connection I thought I'd felt earlier today seems to have been severed.

"So," I say, slurping a strand of linguine between my lips, hoping to lighten things up, "if I can get you to tell me what you're doing in San Francisco, does that initial offer of yours still stand?"

Just call me Mr. Smooth.

"I told you, I don't have sex with men who poach bad luck."

"You want to keep your voice down?" I say. "This isn't exactly information I want to share with my adoring public."

"Sorry." She goes back to her tortellini.

I look around to see if anyone heard. One, because I don't want to get outed as a luck poacher. And two, saying you poached bad luck is like announcing to the world you're a premature ejaculator.

"So how could you tell?" I ask, leaning forward, lowering my voice. "I mean, that, well, you know?"

She stares at me a moment, not answering, giving me a look that once more reminds me of Tuesday, until she finally says, "It was in your aura."

Whatever that means. Auras, energy, astrology. Psychics, crystals, Reiki candles. All that New Age crap and I get along about as well as an alien abductee and an anal probe.

"But I don't poach bad luck," I whisper. "At least, not anymore. And I only did it once."

She shrugs and takes another bite of her tortellini. "It's like herpes. Once is all it takes."

It's bad enough to get turned down for sex by a cute little luck poacher who screwed you over once already. But when you've been compared to herpes, that's when you know you should have stayed in bed.

The emasculation of my ego and the introduction of sexually transmitted diseases puts a damper on the conversation, so we continue to eat in more silence. I watch her watching me, neither of us looking away. It's a battle of wills. And it's not easy to eat linguine and clams without looking down at your plate.

Scooter Girl finally breaks down. "So, Nick Monday. Is that your real name?"

I return her question with a quizzical smile.

"What?" she asks.

"You're the second person today to ask me that question."

"Who was the first one?"

"Barry Manilow."

She stares at me across the table with a single arched eyebrow.

"He's a big fan," I say.

The waiter comes by to check on our satisfaction and to ask if we need anything. I could use a do-over on today, maybe get a nice Thai massage or a lap dance, but I don't think he can help me with either, so I just ask for another Bellini. Scooter Girl asks for the check, which I suppose means she's had enough of my company.

"Do private detectives always drink on duty?" she asks.

"Depends on the day. And I suppose on the detective."

"How long have you been a detective?"

"Long enough," I say, finishing my second Bellini before the third one has arrived. I'd drink some water in the interim to keep myself hydrated, but there's no booze in water, so what would be the point?

"You haven't answered my question."

"Which one?" I say. "I've lost track."

"The one about your name."

The waiter comes back with my Bellini, which I use to wash down the last of my linguine. That my drink and my main course rhyme doesn't help to improve my mood.

"My name's real enough," I say, trying to sound suave and mysterious, but it comes off more like annoyed and petulant. Which I suppose is more honest. "How about you? Do you have a name, real or otherwise?"

"Sorry. Top secret."

"Like your reason for being here?"

She just gives me an innocent smile.

This is how I live. In a world of professional anonymity. A world of people with fake names and false identities.

Or people with no names at all. Faceless people who solicit my services with a phone call or a text message. Customers who meet me in dark alleys or corporate coffeehouses. Strangers who pick me up in unmarked government sedans or who take me out to lunch.

Ciphers. Spooks. Frauds.

My life has so much meaning.

"So, where do you live when you're not trespassing on someone else's territory?" I ask. "Or is that top secret, too?"

"Tucson."

"No kidding. I used to live in Tucson."

"Small world," she says.

Yet another bond we have in common. Poaching and Tucson. What are the odds?

"So what made you leave?" she asks.

"Let's just say I needed a change of scenery."

"Or maybe you got in over your head," she says, giving me another one of her smiles with a cock of her head.

Maybe it's the two and a half Bellinis. Or maybe it's the way she cocked her head. Or maybe it's because I have a dead body in my office while I eat a nice lunch and flirt with another luck poacher. But I decide it's time to let her know what I suspect.

"So," I say, taking a swig of my Bellini and sitting back in my chair. "What's a nice girl from Tucson doing in California working for Tommy Wong?"

"I don't work for anyone."

"Then who sent you to take me to lunch?"

"I wasn't sent by anyone."

"Then why were you at my office?"

She finishes chewing and swallows. No sign of a smile. No twinkling of the eyes.

"I think you need to understand exactly what type of man you've managed to get involved with," I say.

I'm not sure if she thinks I'm referring to me or Tommy Wong. Either way works, I suppose.

"Can I get the check?" she asks the waiter a second time.

"Yes, of course," he says. "My apologies."

He hurries off, leaving Scooter Girl and me with our awkward silence.

"You haven't answered my question," I say.

"Which one? I've lost track."

"The one about why you're here," I say, leaning forward. "Why you showed up at my office door."

"That's two questions."

"There's a dead woman in my office," I say, leaning closer, speaking only loud enough for her to hear. This is probably a mistake, but I'm used to making them by now. Or maybe I've had one too many Bellinis.

She stares at me with no expression, her eyes betraying the calm of her nonreaction as the waiter arrives with the check.

"Can I get you anything else?" he asks.

"No, thank you," she says, flashing him a smile as if

nothing were wrong. When she turns back to me, the smile is gone like a magic trick.

And I'm thinking I've managed to kill any chance I had with her. Oh well.

"The dead woman," I say. "Do you know who put her there?"

"Aren't *you* supposed to be the detective?" she says, pulling out a wad of cash and throwing down more than a hundred dollars on top of the check.

"Tommy Wong put her there. The man who told you to take me out to lunch. The man you came to San Francisco to contract for."

"I told you. I don't work for anyone."

She gets up and walks away from the table and out the front door. Like an obedient dog I follow her. Or maybe it's out of desperation. At this point, I don't care.

Out on Powell Street, the cable car clanks past us heading toward Union Square. Scooter Girl walks in the opposite direction, head down, arms swinging, short hair bouncing as she walks past the Beefeater standing out in front of the Sir Francis Drake.

"Hey!" I yell out, trying to get her attention. It would be easier if I had a name, since I doubt she'll respond to Scooter Girl. But I don't think she'd turn around even if I told her she'd just won an all-expenses-paid trip to Tahiti with Johnny Depp. So I just run after her.

She reaches the intersection of Sutter and Powell and is turning the corner just as I pass the entrance to the Drake.

"Hold on," I shout. "Wait a second!"

Suddenly, a large, white-gloved hand attached to a large, red-clad arm is lowered in front of me like a crossing gate, blocking my way.

"Nice of you to drop by," says the large owner of the large arm.

I look into the Beefeater's face, which is round and friendly and black with a thin, well-groomed mustache. His head is shaved. His arm is as big as my leg. Come to think of it, so is his neck. He looks like he could have played middle linebacker in the NFL. And he looks like he's eaten more than his share of beef.

"Do you know me?" I ask.

"Let's just say that I know enough."

His voice is deep and eloquent and commanding, like that of a practiced actor. Someone who is comfortable onstage or in front of the camera. He doesn't look famous, or like anyone I know, but his voice is definitely familiar.

When I glance back up the street, Scooter Girl is gone. I don't know what I thought I would accomplish by hounding her about working for Tommy Wong, but the thought of her getting away strikes me as a missed opportunity on multiple levels.

I look back at the Beefeater, who is staring at me so hard I'm afraid I might crack.

"You're not going to hit me or drug me are you?" I ask.

"Not unless I have to."

"Have we met?"

He gives a slight shake of his head. "Not in so many words."

Now I can add *cryptic* to the assortment of adjectives to describe what is turning out to be one of my more interesting days.

Another Beefeater, this one white and bald, sans the mustache and the NFL career, steps out of the Drake and nods at us. Rather, he nods at Gigantor, here. I just happen to be in proximity. But even though the second Beefeater doesn't seem to give me a second glance, I recognize him. It's Baldy from Union Square. The guy at Rulli's who was checking out Tuesday and followed her to the bus stop.

Before I can say anything or try to figure out what's going on, Gigantor takes me by the elbow and leads me into the Drake. "If you'll come this way, sir."

"Do I have a choice?"

"Not really."

This not-having-a-choice thing is becoming a habit.

He leads me past the downstairs lounge and around to the bank of elevators, then guides me into one of the cabs and steps in after me, pressing the button for the top floor. Harry Denton's Starlight Room. I don't know who's performing at the club at this time of day on an August afternoon, but I hope I'm not the warm-up act because I haven't prepared any new material.

We ride in silence as the elevator begins its ascent, the numbers counting off one by one, building to a climax that I'm not really interested in experiencing. But since I'm here, I may as well be Buddhist about the whole thing and try to make the best of it.

I take a few deep breaths and glance at Gigantor, my glance turning into a stare as I try to figure out what it is about him that seems so familiar. He doesn't look famous, but I know I recognize his voice from somewhere. Eventually he notices me staring and slowly turns to assess me.

"Did you used to play professional football?" I ask.

"No."

"Any college ball?"

He ignores me.

"How about sumo wrestling?"

He gives me a look that says he's getting annoyed with me. Yeah, get in line.

"You ever do any acting? Movies? Television? Stage?"

Nothing. Not even a sigh.

"What's your name?" I ask.

"I don't really think that's relevant."

I'm pretty sure we've never met. And I know I've never poached his luck. I'd remember someone like Gigantor. But I've definitely heard his voice before. Maybe in animation. Or on commercials or something.

"Do you do voice-overs?"

"I think it would be best if you stopped talking," he says, staring straight ahead, as if even looking at me is too much of an effort.

"You don't like me, do you?"

"Let's just say I find your lack of silence disturbing."

That triggers a memory that eludes me, hovering maddeningly just out of view, until I remember where I've heard that line before. Or something almost like it.

And then it hits me.

"Can you do me a favor?" I ask.

"Doubtful."

"Can you say, 'Luke, I am your father'?"

Nothing. Not even any deep, arrhythmic breathing.

"Okay, then how about 'This . . . is CNN'?"

He looks at me as if he's considering cutting off my hand with a light saber.

What a killjoy.

Before I can ask him to do one of my favorite lines from *Field of Dreams,* the elevator stops on the twenty-first floor. Probably for the best. Having him say *I'm going to beat you with a crowbar until you leave* is a little too close to home.

When the doors open, he gestures for me to exit, then follows me out of the elevator and into Harry Denton's Starlight Room, the nightclub atop the Drake with a 360-degree view and 1930s throwback style. Decorated in ruby reds and Egyptian golds, with deep-velvet booths and rich crimson silk drapes and signed celebrity photos in the bar, Harry Denton's looks like something you'd see straight out of a noir film. Standing at the bar with a half-finished cigarette and a full set of curves is a long-haired brunette in a formfitting, long-sleeve, black shirt; a tight, leopard-print skirt; black stockings; and high-heeled shoes that match her skirt. But I only notice her shoes because they're connected to her long, sleek legs. Which are connected to the rest of her anatomy.

When she sees me, she turns and offers a warm, million-dollar smile. She looks familiar, but I don't know where I've seen her.

"Mr. Monday," she says in a deep, breathy voice as she stands up and extends a hand with long, delicate fingers. "It's a pleasure to meet you."

"The pleasure's all mine," I say, then I fake a sneeze into my hands, which should get me off the hook for shaking hers. "But I'm afraid I'm at a disadvantage, Miss . . . ?"

"Knight," she says, withdrawing her hand. "But please, call me Tuesday."

19

"So, you're Tuesday Knight," I say.

Which explains why she looks familiar. Though it doesn't explain why there are two of them.

"My father's always been a big fan of Tuesday Weld," she says, taking a drag on her cigarette and pointing to several pictures of the actress on display along the walls of the bar. "So he convinced my mother to name me after her."

"I always thought she should have won the Oscar for *Looking for Mr. Goodbar*," I say, not really knowing why I'm saying it. But I have to say something until I can figure out what the hell's going on.

"That was my father's favorite film of hers," she says.

"And your father is Gordon Knight." I turn my attention back to Tuesday. The new Tuesday. The second Tuesday. Whatever.

She takes a drag on her cigarette and blows the smoke off to one side. "You've been doing your homework."

"Well, I wouldn't be much of an investigator if I didn't

know these things," I say, hoping the bullshit police don't show up and arrest me.

"Have you been investigating me, Mr. Monday?"

I let my gaze wander briefly across her breasts and thighs, then I glance over my shoulder, where I see Gigantor standing like a statue by the elevator, shaking his head in disapproval.

"No," I say. "Not exactly."

"Then what, exactly, have you been doing?"

I'm not sure which Tuesday I like better. At least the first one showed more skin and gave me a glimpse down her sweater and the promise of more glimpses to come. Of course, we're just getting started here.

"Just trying to make sure I've got things straight," I say.

"And do you have things straight, Mr. Monday?"

I sit down at the bar. "Nick. Call me Nick."

"Very well." She takes a seat next to me and stabs out her cigarette. "Why don't you tell me what you've been up to, Nick."

"I'm not sure I follow you."

"No. But you've been following someone who looks a good deal like me. Someone who's been using my name and social standing to get free hotel rooms and complimentary meals and pretty much whatever she wants."

Well, that explains why there are two of them. But it doesn't explain why the other Tuesday is pretending to be this one.

"I only met her today," I say, still trying to figure out

what I've gotten myself into. And if there's any chance of turning it into soft-core porn.

"How did you meet her?" says Tuesday.

"She came into my office."

"To hire you?"

I nod.

"What did she hire you to do?"

"That's confidential."

This time it's Tuesday who nods. "Although she's apparently been impersonating me for the past couple of weeks, I didn't know about her until I showed up at the Tadich Grill for lunch last Friday and the maître d' apologized for the misunderstanding about my previous bill. Over the past few days I've learned that she's eaten at more than a dozen restaurants and stayed at two hotels using my name. I wasn't able to track her down until she showed up at Rulli's in Union Square this morning."

That explains why Baldy took such an interest in her. And how I ended up here.

"So it seems," she says, "that you've been hired by an impostor."

I have to admit, this Tuesday seems a bit friendlier than the other one. Her face has softer lines and her shape has fuller curves and she has a scent drifting off her that makes me acutely aware of my own anatomy. Still, I'm technically working for the first Tuesday, so I have to respect that, even if I do want to sleep with both of them. Preferably at the same time.

That thought isn't exactly helping me to stay focused.

"How do I know you're who you say you are? How do I know you're not the fake Tuesday and she's the real one?"

She pulls out a driver's license from some hidden place on her body and shows it to me. The driver's license, not her body.

"This could be a fake," I say, knowing it's not but trying to act like I know what I'm doing. "And so could you."

"You'll just have to take my word for it."

"Yeah, well, in my line of business, I've learned that words don't mean much."

"And how is business these days, Mr. Monday?"

Maybe it's the playful tone of her voice or the way she raises her eyebrows after she says it, but I can't help but feel that she's talking about my poaching business.

I stand up and walk away and pretend to be interested in the collection of signed photos on the walls. "What exactly do you want with me?"

"I want to know who this impostor is."

When I turn around, she's still sitting on the stool at the bar, one leg crossed over the other, one foot bouncing up and down. It's hypnotic.

"I'm afraid I can't tell you that," I say. "She's my client."

"You don't understand. I want to hire you to find out who she is."

"You want to hire me?"

"That is what you do, isn't it? Investigate? Detect? Find things out?"

"On my better days."

"Then consider this a retainer for your services." She reaches into her leopard-print purse and removes an envelope, which she places on the bar and slides toward me.

I walk over to the bar and pick up the envelope, which contains in the neighborhood of two thousand dollars. Not the same neighborhood as what the first Tuesday paid me, but it's still got decent property values. Considering I was going to try to find out who the other Tuesday is anyway, the thought of getting paid for it seems like a bonus.

"All you want me to do is find out who she is?" I ask.

"That's it. And for that information, I'm willing to pay you another twenty thousand dollars. Double if you can deliver my doppelgänger."

The thought of sleeping with both Tuesdays runs through my head again and I wonder if it's something I could propose. I don't think that violates any sense of professional propriety. If it does, it shouldn't.

"Not that I don't appreciate the chance to take your money," I say. "But why pay me when one of your Beefeater goons could just grab her and bring her in like they did with me?"

"I heard that," says Gigantor from down the hall.

"You were an exception," says Tuesday. "And you almost literally fell into our lap. Plus you were rather compliant. Had you made a scene, this meeting would have taken place at your office."

"I take it you prefer to avoid any publicity."

"My father owns this hotel, which I help him to run. Sending out employees of the hotel or the club would lead to unwanted connections and exposure, so we'd prefer to have this taken care of out of house, if you get my meaning."

"I get your meaning. And it seems to me that keeping this hush-hush would be worth more than twenty grand."

She gives me a smile that's more condescending than good-humored. "If you even think about using my father's celebrity as leverage for more money, then the next time you see me, I won't be so accommodating."

The appearance of Gigantor at my side signals that our little meeting has come to an end.

"Sorry about the *goon* comment," I say to him. "I didn't mean any disrespect. Please know that I hold you in the highest regard."

He just looks at me with something that could be exasperation or disdain. It doesn't really matter. I have a way of engendering both.

I grab the money out of the envelope and stuff it into my pockets, then I thank the second Tuesday for her time and generosity.

"I hope this is one of your better days, Mr. Monday," she says, lighting up another cigarette. "I'd hate to be disappointed."

"That makes two of us," I say, walking past her and following Gigantor to the elevator.

"It was a pleasure to meet you, Mr. Monday," Tuesday calls out behind me. "Good luck."

Yeah. I think I'm going to need it.

20

When I get back to my office, the afternoon is halfway gone and so is the dead body. All of it. So I've got that going for me.

After discovering there are two Tuesdays, I almost expected to find two dead Asian double agents in my office, one in each corner like hot, decomposing bookends. It would have made for some nice symmetry.

But at least I have some spending money, which I should really put someplace safe this time so I don't lose it or get it stolen. The bank would probably be a good call, but the last thing I want is to have to report it on my tax return. So instead I file half of it in my filing cabinet under *T* for "Tuesday" and put the other thousand in my wallet. As an afterthought, I take out a hundred and slip it inside my left shoe. Just in case.

My phone rings.

"Nick Monday," I say.

"Why didn't you wait in your office like I told you?" It's Tommy. And he sounds annoyed. What a surprise.

"I did. Then I went out to lunch with the cute little poacher from Tucson you sent over."

"What cute little poacher?"

"I don't know. She wouldn't give up her name."

"I didn't send any girl to take you out to lunch," says Tommy.

"You didn't?"

"No. I sent one of my men. He said you weren't there."

"Then who was she?"

"How the hell should I know?" says Tommy. He pauses. "What did you tell her?"

Just that you're a murderer and an extortionist and a generally unpleasant employer.

"Nothing," I say.

"You better be telling the truth. Or else . . ."

"Yeah, yeah, I know. The whole dead-in-the-alley thing. I got it."

Silence on the other end of the line. I can feel Tommy's irritation pouring out of my phone.

"You need to learn your place," says Tommy.

"Funny, my father used to tell me the same thing."

More silence. My guess is I won't be getting Employee of the Month.

"Call me if you don't understand your instructions," he says.

And then he hangs up.

Instructions? What instructions? Why does everyone have to talk to me in ambiguities? Can't anyone just talk straight and be who they say they are and not threaten to kill me? And what the hell was Scooter Girl doing at my office if she wasn't here to take me out to lunch at Tommy's request? Though I do have to admit, that was a pretty good meal.

I sit down at my desk without turning on the light and pop two more Advil, then I wash them down with two sips of a cold double cappuccino from Starbucks. Although I don't have a headache anymore, I'm expecting it to come back, so I figure I may as well get a head start.

When I lean forward on my elbows with my head in my hands, I notice an envelope propped up against my laptop with my name written on the front in bold, black print. From the masculine shape of the letters, my guess is it's from Tommy. But the way things have been going today, I wouldn't be surprised if it was from Barry Manilow. Or Genghis Khan.

There's a knock at my office door.

If I were Humphrey Bogart, I'd pull my .38 out of my desk drawer and hold it low, pointed at the door, a cigarette hanging from the corner of my mouth. But all I've got is a plastic letter opener and a staple remover, neither of which shoots bullets. And I keep forgetting to take up smoking.

"Come in."

The door opens and Doug walks in, a big grin on his

face as he shuffles over to the chair and parks his multicolored ass. "What up, Holmes?"

"My blood pressure."

While he doesn't show up as often as he used to, Doug still likes to drop by every now and then unannounced. Usually at inconvenient moments, like when I'm in the middle of dealing with the Chinese Mafia. Or surfing porn.

"You need to watch that, Holmes. My dad had high blood pressure."

Doug's father died of a heart attack when Doug was ten, and he was raised by his mom. I think that's part of the reason why he comes around. I have this feeling I'm playing the role of a surrogate father, which is serious miscasting. I'm more like the slacker hedonist with patricidal urges.

"Thanks for caring," I say. "But it'll pass."

"Tough day, Holmes?"

"Nothing I can't handle," I say, scratching an itch in the palm of my right hand.

"Looks like you've got some people to meet."

"What are you talking about?"

"You just got an itch on your right palm. That means you're gonna meet someone new. If it's your left palm, money is on the way."

Figures. Not that I believe him, but like I need to meet anyone else today. And I could have used the money.

"Itching means all sorts of things," says Doug.

"No kidding," I say, eyeing the envelope, wondering what's in it, but I can't open it in front of Doug. He'll want me to play show-and-tell.

"Word. If your feet itch, it means you'll take a trip. If your nose itches, it means you're going to get into a fight."

Yeah, well, that already happened.

"And if your head itches, it means good luck."

I figure it means you probably have lice or psoriasis or seborrheic dermatitis and need a prescription shampoo. But what do I know?

"So what's on your mind, Bow Wow?"

"Nothing," he says, shrugging. Looking nonchalant in a guilty kind of way. "I just saw you cruising back from the Drake and thought I'd check in, see if you needed a hand with your case."

"Were you following me again, Bow Wow?" Every now and then, I catch Doug following me, trying to bone up on his PI skills.

"I was just in the hood, Holmes. You know, checking out the action."

Doug lies about as well as Pinocchio. "You can't keep following me around, Bow Wow."

He doesn't respond but just sits there wearing an expression like a scolded puppy.

I have to admit that in spite of his annoying propensity to insinuate himself into my routine, I've grown fond of Doug. Which isn't necessarily a good thing.

Growing fond of people and developing emotional intimacy is a good way for poachers to end up making mistakes. Or getting someone hurt.

"It's a matter of client confidentiality," I say. "I need you to respect that."

"Yeah. I know. I didn't mean no harm."

"I know you didn't. And I appreciate the enthusiasm. But right now, I've got some things I have to take care of."

We sit there and look at each other, me waiting for him to get the hint, and him nodding his head to some distant drummer. Finally he slaps both of his knees and stands up.

"Well, Bow Wow's got to bounce." He turns around and shuffles toward the door. He raises one hand in the air without looking back. "Later, Holmes."

Then he's gone.

I get up and walk over to the door, open it to make sure he's gone, then I close the door and lock it, smiling as I shake my head. Sure, Bow Wow can be a little exasperating and he needs an extreme makeover from the wardrobe fairy, but his heart is in the right place.

Maybe that's why I don't mind his coming around. He reminds me of what I'd like to be when I grow up.

I walk back to my desk and pick up the envelope, turning it over in my hands, wondering what's inside, not really sure I want to find out. But I don't really have a choice, so I tear it open and dump the contents onto my desk.

There's a single sheet of paper, folded in thirds; a business card for a limousine company with a note that says

Ask for Alex; and a key for a safe-deposit box under an account for Nick Monday at the Wells Fargo on Market Street.

I put the key on my key ring, which might not be the best idea, since the bad luck I poached has a way of making me lose things of value or have them just disappear, and the last thing I need to lose are the keys to my office and to my apartment. But at least this way I know where the key is. Much less likely to slip through a hole in my pocket or fall out when I'm being held upside down over a bridge by my ankles.

You never know.

When I unfold the paper, I find a list of a dozen names and addresses in San Francisco, most of them in Pacific Heights and the Marina, though a couple are in Telegraph Hill and North Beach. At first I'm not sure what I'm supposed to do with the list, until I notice the letters that correspond to each of the names.

H for "high," *M* for "medium," and *L* for "low."

It's a list of marks for me to poach from, and all but three of them are medium-grade good luck. One of them in Telegraph Hill and one in North Beach are low-grade, and the other, the one in Pacific Heights, is top-grade soft.

I stare at the list, wondering where Tommy got the names or how he knows what the grades are. Maybe he has some kind of a service working for him. Or maybe he stole the information from his hired luck poachers. But I guess it doesn't matter as long as the list is legitimate.

I look over the list, my gaze constantly drawn back to the name next to the letter *H,* excitement building inside me. This is the closest I've been to top-grade soft in more than three years, and my right hand is tingling with anticipation, like that of an adolescent boy staring at a *Playboy* centerfold. Only *my* soft-core pornography is names and letters rather than tits and ass.

I'm almost salivating.

For someone trying to give up the lifestyle, I'm not having much luck conquering my demons. It would be a lot easier if people wouldn't put a list of marks in front of me and extort me with dead bodies and threats against my sister.

I pocket the list and pick up the business card for the limousine service and dial the number.

"AAA Limousine," says a male voice. Unthreatening. Masculine. No accent.

"I'm calling for Alex. I was given—"

"One second, Mr. Monday."

That they know who I am doesn't bother me as much as the thought that all of this has been orchestrated without my involvement. I'm just playing along, following instructions, doing what I'm told.

I'm Renfield doing the bidding of Count Dracula.

I'm Igor assisting Dr. Frankenstein.

I'm an obedient dog complying with my master's commands.

Sit. Stay. Come.

Roll over. Speak. Fetch.

Just so long as no one asks me to play dead.

Still, I hate this lack of control. This having to bow down to someone else because he holds some kind of power over me. Ever since my mother died I've been in charge of myself. I had the ability and the confidence to manage my world without having to answer to anyone. Not my teachers. Not my counselors. Not my father.

In spite of his attempts to exert his influence on me, my father eventually realized that you can't have power over someone who has the ability to steal someone's good fortune with a simple, friendly shake of the hand.

Up until the day I moved out, my father refused to be in the room with me unless he was wearing gloves. And he never, ever touched me. Even when my mother died, he didn't offer any physical comfort. To me or to Mandy. When it came to emotional intimacy, my father was about as warm as frostbite.

I'm wondering if I'm more like my father than I want to admit.

"Mr. Monday?" a male voice says in my ear.

"Yes?" I say, trying to remember what I was calling about.

"This is Alex."

"Alex?" I say, still confused.

"I'm your driver."

"Right. My driver. When are you available?"

"As soon as you need me. Are you ready to go?"

"It looks that way. How soon can you get here?"

21

Fifteen minutes later I'm sitting in the backseat of a Lincoln Executive luxury town car, sinking into soft leather and surrounded with air-conditioning while being chauffeured up California Street by a twenty-something dude in a black suit and tie.

We're on our way to my apartment, where I need to clean up, change my clothes, and set up the luck-transference equipment before starting on the list of names Tommy gave me. In spite of my preference for casual-Friday attire, knocking on the front doors of multimillion-dollar homes wearing a sweatshirt and a pair of jeans with blood splattered on them isn't the best way to make a good impression.

Having a chauffeur drive me around town seems a little over-the-top, but I guess Tommy didn't want to trust the San Francisco public transit system to get me from mark to mark. I'm not exactly complaining. I haven't enjoyed this kind of luxury since before I left Tucson.

However, I'm a little disappointed. I was expecting a limo, with a minibar and a privacy window and enough room for me and a couple of strippers from the Hustler Club. Or maybe both Tuesdays, if things worked out.

"Is there something wrong, sir?" asks Alex, looking at me in the rearview mirror. Why he's looking at me and not the road I don't know, but apparently my disappointment is showing.

"I was kind of hoping for a minibar."

"Sorry about that, Mr. Monday. I'm happy to swing by a liquor store if you need anything."

"Actually, I need to stop at a Starbucks or a Peet's. Preferably one near a doughnut store. You like doughnuts?"

"Not particularly."

"I'm buying," I say, feeling generous. "Whatever you want."

"No thanks. I'm vegan."

"That must make it difficult to find a good doughnut."

"As a matter of fact, I just so happen to have plenty of recipes for good vegan desserts," he says. "And they're much better for you than doughnuts."

"Isn't that an oxymoron?"

"What?"

"Good vegan desserts?"

He gives me an irritated look in the rearview mirror. "Have you ever eaten vegan food?"

"Sure. I eat Lucky Charms every day."

"Lucky Charms isn't vegan. It has marshmallows, which contain gelatin, which is made from collagen in cow or pig bones."

"Well, that explains why they taste so yummy."

He continues to stare at me in the rearview mirror. "Maybe it's best if we don't talk about lifestyle preferences."

"Good idea. That'll help us avoid any awkward discussion about the fact that I work at a meatpacking plant." I never was good at letting things go.

"You know that animals raised in factory farms for consumption are pumped full of antibiotics, hormones, and other chemicals to increase production," he says.

"What happened to not talking about lifestyle preferences?"

"And they have vitamins added to their feed so they can be raised and kept indoors year-round, which increases the spread of disease, so they just pump them full of antibiotics to keep them from getting sick."

"That's very thoughtful of them, don't you think?" I say. "I mean, at least the cows don't have to pay for health insurance."

"And dairy cows," he says, blathering on. "The ones who provide the milk for your doughnuts? They're injected with growth hormones to double their rate of production. And they're raised in confinement and suffer emotionally from social deprivation."

"That's not so bad. At least they don't have to sit captive in the backseat of a Lincoln town car and listen to you."

"Plus they're impregnated continuously in order to keep up the flow of milk."

"Kind of makes you want to be a bull on a dairy farm," I say.

We stop at the red light at the top of Nob Hill, between the Fairmont and the Mark Hopkins hotels, and Alex turns around in his seat to look at me. "Don't you care about what happens to these animals? Don't you care about what you put into your body? Don't you care that all of these hormones and steroids pumped into milk and beef are causing girls to reach puberty in the third grade?"

"Don't you care that your parents raised such a douche bag?"

He turns back around and gives me a long, hard stare in the rearview mirror as the signal turns green. I really wish he'd keep his eyes on the road.

"There's a Starbucks and an All Star Donuts right across from each other on Chestnut," I say. "They probably get their milk from factory farming, but it's one-stop shopping before we swing by my apartment."

"Fine. Whatever you say."

I doubt that. But at least I'll get to eat my non-vegan, animal by-product apple fritter.

We ride in silence for several minutes along California through Nob Hill, past Huntington Park, coming full circle back to my first encounter with Tommy. I have a hard time believing that I was sitting on a bench in that same park barely more than four hours ago. It seems more like four days.

As we pass Grace Cathedral, I think about the trip I took in the sedan this morning with Barry Manilow, which gets me to thinking about my botched deal with the Feds about delivering the bad luck to Tommy Wong, which gets me to thinking about Mandy. And I'm wondering if I should fill her in on what's happening.

Part of the lifestyle I've grown accustomed to is only having to look out for myself. Once Mandy decided to eschew her abilities and pretend to be a normal person with a normal life, I figured that was for the best. I didn't need the headache of worrying about someone else or dealing with another person's problems getting in the way of my own happiness. Let Mandy's husband, Bill or Ted or whatever his name is, deal with her problems. Not me.

In the words of Paul Simon:

I am a rock. I am an island.

Except I can't ignore this problem. This is one I created. Or at least was involved in making. And if I'm being honest with myself, after the fiasco in Tucson, after I'd been foolish and lost everything, after I'd run away with the road wide-open in front of me, I could have gone anywhere. I could have started over in Utah or New Mexico.

I could have settled in Tampa or Charleston. I could have made my way up to Portland or Seattle.

Instead, I chose San Francisco, knowing Mandy had started her own life here nearly ten years ago, and that she had a husband and two daughters whom she didn't want exposed to the life she'd left behind.

As we turn north on Franklin and head toward the Marina, I find myself thinking about what I'm doing here. Not in the backseat of a Lincoln town car, though I suppose that's relevant to the situation, but in this particular city. When things went wrong, I found myself drawn to California.

Maybe I need my sister more than I'm willing to admit. Maybe I want to reconcile but I don't know how. Maybe I've been too consumed with my own path to realize that I've lost something important along the way.

In general, poachers aren't predisposed to a lot of self-reflection. It's bad for business. When you take the time to stop and think about the impacts you're having on the lives of those you poach from, about the path you've chosen for yourself, you start to realize what it is you're doing. The choices you've made and the questionable ethics behind them. And despite that I was born with this ability, I have a choice. Like Mom and Mandy, it's a matter of self-restraint.

Just because you have the power to do something doesn't mean you have to use it.

As we drive down Franklin Street toward the San Francisco Bay reflecting the warmth of the midafternoon sun, the sky opening up above us, clear and blue, I think about Mandy and I wonder if my moving here was about finding my way back to the life I'd built for myself, or if it was about trying to find my way back to something else.

22

After grabbing my cappuccino and apple fritter on Chestnut and changing into my charcoal-gray suit with a white shirt and a black tie, I decide to work the list by hitting up the two low-grade marks first, since you don't really want to go backward when you're serial poaching. Start with the lowest grades of luck and then work your way to the top. Otherwise, you end up with a bad taste in your mouth. Like drinking Guinness all night and then finishing off with a Pabst Blue Ribbon.

But before I start poaching, I tell Alex to take me to another address. One that's not on the list and one that I've only been to once before.

I ring the doorbell and stand on the front porch, hoping this time turns out better than the last. Then the front door opens.

"What are you doing here?" asks Mandy. No smile. No warmth. No enthusiasm. Just a suspicious look and a cold stare.

So much for the happy reunion.

"Is that any way to greet your little brother?"

She stands there in the doorway arms folded, lips pursed, not inviting me inside. It's about what I expected.

"Can I come in for a second?"

Mandy stares at me long enough that I wonder if she heard me. Or if she's thinking it over. Or if she's gone catatonic. Then she shrugs her shoulders and shakes her head and turns and walks away without a word.

"I'll take that as a yes," I say, stepping inside and closing the door behind me before walking down the hallway, the walls of which are lined with framed photos of Mandy and Ted and their daughters—smiling and happy and on vacation. Living normal lives. Doing normal things. There aren't any photos on the walls of my apartment. If there were, they'd be of me, alone, poaching luck or selling luck or with a catheter in my penis.

Not exactly Kodak moments.

I stop in front of one family photo at Disneyland where they're all wearing smiles so big they look like a paid advertisement, and I get a twinge of regret at the memories I've missed out on, then I follow Mandy into the kitchen, where I find her leaning back against the kitchen counter by the sink with her arms once again folded, giving me a stare so severe that I'm beginning to chafe.

"What are you doing here?" She doesn't even say anything about how good I look in my suit.

"Can't a little brother swing by to check in on his big sister without being accused of having an ulterior motive?"

"I didn't mention any ulterior motive."

"No. But it's implied in the tone of your voice."

"That's probably just your guilty conscience filling in the blanks."

"Or maybe it's just you jumping to conclusions."

"If I'm jumping to conclusions," she says, "it's only because I know where this is headed and I don't feel like wasting my time trying to get there."

My dad used to say that to me all the time.

"You know," I say, "I think this is probably the longest conversation we've had in the past ten years."

"Maybe that's because we haven't had anything to discuss."

"So let's discuss." I pull out a chair at the kitchen table and sit down, waiting for her to join me. I even nudge another chair out with my foot, but Mandy stays standing by the sink.

"So what do you want to talk to me about?"

"Where are the girls? Stephanie and . . ." And I can't remember.

"Stella," she says. "Stella and Stacy. Wow."

Well, at least I was close on the first one.

"They're at the movies with some friends," she says. "What do you care?"

"Have you always been this hostile? Or do you just reserve it for me?"

"What do you want, Aaron?"

My real name. Or at least the one I was born with. I haven't used it since I dropped out of college. As far as I'm concerned, Aaron died more than ten years ago. Which, I guess, is why I'm here. To see if there might be any chance of resurrecting him.

"I just wanted to see how my nieces are. Make sure they're okay."

"They're fine, considering you don't even remember their names. You asked about them earlier this morning. Or don't you remember that, either?"

"I remember. I was just—"

"Get to the point, Aaron."

This is the tricky part. Letting Mandy know what's going on without having her throw something at me. Like a cast-iron skillet. Or a hive of Africanized honeybees.

"Well, there's this little problem . . ."

"What a surprise," she says with a short laugh. "There's always a little problem with you. Only it's never so little."

"I know. But this time it's different."

"How is it different? Ever since high school it's been the same story, over and over and over. It's all about the money. All the time. Nothing else. The thrill of the score. The freedom. But where has that led you? What do you have to show for it? When are you ever going to grow up and learn that poaching isn't going to make you happy?"

"I know. That's why I'm going to quit."

"*You're* going to quit?" she says, sarcasm dripping and pooling on the floor at her feet.

"Yes. As soon as I take care of a few things."

"Oh, bullshit. I've heard that before."

"When?" I ask.

"Oh, I don't know. After every important event in my life that you missed because you were poaching. My college graduation. My wedding. The birth of my daughters . . ."

"I'm sorry, Mandy."

"You're sorry?"

I nod vigorously.

"For what?"

I realize I'm sorry for so many things that I don't know where to start.

"For not being there for you," I say. "For not being part of your life. For everything I didn't do that I should have done."

She continues to stare at me, only with less exasperation. "Well, that's a new one," she says, her arms unfolding, her palms dropping to rest on the edge of the counter. "You're never sorry."

We just look at each other, neither of us saying anything, but at least when I try on a smile to see if it works, she smiles back. It's just a little one, not much more than a twitch of the lips, but it's a start.

"Are you really going to quit?"

I nod. "Just as soon as I clear up a little problem."

She rolls her eyes. "What now?"

"Well, that's what I came here to talk to you about."

"And why did you come to talk to me?" She folds her arms again, the twitch of a smile waving good-bye.

"Because the little problem involves you."

"Me? How, exactly, does it involve me?"

Alex is outside waiting and my poaching clock is ticking, so I give Mandy the abridged version of Barry Manilow and Tommy Wong and the cylinder of bad luck. I don't tell her about Tuesday Knight, either of them, because, I figure, why upset her?

"Shit," she says, running her hands through her hair, her voice choked. She holds on to her head, staring at the floor, then she looks up and turns her frustration and glare toward me. "How could you do this to me?"

"It's not my fault."

"No, it's never your fault."

"I didn't do anything to bring you into this. Not on purpose."

"It doesn't matter if you did it on purpose," she says, her voice rising. "The fact that I'm involved, that *my family* is involved, is because you're here."

"But I'm trying to help."

"You can help by leaving."

"Mandy, listen—"

"Leave. Get out."

"But I—"

"Go. *Now!*" She raises her right hand and points past me to the front door. "And I'm not just talking about my house."

I know it's pointless to argue. It was pointless to come here. It was pointless to think that I could help. I don't know what I expected to accomplish by telling Mandy she might be in danger. I'd hoped to somehow make things better. Instead, I made them worse.

Which seems to be the flavor of the day.

"I'm sorry," I say, then I get up and walk down the hallway and out the front door, closing it softly behind me. But not before I hear Mandy start to cry.

23

After my failed attempt to reconcile with my sister, I'm not in much of a mood to poach. It's like pretending to enjoy sex when all you really want to do is go to sleep or watch *The Daily Show*. But I don't have a choice. Not if I want my life back. So I figure if I just suck it up and fulfill my debt to Tommy, maybe things will work out. Maybe I can disappear. Maybe I'll be able to find a way to keep Mandy out of this.

Or maybe there's another way.

"Take me to 1331 Greenwich," I tell Alex.

I don't know if this is one of the worst ideas I've ever had or just a really bad one, but I need to find out if young Jimmy Saltzman is carrying Pure. Not that I intend to steal his luck, but I just want to know in case of an emergency. In case I run out of options. In case I discover that I have less character than even my father thought.

Except I wouldn't be poaching Jimmy's luck for personal gain. I'd be poaching it for Mandy and for her family, to keep them out of harm's way. I'd be justified in my actions. Poaching with honorable intentions.

At least that's what I tell myself.

When the car pulls up to the corner of Greenwich and Polk, I take a swig of my cappuccino, then I get out and adjust my tie. Even without good luck in my system, I've been poaching long enough that I approach every mark with confidence. But as I walk up to the Saltzmans' front door, I feel like a nervous teenager going to pick up my date for dinner. Only my date is a ten-year-old boy with an attitude and a vein of pure luck running through him.

Or so I believe.

I realize that the superfluous sweating I experienced the first time I saw Jimmy could have been attributed to any number of factors. The weather. The walk from the Tenderloin. Getting drugged by Tommy. But my hunch tells me Jimmy's the real deal. Which is causing me to perspire just thinking about it.

Imagine that you've known about the existence of a magic elixir, a forbidden fountain of youth, and you're about to get a glimpse of it. To discover if you have the courage to deny yourself the temptation of taking it.

That's how I feel right now.

And, I have to admit, the thought of having another conversation with Jimmy has me a little freaked-out.

So I knock on the door and settle myself down and remind myself that I'm the adult here. I'm the one in charge. Plus this time, I'm more impressively attired.

When the door opens, Jimmy is standing a few feet from the doorway, staring up at me, a look of exasperation on his face.

"Remember me?" I say, all smiles and charm.

"I'm not a moron."

"I didn't mean to imply that you were."

"Then why did you ask if I remembered you?"

I notice I'm already sweating. I don't know if that's because of the suit or if I'm just having an allergic reaction to Jimmy.

"I just thought maybe you wouldn't recognize me because I'm wearing a suit this time," I say, gesturing toward my threads for emphasis.

"Yeah, well, it's kind of hard to forget someone with a fake name who smells like cat pee."

I give him a fake smile to go with my fake name and I wonder if there's any way I can give him a fake kick in the ass.

"Well, it's good to know that I made an impression."

He just stares at me. "What do you want?"

It's only been a few hours, but I've forgotten how adorable he is.

"Is your father home yet?"

"No. He's at work. He has a real job. Unlike some people."

For no good reason I can discern, I let out a nervous laugh.

"What's so funny?" he asks.

"Nothing. I was just remembering something that happened earlier."

"What was it?"

"I can't remember."

"You're kind of a freak," he says.

He has no idea how close to true that statement is.

First sweating, then laughter. Those are two of the symptoms of being in the presence of Pure. But even if I experience a nervous twitch or an unexplained body spasm, I'm going to want something more definitive to prove that he's carrying Pure. A sense of the quality of luck flowing through him. The only way I can get that is to shorten the distance between us, which is currently about six feet.

"When will your father get home?" I ask, taking a small step forward. Jimmy responds by closing the door halfway and watching me from behind its protection.

"It's none of your business."

I sense something that makes the hair on the back of my neck stand up. It could be him or it could just be all of the weirdness of the day coalescing into this moment. But I don't need to be psychic to know that Jimmy Saltzman is seconds away from calling out for his mother or closing the door.

So I decide to see if I can get a better reading and see what happens.

"How about your mom?" I say, taking another step toward the front door until I'm inches from the threshold. "Is she home?"

"She's busy," he says, and slams the door in my face. But not before I pick up on something that nearly knocks the breath from my lungs. A grade of luck more powerful than anything I've ever sensed before in a mark. An intensity and purity that surpasses anything I've ever poached.

The Holy Grail of good luck.

24

On February 25, 1999, Virginia Rivero from Misiones, Argentina, went into labor at her home and walked out to a nearby road to hitchhike to the hospital. Two men offered her a lift in their car, though Rivero was so far along in her pregnancy that she ended up giving birth to a baby daughter in the backseat. But she wasn't finished.

When Rivero told the two men she was about to have a second baby, the driver sped up, overtook the car in front of him, and collided with another vehicle. Rivero and her newborn daughter were ejected through the back door of the car, suffering minor injuries. Rivero flagged down another car and finally made it to the hospital, where she gave birth to a baby boy.

Virginia Rivero's daughter holds the record as the youngest survivor of a car accident.

Chances are, both Rivero's daughter and son were tracked down by luck poachers and relieved of their good fortune at some point before they reached the age of ten. I can only imagine what it would have felt like to have such virginal good luck flowing through me. The euphoria and the sense of power. The wonder of absolute purity.

I'm thinking about my grandfather and the look he would get when he told me his stories about Pure. How his cheeks would flush with color and the corners of his mouth would turn up into a soft, wistful smile. How his eyes would grow distant and misty, as if staring off at some fond memory.

Even though I don't have a mirror in the backseat of the Lincoln town car for me to see my reflection, I know now what it means to own that look.

Problem is, right now, the look is all I have. While poaching Jimmy's luck could conceivably help me find a way to keep Mandy and her family safe, there's no guarantee things would work out the way I hoped. Even if they did, I'd have to live with the shame of what I'd done. Plus there's the problem of actually getting close enough to grab his hand. So it's not like I have a valid dilemma. Still, it's tempting to think that if I could find a way to poach the Pure from Jimmy, I could solve all of my problems, get the half million from Tommy, and then live happily ever after in personal disgrace.

At least I'd have my health.

Instead, I'm poaching luck from people on a list given to me by a power-hungry Mafia sociopath while being chauffeured around by a militant vegan douche bag with a superiority complex.

"Hey, you know that factory-farmed pigs are confined in narrow cages and become crazy with boredom?" says Alex. "They're very social, affectionate, and intelligent, and they spend their lives in a space so small they can't even turn around."

"Why don't we play the quiet game?" I say. "You stop talking, and that way I won't have to scream at you to shut up. How's that sound?"

He gives me a quick glance in the rearview mirror, then stares straight ahead, sulking.

I'd give anything right now for a pulled-pork sandwich and a side of bacon.

Yummy.

We drive through Pacific Heights, past Lafayette Park and the Spreckels Mansion, home to romance novelist Danielle Steel. I tried to poach her luck once, but you seldom see her out in public without a pair of gloves.

I don't know if it's just a fashion statement or if she believes the tabloid stories about luck poachers, but it seems as though more people today are wearing gloves than they used to. Mostly movie stars and high-profile professional athletes, along with the occasional career politician. But not your average Joe or Jane. Even if they believe in the stories about us, they can't be bothered to take the necessary precautions. After all, people believe in earthquakes and epidemics and venereal diseases, too.

When it comes to disasters and tragedies and personal health, most people don't believe that whatever *might* happen *will* actually happen to them. It's just human nature. So they don't take precautions. They don't plan for the worst.

They don't get vaccinated. They don't practice safe sex. They don't keep an emergency supply of food and water.

So expecting everyone to walk around wearing gloves to protect themselves against luck poachers is about as realistic as expecting everyone to use a condom.

After the fiasco at my sister's and my encounter with Jimmy, my mood is subdued, so I decide to try to cheer myself up by altering the order of marks on the list. Instead of saving the best for last, I figure I could use a little pick-me-up right now.

Donna Baker, thirty-nine years old, lives in a blue, two-toned Victorian at 2470 Broadway, between Steiner and Pierce in the heart of Pacific Heights. According to Tommy's list, her luck is top-grade soft.

That's about the extent of what I know about Donna Baker.

I don't know what attributes she exhibited to warrant her grade of good luck. I don't know her history—personal, health, sexual. I don't know if she's liberal or conservative. Religious or spiritual. Vegetarian or carnivore.

All of these details make a difference. Not so much from a philosophical standpoint but from a physiological one. Political, religious, and dietary preferences have a significant influence on a person's mental and physical health and, consequently, on his or her luck. You get a conservative Republican and you end up with good luck contaminated with self-righteous hypocrisy. Poach from a fanatic born-again Christian and you get luck polluted with intolerant irony. And if you take your chances with a blue-collar noncarnivore, you could end up with someone like Alex the Vegan Douche Bag.

The last thing I want to do is poach luck from some uptight Christian conservative who doesn't get enough protein in her diet.

Unfortunately, I don't have the time or option to find out any of this, so I just have to hope Donna Baker is a moderate liberal, does yoga, and eats bacon every once in a while.

Still, in spite of everything, I have to admit I'm excited and even a little anxious. It's been a long time since I've poached top-grade soft. It would be like not having sex for three years and then meeting someone special and hoping you remember what you're supposed to do and how you're supposed to do it and that you don't do it too soon.

Nothing screws up your confidence like a premature poaching.

WE'RE PARKED ACROSS the street from Donna Baker's. Alex sits in the front seat and alternately stares at me in the rearview mirror while reading a copy of *Vegetarian Times* as

I drain the last of my cappuccino and finish off my apple fritter with a smile and a long, drawn-out "Mmm."

"Animal killer," he says.

"Douche bag."

I climb out of the car and walk across the street, stopping beneath the shade of an elm tree to collect my thoughts and put on my game face. Poaching luck is a lot like a job interview—if you don't make a good first impression, you're probably not going to get what you came for.

Grandpa used to tell me that. Said poaching luck was like any artistic endeavor. The more you practiced, the better you got. It was a gift, he said, to be nurtured and not taken for granted. Bad habits bred bad results.

Grandpa was always full of useful information.

Whenever possible, he would coach me on different techniques and approaches and the dos and don'ts of poaching:

Always act like you're in charge.

Keep your head clear and your eyes open.

And never poach under the influence of a woman.

Needless to say, my father tried to keep Grandpa away from me and my sister as much as possible, limiting my grandfather's visits after my mother died in the hopes that he could prevent us from following the poacher's path. But even though I only saw my grandfather a few dozen times and I was only twelve years old when he died, I still remember everything he told me.

That doesn't mean I always put it into practice.

After a few deep breaths and a quick adjustment of my tie, I walk up to the front door and ring the bell, hoping Donna Baker isn't married and doesn't have any children. Or at least if she does, that she's home alone. The last thing I want is another encounter like the one I just had with Jimmy Saltzman. Plus, parents are more wary and distrustful of strangers when their children are present. If her husband answers instead, then I'm going to have to abort, which means I won't be able to come back.

That thought almost ruins the good mood I've manufactured for myself. But when Donna answers the door alone, I'm confident this will be an easy score.

"May I help you?" she asks.

"Good afternoon," I say, extending my right hand. "My name is William Kennedy and I'm setting up a local Neighborhood Watch program."

People tend to trust someone trying to do something for the safety of the neighborhood more than they do a door-to-door salesman or a special-interest representative or a religious solicitor. And William is a name everyone seems to trust. It's nonthreatening and has a formality to it that puts people at ease. Likewise, Kennedy has a presidential appeal that still runs strong nearly fifty years after the end of Camelot.

When you're poaching luck door-to-door, trust is everything. You can't just pick a random name or crusade and expect people to relax when they live in a multimillion-dollar house and a stranger knocks on their door. Poaching is an art form, not unlike being on the stage. All you have to do is convince your audience that you are whom they want you to be.

"Nice to meet you," she says. She still doesn't trust me enough to offer her own name, but I'm not looking for that level of acceptance. All I need is her hand, which she gives to me.

Easy as pie.

Most people don't notice when their luck runs out, so to speak. It leaves without fanfare, like sweat through your pores or air from your lungs. Donna Baker might notice a slight temperature change or a momentary acceleration of her heart rate, but it's nothing the human body doesn't go through multiple times each day.

I, on the other hand, feel a surge of adrenaline through my arteries and organs and tendons. My lungs expand and my pulse quickens. I can feel my pores opening and my face flushing and the blood pumping through my veins. I feel all of this happening in the span of just a few seconds.

The problem is, it's been more than three years since I've poached top-grade soft and I'm out of practice. The sensations overwhelm me and I stagger back a step from the front door with Donna Baker's hand still clasped in mine.

"Hey, let go of me!" She yanks her hand away. Before I can offer up an apology or try to calm her down, the front door slams and the dead bolt clicks into place. But I'm too busy enjoying the thrill of scoring top-grade soft to worry about what happens next.

The initial moments after a successful poaching of top-grade soft are intense. Colors turn rich and vibrant and full of texture, like an IMAX movie in 3-D or a Van Gogh painting on acid. Half a block away, you hear a crow take flight, hear its wings flap, then a car engine comes to life. You smell the oil on the street and the coffee on your breath and the honeysuckle in the yard next door. Your pores release perspiration to cool your skin as the sun heats the air around you. You feel this. You experience every moment, every fraction of time. It's as if existence has slowed down and you're moving at twice your normal speed.

It doesn't last forever, this heightening of the senses. This immersion in perception. Being engulfed by colors and sounds and aromas. But for the moment, I'm a walking paradox.

I'm buoyant and grounded. Distracted and focused. Yielding and invincible.

Poachers have used a term over the years to refer to what we experience after scoring top-grade soft. How we feel. Where we go. Our personal nirvana.

A place we call Softland.

I don't know who coined the term, but it's been around since before my grandfather, and it's been used in a number of ways to describe the rush of having high-grade good luck flowing through your system.

Going to Softland. Tripping in Softland. Riding the Softland Express.

Though it isn't a good idea to let good luck, especially top-grade soft, stay in your system for more than an hour. The longer you have it, the more you crave the high of something you can't keep. Something that doesn't belong to you. Something that can become an all-consuming obsession.

More than a few poachers have gotten lost on the road to Softland and never found their way back. Good luck is like any drug. You need to know how to control it rather than allowing it to control you. I've never had a problem. I've never allowed myself to get swept up in the high or surrender myself to the ride.

But right now, after more than three years of waiting to get a ticket on the Softland Express, I don't want to get off.

In spite of the flood of invincibility that accompanies poaching top-grade soft, I know I'm pushing my luck by sticking around. So after one last deep inhale of honey-suckle, oil, and coffee, I turn around and head toward the Lincoln town car, feeling the pavement through the soles of my shoes and the blood rushing through my veins.

I don't pay attention to the approaching hum of tires on asphalt until it's too late.

25

A black, unmarked sedan with tinted windows brakes to a sliding stop in front of me. Both passenger-side doors open and two men who look like Jake and Elwood Blues, complete with sunglasses and ties but sans the fedoras, emerge from the sedan. I'm half expecting them to start dancing while singing "Soul Man" or "Shotgun Blues." Instead, each grabs hold of one of my arms without so much as a shuffle or a note.

As I'm being escorted toward the back of the sedan, I hear tires squealing and I look to see the Lincoln town car with Alex behind the wheel take off down the street.

So much for his tip.

Moments later the door is closed and I'm inside the sedan on a bench seat with my back toward the windshield, sitting next to Elwood Blues and facing Barry Manilow.

"What are you doing here?" asks Barry.

"Are you talking in an existential sense?" I ask as the sedan drives away from Donna Baker's house. "Why are we here? The whole philosophy-of-the-cosmos thing? Or are you being more specific?"

"Why are you here? At this address? Poaching luck?"

"Well, I *am* a luck poacher. Asking me why I'm poaching luck is kind of like asking a prostitute why she's having sex. It's just . . . wait a minute. That's not the right analogy. Let me come up with a better one."

"I don't want to hear your analogies," says Barry. "I just want you to answer the question."

"I thought I just did."

He lets out an exasperated sigh. "What the fuck have you been doing?"

"That's a long story." I lean my head back against the soft leather of the bench seat and close my eyes, relaxing into the luxury. "You wouldn't believe the day I've had."

The interior of the car smells like leather and sweat and body odor. Someone had a lot of garlic for lunch. Either that or they're warding off vampires.

"I'm not interested in your day," says Barry. "All I want to know is did you deliver the bad luck to Tommy Wong?"

"Sort of," I say, my eyes still closed.

"What the hell do you mean, 'sort of'?"

I wish he would stop talking. Or at least speak in hushed tones. His voice is like a cannon booming inside the interior of the car.

I can feel the car engine vibrating through the sedan's frame like a racing pulse. The sound of the tires humming on the asphalt is an angry swarm of bees.

"I mean he sort of drugged me and took the bad luck," I say, opening my eyes. "So theoretically I delivered it to him. It's really just a matter of semantics. How about we call it even?"

"God damn it!" Barry looks out the window with his lips pursed for a few moments before turning back to me with a scowl. "This is not the way things were supposed to go down. You've managed to turn this into a complete clusterfuck."

"So now we're pointing fingers?"

He continues to stare at me, unamused.

I think about breaking into "Can't Smile Without You" to cheer him up, but I can't remember the melody. So I run through the library of Barry Manilow tunes in my head, trying to come up with an appropriate icebreaker, then realize one of the songs is "Mandy," which I find kind of funny. Though I don't think either Barry or Mandy would appreciate the humor.

"Where did you get the ride?" he asks.

"What ride?"

"The one that drove you to your sister's and then to a house in Russian Hill, then pulled out of here like Mario Andretti when we showed up."

"Oh, that. I just felt like treating myself a little special today."

I look at Barry and notice that he has dandruff on his eyelashes. And he needs to exfoliate. And the pores on his nose are like tiny open mouths sucking for air.

He could really use a facial.

"Are you working for Tommy Wong?" asks Barry.

"Define *working*."

Barry gives me a look that tells me he doesn't have a dictionary. Either that or he has a limited vocabulary.

"Search him," says Barry.

Elwood reaches into the pockets of my suit jacket, both the exterior and the interior, and digs around, removing items, patting the pockets of my pants, then searching those, too. In my current frame of mind, it's more than just a simple patdown. His hands this close to me, searching through my clothes, fills me with a sense of being violated. Assaulted. Invaded.

I'm Normandy. I'm Palestine. I'm a rectum at a proctologist convention.

When Elwood finishes searching me, he's removed a Starbucks gift card, a roll of Mentos, a pair of Ray-Ban sunglasses, my keys, wallet, phone, and the folded list of marks, which he hands to Barry. Not that he hands everything to Barry. Just the list. The Ray-Bans, keys, wallet, and phone he gives back to me. The Mentos and Starbucks gift card he pockets. Asshole.

"Your brother's a more talented singer," I say to him.

"What?" says Elwood.

"Jake," I say, nodding toward the front passenger seat. "He's got a better voice."

"Who's Jake?"

"Though I thought you were great in *Ghostbusters*."

"What?"

"But *Caddyshack II* sucked."

The smell of garlic is definitely coming from Elwood. Which is probably why he took the Mentos. So I'll cut him some slack. Plus the joke's on him—the gift card from Starbucks only has seventy-five cents left on it.

"This is a list of poaching targets," says Barry, holding the list up for me to see, as if I didn't know what it was. I always appreciate a good demonstration of the obvious. "Where did you get this?"

"From an envelope on my desk."

He looks at the list again as if to confirm I'm telling the truth.

"Okay, how about this for an analogy?" I say. "Asking me why I'm poaching luck is like asking the mailman why he's delivering the mail."

Barry and Elwood don't respond but just stare at me.

"You're right," I say. "That one doesn't work, either."

The sedan continues along Broadway and across Polk Street. Outside, I see men and women walking past the Little Thai restaurant, crossing the street. I hear snippets of conversation through the windshield, and I see faces as clearly as if I were standing next to them. For an instant I think I see Scooter Girl standing out in front of Shanghai Kelly's Saloon. Then we're through the intersection and she's gone.

"What are you looking at?" says Barry.

"Nothing. Just enjoying the scenery."

"Well, you won't be enjoying it much longer. My partner is missing and we have reason to believe Tommy Wong has something to do with her disappearance."

I consider telling Barry about how his dead partner ended up in my office and that she was double-crossing him, but that would probably make things awkward.

I never was good at breaking bad news.

"The fact that you're apparently working for Tommy makes you an accessory to conspiracy, racketeering, fraud, extortion, bribery, kidnapping, and possibly murder."

"Is that all? What about global warming?"

"This isn't a joking matter," says Barry. "So you might want to change your attitude before you make things worse for yourself."

Honestly, why is everyone I'm meeting today channeling my father?

The late-afternoon sunlight outside the sedan is replaced by the artificial lights of the Broadway Tunnel as we hurtle under Russian Hill toward North Beach. I don't know how long this ride is going to last or where I'm going to end up when they decide to let me out, and I know I should be concerned. But when you've got 100 percent top-grade good luck pumping through your system, everything seems to take on a Bobby McFerrin quality.

Don't worry. Be happy.

Still, I realize I need to make a play here. Come up with something that will get Barry off my back and allow me to focus on dealing with Tommy. And keep Mandy from getting hurt.

"Tell you what," I say. "Let's make a deal."

"What do I look like?" says Barry. "A game show host?"

"Actually," I say to Elwood, "I think he looks like Barry Manilow."

Elwood looks at Barry, pushes his sunglasses down and looks over the top of them, and says, "Now that you mention it . . ."

Barry points his finger at Elwood and says, "Not another word from you." Then he turns his finger toward me. "What kind of deal?"

I don't know if what I'm about to propose will make a difference, if it will help to fix anything, but at this point, unless I decide to poach good luck from a ten-year-old kid with an attitude problem, I don't really have any other options. Or at least if I do, I haven't figured them out yet.

"I want you to leave my sister alone," I say.

A few days ago, even a few hours ago, I would have asked for immunity. For a new identity. For a house on Martha's Vineyard and season tickets at Fenway. Maybe even a lifetime membership to the Playboy Mansion. Actually, let's put that one at the top of the list. But all I want now is to try to make things right before they get any more wrong.

"You're not exactly in a position to name your price," says Barry.

"Neither are you."

I don't know if that's true, but it's what comes out of my mouth. Another side effect of poaching top-grade soft is that it makes you say stupid things with complete confidence.

Like politicians. Or professional athletes accused of taking steroids.

We emerge from the Broadway Tunnel into Chinatown and come to a stop at Powell Street, which ascends toward Nob Hill on one side and drops down to Fisherman's Wharf on the other. Barry sits across from me staring, waiting for me to blink first. But I'm not going to let him win this one. I can't afford to.

"Your sister is my leverage," says Barry.

"Does that mean she's the fulcrum?" I ask. "Or is she the lever and I'm the fulcrum? Or is one of us the mechanical force? And does that make you the load?"

I never was good at physics.

"I was thinking more along the lines of business operations," says Barry.

"I don't know about that. But I'm still thinking you're the load. A really big load."

Next to me, Elwood smirks.

"Think of yourself as the equity and your sister as the debt that has to be paid off to supplement my investment in you," says Barry, ignoring my comment. "She's what I'm using to maximize my gain."

"Well, the way I see it, without my help, you're going

to have a hard time building any equity. So if you keep leaning on your debt, you're not likely to get a return on your investment. Which means eventually you'll end up bankrupt." I don't know if that's right, but it sounds good to me. "Or another way to look at it is that my sister isn't any good to you as bargaining power if dangling her safety over me just pisses me off."

Next to me, Elwood fights to suppress a smile.

"You're pushing your luck," says Barry.

"I've been pushing luck most of my life. Why stop now?"

The sedan crosses Columbus and pulls over in front of the Garden of Eden strip club, across from the Hungry I Club, the Roaring 20's, and Big Al's Adult Super Store. If this is where they're kicking me out, it's a big improvement over Grace Cathedral. Not exactly the Playboy Mansion, but I'll take it.

"Let's say I agree," says Barry. "What are you going to do for me?"

Somewhere in the back of my head, my father is telling me I don't have the balls to behave like a real man. To accept my responsibilities. To suck it up and take what's coming to me.

"I'll agree to do whatever you want." I never was good at negotiations. "You want me to poach for the CIA or the FBI or whoever the hell you are? I'll do it. You want to use me as a scapegoat for whatever you have on Tommy Wong? Go ahead. You want me to tell you about the secrets of the poaching trade? I'm your man. Just back off my sister."

Nothing like agreeing to give up everything in order to try to win back your self-respect.

Barry stares at me across his pore-gasping, Transamerica Pyramid of a nose, his eyes blinking once, then twice, so slow it's like his eyelids are low on batteries.

"We're going to give this one more try," he says, pulling out a pen and a white business card and writing something down on the back of it. "You think you can follow directions this time?"

"I don't know. You think you can learn how to say *please* and *thank you*?"

Elwood coughs once into his fist in a valiant effort to cover up a brief explosion of laughter.

"Go to this address," says Barry, handing me the card and giving Elwood a glance of disapproval. "Show this card and try not to say anything stupid."

That's like asking a fish to try not to swim.

On one side of the business card is a handwritten address for 636 O'Farrell, and under that is what looks like someone's license plate: 2OZ LGH.

Two ounces low-grade hard.

While your run-of-the-mill bad luck can be offset with a healthy dose of top-grade soft, only an infusion of Pure can remedy the effects of low-grade hard. So despite the rush of the top-grade soft from Donna Baker flowing through my system right now, this doesn't exactly sound like my idea of a fun time.

"Just make sure you don't lose that," says Barry, pointing to the card.

I flip the card over. On the other side are just three black letters, raised and embossed on the white background: BGS.

I don't know if they're the initials for Barry's real name or if they're an abbreviation for whatever government agency he works for or if they stand for Bozo Goon Squad, but he still hasn't given me an answer.

"What about my sister?"

"I'm not in a position to make any deals. But just deliver the bad luck to Tommy Wong and you won't have any problems."

"You didn't say *please*."

"Pretty please. With sugar on top. Whipped cream and a fucking cherry, too. Now get out."

Then Elwood is opening the door and getting out of the sedan.

I step out onto Broadway, the sound of traffic and tourists and the smell of exhaust and sweat assaulting my heightened senses. I put on my sunglasses to block out the brightness of the colors and try to breathe through my mouth as Elwood slides back into the sedan. Before he can close the door, I lean over and look past him into the backseat at Barry.

"Hey, how's this for an analogy? Asking me why I'm poaching luck is like asking a federal agent who looks like Barry Manilow why he's such a complete dickhead."

Elwood smirks, then regains his impassive expression and closes the door. The sedan drives off, turns right on Kearny, and disappears around the corner, leaving me standing on the sidewalk in front of the Garden of Eden.

Some Italian huckster with slicked-back hair and a cheesy mustache is trying to talk me into coming inside to check out the merchandise. I have to admit, getting a lap dance while high on top-grade soft is tempting. You haven't experienced physical pleasure until you've indulged in carnal delights while riding the Softland Express. Yet another reason why so many poachers end up addicted to their product. It's like discovering the joys of first class and realizing you can never go back to coach.

So here I am, being tempted by the fruits of the human flesh in front of a strip club named after the paradise that man was allegedly thrown out of for eating the apple from the tree of knowledge, and I can't help thinking about the symbolism of my getting dropped off here.

As far as I'm concerned, Christian mythology is just that. Myths. Stories. Fables. Parables and metaphors designed to teach lessons about what it means to be human. And the lesson of the original sin is the curse of knowledge.

When that first apple was eaten, we absorbed its nutrients and it became a part of us. All of that knowledge of what we were capable of. The good and the evil. Once we've eaten from it, we can't uneat it. We have to live with the consequences of what we've done. There's no turning back.

Sounds familiar.

Personally, I've never subscribed to any kind of religion because, well, when you have the ability to manipulate luck and influence the lives of every person you touch, you tend to develop a belief in yourself as some kind of superior being. It just goes with the job description. You can't do what I do and think of yourself as normal. I exist in a different universe. The rules don't apply to me.

You can see why it's easy for me to get into trouble.

No one wants to confront his own shortcomings. Least of all me. I hate taking responsibility for my own actions. It's so much easier to pretend that the things I do have no consequences or ramifications.

Which is how I got into this mess in the first place.

With the late afternoon slipping into early evening, I don't have time to get a lap dance or stand here philosophizing about the moral implications of my lifestyle choices. I need to catch a cab to the Tenderloin and pick up some bad luck so I can prevent my sister from becoming collateral damage for my own hubris and desire.

I have a busy schedule.

I flag down a cab heading toward the Embarcadero and climb in the back.

"Where to?" says the driver.

I pull out the card Barry Manilow gave me, but before I tell the driver to take me to the address on O'Farrell I need to find out if the woman I thought I saw a few minutes ago was Scooter Girl, and if it was, I've got a few questions I want to have answered first.

"Shanghai Kelly's on Broadway and Polk," I say. "And if you flip a bitch and make that green light, there's a hundred in it for you."

The driver pulls away from the curb and makes a quick U-turn that gets us through the light before it turns red. I pull a hundred from my wallet and drop it on the front seat.

"Thanks," I say. "By the way, you're not vegan, are you?"

26

Another thing about high-quality good luck is that it helps you to make green lights all the way to your destination, so you get to Shanghai Kelly's just in time to see who you thought was Scooter Girl, and who turns out to be Scooter Girl, get on her scooter and drive off in the direction from which you just came.

"Follow that scooter," I say to the cabdriver.

"We're not really supposed to do that."

I throw another hundred on the front seat next to him. "How about now?"

After scooping up the cash, the cabdriver flips an illegal U-turn on a yellow light and heads back toward Chinatown. As we're driving down Broadway again toward the tunnel after Scooter Girl, my phone rings.

"Nick Monday," I say.

"What the fuck happened to you?" says Tommy.

"You'll have to be a little more specific there, Tommy. It's been one of those days."

"I got a call from your driver. He told me some men grabbed you in Pacific Heights."

"The driver's vegan. And he's a douche bag. Don't believe a thing he says."

"I believe who I want to believe," says Tommy. "Where's the product?"

"It's in a safe place," I lie. Other than Donna Baker, I didn't poach from any of the marks on the list.

"Have you deposited it at the bank?"

"It's on my list of Things to Do."

"Why haven't you made a deposit?"

What, where, why? It's always questions with these Mafia kingpins. And it's never anything like *How are you?* or *What's up with the ladies?* or *Did you enjoy the fruit basket?*

A little appreciation goes a long way.

"I wanted to complete the list first," I say.

"You haven't completed the list?"

"Still working on it," I say as the cab enters the Broadway Tunnel. "By the way, can you e-mail a copy of the list to me?"

"A copy? Why do you need a copy?"

"Just as a backup."

In the brief moment of silence on the other end, Tommy is probably realizing that I don't have the list. Either that or I lost reception.

"You lost the list?"

"It's in the car with the douche bag," I say. Which is

the truth. It's just in a different car. With a different douche bag.

"Where are you?"

"In a cab. On my way to North Beach."

"I don't like this, Monday."

"I don't like this Monday, either. Or is this Tuesday? What day is this anyway? I've lost track."

"You better make a deposit before the bank closes if you want to stay out of my doghouse," says Tommy.

And by *doghouse* he means *body bag*.

"Since when do I have a deadline?"

"Since now."

Then he hangs up.

It's already after five. I don't have time to properly process Donna Baker's luck out of my system and make it to the Wells Fargo on Market before six o'clock. My only other option is to give Tommy the stash of luck in my refrigerator and hope he doesn't know the difference.

Up ahead of us, Scooter Girl is out of the Broadway Tunnel and turning left onto Powell. I throw another hundred on the front seat for the cabdriver to beat the light.

My phone rings again.

"Nick Monday."

"Mr. Monday, this is Tuesday Knight."

"Which one?"

After a slight pause she says, "I'm not sure what that's supposed to mean."

It's the first Tuesday. The fake one with real breasts. At

least they looked real. But I'm not discriminating when it comes to breast implants. If it's a mammary gland, I'm a fan.

"Never mind," I say. "I'm just having trouble keeping track of the days."

"I'm afraid I don't understand."

"That's okay. Neither do I."

Scooter Girl turns right a block ahead of us. When the cab pulls up to the stop sign at the corner of Powell and Green ten seconds later, Scooter Girl is getting off her scooter in front of the Green Street Mortuary.

Even the symbolism isn't working in my favor.

"What can I do for you, Miss Knight?"

"I wanted to talk to you about my father."

And I'm thinking, that makes two of us. Instead I say, "I'm all ears."

Half a block down from us, Scooter Girl is locking up her helmet and fluffing up her hair.

"I was hoping we could meet," says Tuesday.

"Sure. My schedule's wide-open."

I don't know why I say it. I don't have time to meet with a woman who's apparently pretending to be Tuesday Knight. I'm following Scooter Girl. I have bad luck to pick up and good luck to deliver. Not to mention that I should really transfer the good luck out of my system before I end up addicted to it. Or pissing it into a urinal.

I can feel the two cappuccinos I've had since my last luck transfer already starting to bully my bladder into submission.

"Why don't we meet at my office in forty-five minutes?" I say.

That should give me enough time to get home and process Donna Baker's good luck. I don't know how I'm going to get to the bank in time to deposit anything into the safe-deposit box, but I'm sure I'll figure something out.

If not, then I'll probably be back here at the Green Street Mortuary on business.

"I was thinking we could meet for a drink," says Tuesday. "Do you know O'Reilly's?"

I watch Scooter Girl walk across the street, toward the sidewalk tables filled with the early-evening work crowd enjoying happy hour out in front of O'Reilly's Irish Pub.

"I know the place," I say.

"Good," says Tuesday. "I'll meet you there at six."

27

"Hey!" I shout as I run from the cab.

Several of the patrons out in front of O'Reilly's turn and look my way. When Scooter Girl sees me, she walks away from the entrance and meets me in front of the alley next door.

I probably don't have time to do this, but I don't know when I'll get another chance to confront her. Or ask her out on a date.

"What are you doing here?" she says.

"Top secret," I say, catching my breath. "I'd tell you, but then I'd have to . . . well, you know."

I give her my most charming smile and hope she reciprocates, but all I get is a cock of her head as she looks past me and sees my cab waiting at the corner.

"Were you following me?"

"No. I just happened to be in the neighborhood and saw you."

"Uh-huh. What do you want?" She's still angry about lunch.

"I'm sorry about lunch. I was out of line. It's none of my business who you work for."

"I told you, I don't work for anyone."

"Okay," I say. "It doesn't matter. You're a poacher. I'm a poacher. We should be on the same side. Let me take you out to dinner so we can talk."

"I don't think that would be a good idea."

"Come on. It's just dinner. It's not like I'm going to kidnap you."

She smiles. "Look, Nick. In spite of everything, you're kind of cute, and if the circumstances were different, I might consider having dinner with you, but it would never work out between us."

"Why not?"

"Let's just say it's complicated and leave it at that."

"But—"

"Good-bye, Nick," she says, waving her fingers at me. She doesn't move but just stands there, looking at me, her head cocked to one side.

I finally get the hint and walk back to my cab, feeling like the high school nerd who just asked out the prom queen and got totally rejected. When I slide into the backseat of the cab, Scooter Girl is walking into O'Reilly's.

I consider going after her to find out what she meant by *it's complicated*. And what was that *in spite of every-*

thing crap? But I can't afford to miss getting to the bank before it closes, not if I want to avoid ending up at the Green Street Mortuary, so I give the cabdriver my address and throw another hundred on the front seat.

Less than ten minutes later I'm at my apartment, where I fill another backpack with the bottles of low- and medium-grade good luck from my refrigerator, though I leave one bottle of lemonade because Tommy only had two on his list. Then I release Donna Baker's luck into a plastic water bottle half-filled with a mixture of water, ice, and sugar. The reason for the water is to dilute the urine. The reason for the ice is to keep the luck from overheating. And the reason for the sugar is to make the mixture sweeter going back down.

As a luck poacher, you never want to have to resort to emergency measures or quick fixes. It's always best to have a plan. But when you're making up the plan as you go, you have to improvise, and I can't afford to be out there unarmed while dealing with greedy Chinese Mafia overlords and dickhead Barry Manilows and multiple Tuesdays. Which means that sometimes, you have to do things you'd rather not admit to.

Like drinking your own urine.

When you don't have the time to properly process good luck or when you don't have access to transference equipment, drinking your own urine is one way to keep from wasting the good luck you've poached. If you weren't born with it, it's not meant to stay in your system and will eventually find its way out. But you can prolong the beneficial effects of the luck by reconsuming it.

If you're not interested in drinking it straight or mixed with sugar and water, you can run it through a carbon-based water filter to help remove the acid, the color, and even improve the flavor. You just don't want to let it sit because that's when it can start to breed bacteria.

Some poachers practice urophagia regularly, rationalizing that by consuming their own urine they're not only prolonging their luck high, but re-ingesting their own abilities. While no hard evidence backs up their claims of urinary self-actualization, the concept of extending the beneficial effects of poached luck through urine consumption isn't without precedent.

A tribe in Siberia that uses psychoactive mushrooms for ceremonial purposes often engages in the sharing and drinking of urine. Since the urine retains the intoxicating effects of the mushrooms, some tribesmen who can't afford the mushrooms drink the urine of those who can, while other tribesmen drink their own urine to prolong the experience.

Nothing like passing out cups of warm pee to get a party started.

Although this practice isn't observed regularly in most cultures, urine has been used for all sorts of purposes throughout the centuries.

In China, the urine of young boys is considered a curative.

In seventeenth-century France, women used to bathe in urine to beautify their skin.

In ancient Rome, urine was used to whiten teeth.

Just to name a few.

And I won't even go into the people who drink it for sexual pleasure or who get off by getting pissed on.

Other than a bacterial infection in the urethra or the high salt content, there's not much risk in drinking your own urine, so long as you don't drink it while you're dehydrated and you make sure to dilute it with water. Poachers who don't dilute their urine with water have been known to develop receding gums due to the high acid content.

Drinking my own urine isn't something I've ever had to resort to before now. But I don't have the time to properly process the luck into a consumable form, and as the saying goes, desperate times call for desperate measures.

Over the lips and past the gums . . .

It's not as bad as you might think. A little tangy, and I regret having had steamed asparagus last night, but I just pretend it's really bad lemonade and that helps to justify the aftertaste.

I need a breath mint.

When I get back to the cab, it's a quarter to six, and if I'm lucky, I can make it to the Wells Fargo on Grant and Market before it closes, which I hope will get Tommy off my back while I figure out how to infect him with the bad luck I'm supposed to pick up in the Tenderloin.

And I thought sleeping with multiple baristas was complicated.

We pull away from my apartment and race down Lombard and I'm sitting in the backseat with my backpack full of good luck, thinking about Tuesday's phone call and Scooter Girl going into O'Reilly's, and I wonder if there's a connection between the two of them. I wonder if they know each other. I go back over the day's events, trying to play detective. Find a clue. Discover something I missed.

In addition to heightening your physical senses, poaching good luck, especially top-grade soft, often provides moments of omniscient clarity; an almost godlike perception into situations that would otherwise be muddled or confusing. Moments and circumstances that seemed disconnected at the time suddenly become related, a series of events leading up to right now.

Except it's not always the same when you reconsume the luck.

I'm not getting that aha moment. I'm not having any epiphanies.

So maybe there's no connection. Maybe they don't know one another. Maybe it's just a circumstance diverting me from something else I should be focusing on. A smoked herring. Or is that a red herring?

I never was good with idioms.

I figure it must just be a coincidence that they were both going to be at O'Reilly's. Except the one thing I've learned over the years is that there's no such thing as coincidence. Scratch that. I've learned two things:

One, there's no such thing as coincidence.

Two, a lot of women like to be spanked.

Now that I think about it, I'm pretty sure there's one or two other things I've learned, but my memory isn't what it used to be.

Part of me wishes I'd stayed at O'Reilly's to wait for Tuesday to show up and see if she and Scooter Girl got together. Not in a lesbian-porn kind of way, although I wouldn't mind watching that, either. But I was thinking more along the lines of listening to them have a conversation. Not as entertaining, obviously, but more relevant to the situation.

But had I waited around, that would have meant risking the wrath of Tommy, and I couldn't risk having him more pissed off at me than he already is. Plus I really needed to pee. And I doubted I was going to see any girl-on-girl action. So I'm hoping I made the right decision. With my recent track record, I wouldn't lay down any bets.

The cabdriver gets me to Wells Fargo in record time and with another C-note in his pocket. Since there's no place to park on the street, I tell him to grab a cup of coffee or a burger or a quickie and come back to pick me up in five minutes, then I head into the bank to deposit my bottles of luck.

When I step inside the door, a tall, male employee approaches me in a canary-yellow shirt, black slacks, and a coordinating tie. He looks like an anorexic bumblebee. His name tag identifies him as Oscar.

"Welcome to Wells Fargo," he says. "How may we help you?"

"I need to access my safe-deposit box," I say.

He motions to the queue, which is five people deep waiting for two open tellers. "If you'll just wait over there, someone will be with you as soon as they're available."

I'm not interested in waiting. I have a date with a femme fatale.

"Look, Oscar," I say, hoping Donna Baker's good luck and Tommy Wong's reach have some influence here. "I'm supposed to meet someone and I'm in a bit of a rush. My name's Nick Monday and I—"

"Oh, of course. Right this way, Mr. Monday."

Well, that was easier than I expected.

Oscar leads me back to the safe-deposit boxes without signing in, takes my key, opens up one of the large boxes on the lower shelf, then leads me to a booth and stands guard outside while I fill the box with plastic bottles of liquid luck. Sixty seconds later, I'm done and walking out with an empty backpack while four of the five people are still standing in line giving me dirty looks.

Apparently, working for the Chinese Mafia has its perks.

When I step outside, my non-vegan cabdriver hasn't yet returned, so I stand on the corner of Grant and Market to wait for him, hoping he shows up soon so I don't end up missing my drink with Tuesday and her breasts.

Sometimes I just can't control my fixations.

I'm standing there less than a minute when someone calls out to me.

"Hey, Holmes!"

I turn to see Doug shuffling toward me, doing his best gangsta-rap walk with his pants halfway down his ass and a big grin on his face.

"I thought that was you," he says, giving me a knuckle tap. "What's the word?"

"Grease."

"Grease?" says Doug, looking completely baffled.

"Sure. It's the word that you heard. It's got groove, it's got meaning."

"I got no idea what you're talking about, Holmes."

"That makes two of us."

A cab comes driving down Market with its light off. It's not my cab. Apparently, the driver of my cab doesn't understand the meaning of a quickie.

"You look sharp, Holmes," says Doug with a big, ridiculous grin. "What's up with the threads?"

"I've got a hot date."

A streetcar rolls past, traffic moves east and west, everyone's going somewhere, and I've got someplace to be but I'm standing still.

A crow lands on the top of the street sign next to me and Doug lets out a whistle.

"What?" I say.

"That's bad luck, Holmes."

"What is?"

He points at the crow. "If it was two, it would be good luck, but a single crow means bad luck."

What a surprise.

"Three crows means health," he says. "Four means wealth, five means sickness, and six means death."

Well, at least there aren't six of them.

"But maybe there's another one around here somewhere," says Doug, looking up and down Market Street.

I don't care how many crows there are. It's after six o'clock and my cab hasn't returned and I don't see an off-duty one anywhere. If I don't get to O'Reilly's soon, my window of opportunity with Fake Tuesday is going to close.

"Hey, Bow Wow, you got any wheels?"

"Shit yeah. Right around the corner. You need a ride, Holmes?"

28

Doug's ride turns out to be a lemon-yellow Toyota Prius with a rear spoiler, mag wheels, and a vanity license plate that says BOWWOW. The custom eight-speaker stereo system with a subwoofer in the trunk is currently thumping out some unidentifiable rap song with a heavy bass line and lyrics that would make a cockney whore blush.

"I didn't know you could get a Prius in this color," I shout over the thumping.

"Custom ordered, Holmes," he shouts back at me. "It's a sweet ride, right? All the brothers think it's da bomb."

Doug has a way of peppering his urban speak with out-dated suburban-hipster lingo.

As far as I'm concerned, the car isn't so much of a bomb as it is a public nuisance. The thundering stereo system has me looking around to make sure we're not being stalked by dancing elephants. Fortunately, it's just a five-minute ride to O'Reilly's. But I've still got three minutes to go and Doug is trying to sing along to the lyrics in a way that makes me realize he could use a coolness intervention.

"Hey, Doug."

"Bow Wow, Holmes. Ain't no Doug around here."

"Right. Sorry. Bow Wow," I say, turning down the volume until the dancing elephants become gorillas at a ballet recital. "Can I ask you something?"

"Say what's on your mind, Holmes. Dr. Bow Wow is *in*."

"Right," I say, wondering how the doctor is going to react to my analysis. "Look, I know it's probably none of my business, but why are you doing this?"

"Because Bow Wow's got your back," he says, making a fist in a show of solidarity. Either that or he just had a seizure. "You're on the case, Bow Wow's gonna back you up."

"I don't mean giving me a ride. I mean this," I say, gesturing to everything inside his car.

He shrugs and smiles. "I'm not diggin' your meaning, Holmes."

"I mean this persona you've created. The clothes. The voice. The car."

It sounds harsh coming out of my mouth, even to me, but this has to stop.

"What's wrong with the car?" he says, his smile faltering.

"It's a little bright. And this music. It can't be good for you. I think it's taken three years off my life already. Have you ever listened to Green Day or the Pixies?"

"I don't know what you're talking about, Holmes," he says, his shoulders sagging more than normal, the perpetual smile gone from his face. He reaches over and turns the volume up and brings back the dancing elephants.

Maybe this isn't a good idea. Maybe I should just leave it alone. But now that I've started it, I can't let it go.

I turn the music back down.

"Listen, Doug."

"It's Bow Wow," he says, like a scolded child, sulking and looking straight ahead.

"How long have we known each other?"

"I don't know. Couple of years."

"And in that time have I ever steered you wrong?"

"I don't know," he says. "I guess not. Though there was that time you told me women liked it when men waxed their nuts."

"I mean besides that?"

"No, not that I can remember. But that really hurt."

"I'm sure it did," I say. "But what I'm trying to say is that this, the clothes and the bling and the car, it's not a good look for you. To be honest, it's not a good look for anyone. And while I admire the effort you've put into it, I don't believe it's who you are inside."

The car suddenly comes to a stop.

"We're here," he says.

I look out the windshield and see the crowd of happy-hour revelers gathered out in front of O'Reilly's. It's ten after six. Scooter Girl's ride is gone from in front of the mortuary and I'm hoping Tuesday is still somewhere inside.

Bow Wow just sits there, staring straight ahead, thumbs tapping on the steering wheel to the beat of some song about bitch-slappin' and cop-killin'. Good, wholesome lyrics. The kind of music you hope your kids grow up listening to. I figure Doug's not going to answer me, so I open the passenger door and get out.

"You're wrong, Holmes. This *is* who I am."

I look in at him, still staring straight ahead, and I realize I don't have a valid response.

"Thanks for the ride, Bow Wow."

Then I close the door and he's driving away and I'm walking through the horde of happy-hour drinkers into O'Reilly's.

29

Inside O'Reilly's, the cacophony of conversations is almost enough to make me appreciate Doug's choice in music, but I manage to avoid concentrating on specific voices, and all the conversations blend into a constant background murmur.

On the bar's stereo system, Jimmy Buffett is singing "Why Don't We Get Drunk and Screw?"

The left side of the wraparound bar is dominated by a mahogany back bar with a canopy supported by pillars and illuminated stained-glass panels. Opposite the bar, the walls and drinking nooks are plastered with old photos and framed pictures of Ireland and Irish celebrities, while covering the corner walls at the back of the bar is a hand-painted mural of famous Irish writers, including Oscar Wilde, W. B. Yeats, and Samuel Beckett.

At the moment, I feel a bit like a character out of a Beckett play, looking for meaning in the obstacles and distractions of my existence. I don't know if my coming here is a fruitless attempt to find some answers, if I'm only waiting for Godot, but I have my doubts that anyone here is going to be saved. Either way, today has most definitely been the theater of the absurd.

One of the characters in *Waiting for Godot,* Lucky, was apparently so named because, according to Beckett, he was lucky to have no more expectations.

If only I was so fortunate.

I find Tuesday, the fake one, sitting at the far end of the bar near Oscar Wilde with a half-empty beer in front of her. I glance around the bar, but Scooter Girl is nowhere to be seen.

The thought that the two of them might be connected continues to knock around inside of my head, and I'm more than curious as to Scooter Girl's motivations. What is it about her situation that's so complicated she couldn't have dinner with me? But at the moment, I'm more interested in finding out what Tuesday wants and why she's pretending to be the mayor's daughter.

"Sorry I'm late," I say, sitting down on a stool next to her. "Something suddenly came up."

"That's the same thing I say when I want to get rid of men like you," she says, taking a sip of her beer.

On the bar's stereo system, Jimmy Buffett has better odds of getting laid than I do.

"Maybe I misunderstood," I say, stealing a glance down her V-neck sweater. "But didn't *you* invite *me* out for a drink?"

"To discuss business. Not for your company."

"Well, they say honesty is the foundation of any good relationship. So at least we're off to a good start."

She laughs and takes another drink. "Nice suit, by the way."

"You dig me. You just don't know it yet."

In front of me on the bar is a small brass plate that says THIS SEAT IS RESERVED FOR CHOCOLATE DICK. I don't know who Chocolate Dick is, but I bet he's popular with the ladies.

I order a Guinness from the bartender, then I turn back to Tuesday and catch her watching me before she looks away. Not with a look of desire, but more with a look of distaste. Which doesn't bode well for my chances of getting more than a glimpse of her cleavage.

"I figured you as more of the martini type," I say, indicating her pint of beer. "Fund-raisers, box seats at the symphony, stiffs in tuxedos."

"Never acquired a taste for them."

"Martinis or stiffs in tuxedos?"

"Both," she says.

"So you prefer beer and detectives in suits?"

"Just beer." She finishes off the rest of hers in two swallows.

I take the opportunity to steal another peek at her breasts. Actually, it's more like a lingering stare than a peek. Long enough for me to determine that she has a mole on the inside of her left breast. Long enough for me to notice the outline of a nipple in the fabric of her sweater. Long enough for her to notice me staring.

"So about your father," I say, getting down to business as my Guinness arrives and Tuesday orders another Stella.

"What about him?" says Tuesday.

"I thought you wanted to talk about him. Discuss your case."

"Not here. This place is too public. Too many eyes and ears."

I glance around at the people at the bar and sitting at the tables in the handful of nooks, drinking their beers and having normal conversations about normal lives. I bet some of them are even going to get laid.

"Then why did you ask me to meet you here?"

"Because I was thirsty."

Her second beer arrives, which apparently turns out to be her third, and I notice for the first time that Tuesday's a little tipsy. I also notice that her sweater is sliding off one shoulder, revealing a glimpse of her black bra strap.

When it comes to women, men love to catch glimpses of three things: bra straps, panties, and tattoos. They create a sense of discovery about what other treasures might be hidden. Which is half the fun of undressing a woman, both physically and mentally. The anticipation of what you might find. When you see a man checking out a woman, he's either storing up information for a masturbation session or he's hoping her clothes will miraculously fall off.

Right now, I'm multitasking.

"So tell me about yourself, Mr. Monday," she says, taking a drink, oblivious to the effect her exposed bra strap is having on me.

"What do you want to know?"

"Oh, I don't know." She gives me a sultry glance that makes me wonder if she's bipolar or just playing hard to get. "Amuse me with your personal history."

So we spend most of her third Stella and my first Guinness discussing my childhood, where I grew up, where I've lived, how long I lived in Tucson, why I moved to San Francisco, what made me become a detective. I fabricate most of the answers because I'm not about to tell her the truth since I don't trust her. She doesn't seem to notice. Just orders up another round of drinks and keeps asking me questions and I keep answering, both of us ignoring the white elephant in the room.

Wait. That's not right. A white elephant is a party where you bring a used or worthless gift to exchange for another used or worthless gift. This is just a regular elephant we're ignoring. Lingering about, waving its trunk, batting its eyes, then leaving a big, steaming pile of excrement on the floor.

Or maybe I'm the only one ignoring the elephant since Tuesday doesn't know that I know the truth about who she is. Or rather, who she isn't. Except I'm not even sure what the truth is, only that she's apparently not who she claims to be. I don't know why she's here or how come she's impersonating the mayor's daughter. And since I'm the only one of us who's aware of this information, then technically

I'm the only one avoiding it, so maybe there isn't any elephant to ignore.

Stupid idioms.

By the time I've finished my second Guinness and Tuesday's almost drained her fourth Stella, it's seven o'clock and happy hour's over and I'm still no closer to figuring out who she is or what she wants or how I can get my hands on her breasts.

I can't help it. It's just innate. Like breathing.

Some men like legs. Others prefer butts. Some are tits-and-ass men, which I can respect, but you should really make up your mind. Choose a body part and stick with it. I've heard a few men have a thing for necks. Which I find completely baffling.

I've always been a breast man. Big breasts. Small breasts. Real breasts. Fake breasts. Breasts of any shape, size, or color. I even prefer them when it comes to dinner. If it's a turkey, give me a breast. If it's a chicken, ditto. A duck? You bet. I've never had a pig breast, but if someone ever served one up, I'd be first in line.

"Would you like to go someplace more private where we can discuss my father?" asks Tuesday. "Or would you prefer to stay here and stare at my breasts?"

At least I'm predictable.

"How about we go someplace more private where I can stare at your breasts."

"I'm sure you're going to stare at them no matter the venue. So I suppose it doesn't really matter."

"How about my office, then?"

I'd take her back to my apartment, but that would be breaking one of the cardinal rules of poaching: never let anyone know where you live. Or maybe that's just my rule. Besides, I don't think she'd appreciate my six hundred square feet of drug-infested heaven.

"Fine." She pulls out her cell phone. "I'll call a cab."

I settle the tab while Tuesday calls a cab, then she goes to use the restroom and I try to figure out my next move. I could continue to play along, pretend I don't know that she's impersonating the mayor's daughter, and see where it leads. Plus she's had enough to drink that I'm pretty confident sex isn't entirely out of the question. I'd give it a better than fifty-fifty chance. But sex isn't a good idea for all sorts of reasons.

One, I don't have time.

Two, I can't think of a good second reason. And the first reason is negotiable.

"I told the cab to meet us at the corner," says Tuesday, returning from the restroom.

"Perfect." I offer her my arm, which, oddly enough, she takes.

We walk out of O'Reilly's into the relative tranquillity of the early San Francisco evening, the shadows stretching across the city, and head away from the crowds and traffic of Columbus Avenue toward Powell Street. A cab is already sitting at the corner on the opposite side of the street, so we cross over until we're passing in front of the Green Street Mortuary parking lot, which sits deserted. No one is within a block of us. It's just Tuesday and me, weaving down the sidewalk. More than once she stumbles and falls into me, so I, being the perfect gentleman, put my arm around her waist to hold her up and cop a feel.

"I think I had too much to drink," she says.

She staggers again, one hand reaching around and grabbing on to me, and I smell the beer on her breath and the shampoo in her hair. Her body presses against mine and I feel her soft curves, the warmth of her flesh, and her heart pounding, fast and rhythmic, like a long-distance runner's.

Even without the heightened perceptions of Donna Baker's high-grade good luck, being this close to Tuesday is intoxicating. It's all I can do to maintain my self-control. I know I'll probably kill any chance I have of discovering her hidden treasures if I divulge that I know she's a phony, but I need to find out what she wants from me and why she's pretending to be someone else.

"You know," I say as we approach the front bumper of the cab, "for someone impersonating the mayor's daughter, you should really learn how to hold your—"

Before I can react, Tuesday pivots around and knees me in the balls. I let out a sound like a baby seal calling out to its mother and I fall over as the driver-side cab door opens and Scooter Girl steps out.

I wonder if this is what she meant by *it's complicated*.

I'm on the ground, curled up in a fetal position, whimpering, with Tuesday leaning over me, her breasts hovering above my face. But I'm in so much pain, I can't appreciate the view.

Tuesday grabs a handful of my hair, pulls my head off the sidewalk, leans in close and whispers, "That's for my father, you son of a bitch."

Then my head is slamming into concrete and everything goes black.

30

When I wake up, I can barely move. Part of the reason is that the slightest movement sends tendrils of ball-tugging agony snaking through my groin and up into my abdomen and causes me to throw up a brown, foamy liquid that looks too much like Guinness to be anything else. My lack of mobility isn't helped by the fact that my hands and ankles are bound with zip ties.

This getting-kidnapped thing is becoming a habit. And not nearly as enjoyable as apple fritters or corporate-coffeehouse baristas.

I'm on my side on a concrete floor in what I'm guessing is some kind of a warehouse, which from my limited vantage point appears empty except for me. Fluorescent lights hang from the ceiling, but they're turned off. Fading daylight filters in through the skylights. I hear something that sounds like water, waves lapping at a building, which makes me think I'm in a vacant warehouse on one of the piers. I don't know how much time I've lost, but from the soft, orange light coming in through the skylights, I'm guessing it's pushing sunset.

My head is throbbing and my throat is burning and my mouth tastes like the inside of a Dumpster. Not that I've ever tasted the inside of a Dumpster, but I imagine it would probably taste something like what my mouth tastes like now.

I'm cursing Elwood for taking my Mentos.

I try to get my knees under me so I can sit up, but the effort is more than my testicles can handle, so I just lie on the concrete and let out a groan.

"Good, you're awake," says a woman's voice from somewhere behind me. Then I hear shoes clicking on the concrete, and a moment later a pair of red heels and creamy-white feet come into view. The feet are attached to legs, which disappear into a red circle skirt, and before I get to the bountiful cleavage inside the black V-neck sweater, Tuesday crouches down and looks at me. Only instead of a brunette, she's now a blonde.

"Sorry about smacking your head on the sidewalk," she says. "Chalk it up to a lot of repressed hostility."

"I notice you're not apologizing for turning me into a eunuch." The words come out in a raspy whisper. I sound like Louis Armstrong with laryngitis. Or Don Corleone with strep throat.

"No, that you had coming." Tuesday stands up and walks past me. She comes back a moment later with a folding metal chair, which she sets in front of me before sitting down on it, crossing her legs.

I'm still lying on my side, my face inches from the pool of regurgitated Guinness and something that looks like peanuts. I don't remember eating any peanuts, which bothers me, but I suppose I should be worrying about other things at the moment rather than what I had for dinner.

Tuesday just sits there, watching me, wearing a faint smile, one ankle bouncing up and down to the beat of some distant, unheard music.

"Isn't this kind of cliché?" I ask, my voice slowly returning.

"Which part?"

"Good point. But I was referring to the hero tied up in an empty warehouse. Where are the implements of torture and the briefcase full of money?"

"First of all, you're no hero," says Tuesday. "As for the implements of torture, let's just say you'll get what you deserve. And if you're thinking you can buy your way out of this, forget it. This is where it ends for you."

I'm hoping she's wrong. I've got tickets to the Giants and Dodgers game on Friday night. And I still haven't seen *Wicked*.

"I liked you better as a brunette," I say.

She smiles and runs a hand through her hair. "It served its purpose. Besides, we really do have more fun."

I should have known from her blond eyebrows the first time we met that she was a fake, but I was too distracted by her breasts. And the jury's still out on those.

"So who are you?" I ask.

"Doesn't matter. It wouldn't mean anything to you anyway."

At the moment, the only thing that means anything to me is making it to my next birthday.

"Then I take it you weren't interested in retrieving your so-called father's luck."

"Gordon Knight's political tailspin just provided my cover. If the last person anyone saw you with was me, they'd identify the mayor's daughter. No one would even know who I was."

"So what do you want from me?" I ask, half into the concrete. It's not easy talking when you're lying on your side with your hands and ankles bound while your testicles feel like they've been pounded with a meat tenderizer.

"For a detective, you're not very perceptive."

"Yeah, well, for a hot-looking chick you're not very personable." It's all I can come up with on short notice.

Tuesday just laughs at me.

"Okay, for starters," I say, trying to redeem what little pride I have, "I know you and Scooter Girl are working together."

"Scooter Girl?"

A door opens and closes somewhere behind me, followed by the approach of footsteps. Moments later, Scooter Girl is standing next to Fake Tuesday in jeans, sweatshirt, and tennis shoes and wearing a small leather backpack.

"Everything taken care of?" asks Tuesday.

Scooter Girl nods, then looks at me and cocks her head, as if she's empathizing with my current horizontal position. "How are you feeling?"

"I've been better."

She gives me a smile, and in spite of my current predicament, I still can't help but think that there's something here worth pursuing. Sure, she lied to me and got me beat up by a bunch of teenage skate punks and helped to kidnap me, but every relationship has issues that need to be worked out.

"I guess this is what you meant when you said it was complicated."

Scooter Girl smiles, then cocks her head again. "You know, it's kind of a shame. He *is* kind of cute."

"Please," says Tuesday. "Don't make me gag. And speaking of gags, get out the duct tape and let's get on with it."

"Wait a minute," I say. "Can't we talk about this?"

"There's nothing to talk about," says Tuesday. "There's nothing you can say that will change what you did."

"Look," I say, "I know you're both working for Tommy Wong—"

"We don't work for Tommy Wong," says Tuesday.

"Then why did you take me out to lunch?" I say to Scooter Girl.

"I didn't say anything about lunch. You did. I just played along."

I think back to the conversation, replaying it in my head, but I can't remember who said what first. No surprise, considering I was still coming to terms with having a dead body behind my desk.

"So why were you at my office?"

"Following up. Finding out where you were from. Making sure we had the right guy."

"The right guy for what?" I ask. "What the hell kind of poachers are you?"

"We're not poachers," says Tuesday.

"You're not?"

Scooter Girl shakes her head.

"What about the skateboarder on Lombard? I saw you poach his luck."

"I just shook his hand. You presumed the rest. Like the lunch."

If I wasn't confused before, I'm completely lost now.

"I've studied poachers for the last three years," says Scooter Girl. "Learning what you do and how you do it. All I had to do was make you think I was stealing his luck. It was all part of the act."

"Act?"

Tuesday looks at me and laughs. "Oh my God. You don't really think she likes you, do you?"

I look at Scooter Girl, who just smiles and shrugs. "I spent three years in the theater program at U of A."

So much for my instincts.

"But if you weren't there to poach that kid's luck, then why were you there?"

"I was keeping an eye on you," she says. "And confirming our suspicions."

"Suspicions?"

"Of who you were," says Tuesday.

"You were following me?"

Scooter Girl nods. "Ever since my sister left your office."

"Your sister?" I say, looking from Scooter Girl to Fake Tuesday.

"We're from Tucson," says Tuesday. "We grew up there."

"Tucson?" I look back and forth between the two of them, trying to figure out what I'm missing. "So I take it you didn't come to San Francisco to work for Tommy Wong?"

"No," says Scooter Girl. "We came here to find you."

"To find me? For what?"

Tuesday gets up and walks over to me, then squats down and grabs me by the hair. "For what you did to our father."

"Your father?" I say, my eyes closed and my face scrunched up, hoping this isn't going to be a repeat of having my head slammed against the ground. "Who's your father?"

Tuesday lets out a bitter laugh and lets go of my hair. I open my eyes as she walks out of view, then Scooter Girl walks over to me in her sneakers and jeans and leans down.

"What did I do?" I ask.

"You killed our father."

"What? I didn't kill anyone. You have the wrong guy. I don't even know who your father is."

"No, but the person you poached bad luck for in Tucson does. Or should I say, he did." Scooter Girl gives me a wicked smile.

And then it finally dawns on me.

The bad luck I poached three years ago in Tucson was used to kill their father, and they found me through my buyer, who I'm guessing is no longer in the present tense. And I'm about to join him. Not that I have anything against the past tense. He said. She said. They were. I was. People get along just fine with the past tense. But I prefer the present tense, especially when there's a possibility I won't have any future tense.

I never was good with grammar.

"We spent the past three years tracking down your buyer and then you," says Scooter Girl. "It wasn't easy. But my sister refused to give up. Said we owed it to Dad. And she was right."

No matter how far you go, sooner or later, your past is bound to catch up with you.

"It's too bad," she says. "You really are kind of cute. But like I said, I don't have sex with men who poach bad luck."

Somewhere behind me, I hear a door open and the sound of water increases in volume.

"Look, I didn't know what the bad luck was going to be used for," I say. "I never know what my buyers are going to do with the luck they purchase."

Scooter Girl shrugs off her backpack and opens it. "That's kind of like a gun dealer not taking responsibility for the people his merchandise kills, don't you think?"

Before I can offer up a rebuttal and grovel for my life, Tuesday is behind me and Scooter Girl is ripping off a piece of duct tape and taping my mouth closed.

This is another reason why you don't get involved with women. Eventually you end up bound and gagged in an abandoned warehouse.

Chalk it up to bad judgment.

Once I'm taped up, they grab me by the feet and drag me across the floor toward an open door. The sun has almost set and I can see the lights of the Bay Bridge and Treasure Island in the distance.

This isn't exactly how I saw things playing out for me long term. I always envisioned poaching enough luck until I could retire and then spend the rest of my life on a tropical island lounging in a hammock between two palm trees, drinking piña coladas and getting caught in the rain. Instead I'm beat up, tied up, and gagged while being dragged toward what I can only presume is a plunge into the cold waters of the San Francisco Bay. Plus my shirt is riding up and the concrete is skinning my lower back.

I'm thinking now is probably too late to start over with a clean slate.

Tuesday and Scooter Girl drag me out the door and to the end of the pier, which is dark and deserted. Water laps at the pillars below us. From the far end of the building I hear the street noise of the Embarcadero, people and traffic and streetcars. I don't know which pier this is, but from the view of the Bay Bridge, I'm guessing somewhere just south of Pier 23. Maybe Pier 19 or 17. It doesn't really matter. I'm about to become what my father always said I was. Deadweight.

They drag me over to the railing, which I can't fit through, so they're going to have to pitch me over. Either that or chop me up into pieces and shove me through the railing. I'm kind of hoping it's the first option. Not that I'm looking forward to drowning, but I figure I have a better chance of getting out of this if all of my appendages are still attached.

Tuesday leans over me as Scooter Girl walks around behind me. "Dee thought we should knock you out before we dumped you over the side," says Tuesday. "But I'd rather you experience the terror of drowning and knowing that your life is going to end. It won't be as bad as an acetylene torch, but at least you'll suffer. And that'll have to be enough."

I plead for mercy. I apologize for my sins. I offer to poach them top-grade soft at a discount. But when you're begging for your life through duct tape, no one really pays attention.

Scooter Girl grabs me under my arms while Tuesday grabs my ankles. I figure this is my only chance to make an escape, though with my hands and feet zip-tied, my options are pretty limited. But I've still got Donna Baker's good luck flowing through me, so I'm going to trust in that and see what happens.

Just as they lift me up, I swing up and back with my bound hands and smack Scooter Girl in the face and she lets go, dropping me onto the pier, my head smacking against the wooden planks and briefly knocking me out. When I regain consciousness, my arms are pinned to my sides with duct tape that's wrapped several times around my chest.

So much for my escape attempt.

Scooter Girl once again grabs me under the arms while Tuesday handles my lower extremities, and the two of them are lifting me up to toss me over the side and into the water when I hear footsteps running on the pier, followed by the sound of something hard hitting something soft. There's a feminine grunt behind me and suddenly Scooter Girl lets go of my arms and falls on top of me, pinning me to the ground like a WWE wrestler.

With her body draped across my face I can't see anything and all I hear is Tuesday shouting, "Dee!" and more footsteps. Whose, I don't know. It sounds like more than one set of feet. Maybe a struggle. Maybe a brief pursuit. Maybe a waltz. There's breathing and scuffling and the sound of something swishing through the air. Meanwhile, I'm trying to roll over to get Scooter Girl off me, but I can't get any leverage. However, I have managed to adjust my position so that my face is pressed right between her breasts. They're not as nice as Tuesday's and she's wearing a thick sweatshirt, but any port in a storm.

Before I can manage to shove Scooter Girl aside, I hear something that sounds like a body slamming up against the railing, followed by flesh hitting flesh, an explosion of air, a grunt of exertion, the sound of fabric tearing, then a brief silence that's broken by a loud *splash*. Moments later, Scooter Girl's breasts are rolled away from my face and I'm staring up into the wide-eyed, adrenaline-pumped face of Doug.

"Hey, Holmes," he says, his voice high and shaking, his hands trembling as he reaches down to help me out of the duct tape. "What do you say we bounce out of here?"

31

We're driving down Market Street to my office in Doug's lemon-yellow Prius. People keep trying to flag us down, thinking we're a cab, as Doug explains how he ended up at the warehouse on the pier.

"After I dropped you off, I was pretty upset," he says, his head nodding to the thumping bass line coming out of the speakers. "All the stuff you said really hurt my feelings, Holmes. But then I figured you didn't mean nothin' by it."

"I'm sorry, Bow Wow."

"It's all good. Anyway, I figured you were on a case so I decided I should stick around, make sure you had everything under control."

Which I didn't.

"When I saw you come out of the bar with that hot number, I figured you was just out tapping the talent. So I decided to cruise. Then I saw you get taken down by those two bitches and I followed you out to the piers."

"Thanks, Bow Wow. I owe you one."

"I told you I got your back. Bow Wow is on the case!" Apparently, the initial shock of battle has given way to a postcombat testosterone rush. "I almost left. You're lucky I didn't leave, Holmes."

Lucky. Yes. Definitely.

Color me leprechaun green.

I'm a regular human rabbit's foot.

"That one I laid out," he says. "She drove off in the cab right after they got there, then came back on her scooter. Cracked that bitch a good one!"

I think Doug's been listening to too much rap.

Before we left, I checked on Scooter Girl to make sure she was still breathing, then I found the keys to her scooter and tossed them into the bay. The metal flashlight Doug used to knock her out with was on the ground a few feet away, next to what turned out to be Tuesday's black sweater, which was torn down the side.

"I tried to grab her when she started to go over the railing," says Doug. "But all I got was her sweater and a handful of one of her breasts."

Some guys have all the luck.

Apparently Fake Tuesday was still conscious when she went into the water, but neither of us heard her moving around below us and we didn't exactly stick around to help her out.

I'm just happy to be alive, though my balls are still throbbing and my head is filled with cement that someone is trying to break up with a jackhammer. I feel like

I've been kicked and beaten and dragged around, which I pretty much have. I'd like to think I could have avoided all of this had I not allowed myself to get so distracted by the charms of two women that I failed to realize they were planning to kill me.

These are the kind of details you'd think I'd notice.

Grandpa always told me I needed to learn how to read people, to see through to their true intentions. A good poacher nurtures his intuition, he used to say. A bad poacher nurtures his desires. Eventually, they both end up nurturing the soil, but the bad poacher gets there first.

Had it not been for Donna Baker's good luck, Doug wouldn't have shown up in time and I'd be dead. You'd think that having her luck would have prevented me from being in that situation in the first place. But good luck doesn't affect your decision-making. It just helps to save your ass when you make bad choices.

When we reach my office, I thank Doug again for coming to my rescue. "And sorry about the whole dissing of your lifestyle. My bad."

"No worries, Holmes. We're cool."

I reach out with my left hand and put it on his shoulder, a small display of man affection that won't pose any risk of my poaching Doug's luck, since all I'm touching is his New York Jets throwback jersey. That's when Doug's facade crumbles a little and I see the emotion of what we've been through building up in his eyes. He's about to cry and I don't know what to do.

Before I realize what's happening or have a chance to react, Doug reaches out and grabs my right hand with his in a soul handshake and gives me a bro hug, pulling me close. I try to pull back and let go, to stop things before it's too late, but as soon as our palms touch, Doug's luck is suddenly flowing into me through our clasped hands.

I've never mingled luck before. It's not good practice as it tends to dilute the value of each score. Especially when you're dealing with different grades. Mixing top-grade soft with low-quality good luck would be like mixing a hundred-dollar bottle of merlot with a twenty-dollar bottle of chardonnay and expecting it to taste like sangria. Or like mixing LSD with crystal methamphetamine.

You never know how the two are going to interact.

But Doug's luck is higher quality than I thought—not top-grade like Donna Baker's but still pretty good. And because Doug is so emotional, his luck surges into me with the force of an ocean wave crashing to the shore.

I nearly gasp as I pull my hand away, hoping that somehow by letting go I can stop the flow of luck. But it's too late. The damage has been done and there's no way for me to give Doug's luck back to him.

"You okay, Holmes?" he asks, sitting there looking hurt and confused.

"Yeah. I'm just a little weird about touching people, you know?"

"You mean like OCD and shit?"

"Something like that."

I sit there with Doug's luck pulsing through me, mixing with Donna Baker's top-grade soft, filling me with adrenaline, cranking my perceptions up to eleven.

I smell beer and sweat.

I see the whiskers on Doug's chin and I hear his heart thumping.

I taste the garlic hummus falafel he had for lunch.

I feel strong and fragile. I feel elated and subdued. I feel hungry and satiated.

I feel more alert and attuned than I've ever felt before.

And for the first time in my life, I feel dirty. For the first time in my life, I wish I didn't have this ability.

I should have warned him. I should have told him the truth so he knew not to grab my hand. I should have worn gloves. I should have done something to prevent this from happening. Instead, I've stolen the luck from the only person I consider a friend.

Except who am I kidding? I don't have any friends. No one I hang out with or call up to grab lunch or to catch a movie. All I have are acquaintances. And distant ones, at that. I don't even have a relationship with my sister or my nieces.

I don't know if Doug is a friend or just a temporary acquaintance, but he deserves better than this. Especially after saving my life.

"I'm sorry, Bow Wow."

"Sorry for what, Holmes?"

"For getting you involved in this. For . . . for . . ." I almost say, *For poaching your luck,* but I'm too much of a coward to admit to that. "For making a mess of things."

"Ain't no mess, Holmes. It's cool. It's all good."

I only wish it were.

I'm trying to think how I can fix this. How I can put things back the way they were. But Doug's like Humpty Dumpty and I'm all the king's men. I don't know about the king's horses. How they would be able to work a jigsaw puzzle is beyond me.

"Look," I say. "You need to do me a favor."

"Anything, Holmes. Just name it."

I know he means it. It's not just hyperbole. I could ask him to hit me. I could ask him to loan me his car. I could ask him to sing "I Will Survive" by Gloria Gaynor while wearing a feather boa. He'd do it.

This realization doesn't make me feel any better.

"I need you to go home," I say. "I need you to get someplace safe, preferably away from any electrical wires or sharp objects."

"I don't understand, Holmes. I thought we were a team."

"We are."

"Then let me help, Holmes. Let me be your Watson."

Which is sweet, in a weird, male-bonding kind of way.

Doug isn't making this any easier for me.

Problem is, I can't let him stay in the city or be any-where around me, not if there's a chance he could get hurt. And since I don't think Doug would understand why I would want him to drink my urine, this is the only way to keep him out of danger.

"Just do it for me, okay?"

"Okay, Holmes," he says, obviously disappointed. "Whatever you say."

I feel like an ungrateful bastard, sending Doug away as a reward for saving my life, but I'll feel a lot better know-ing he's off the streets.

I get out of the car and then lean back in to apologize again. Maybe even tell him the truth so he knows why I'm doing this. What comes out of my mouth instead is "And no speeding, okay? Pay attention at intersections. And no talking on your cell phone while you're driving. And keep your eyes on the road."

"What are you, my mother?"

"I just want to make sure you get home safe."

"You want me to call you when I get home, too?"

"That would be nice."

He shakes his head in disgust and drapes one arm over the steering wheel, looking straight ahead.

"And, Bow Wow?"

He looks at me with the exasperation of a put-upon twenty-one-year-old who doesn't want to be bothered with my point of view. "What?"

"Thanks. I owe you. More than you can imagine."

Then I close the door and watch him drive off toward Chinatown before he hangs a right on Bush, his lemon-yellow Prius disappearing around the corner.

I stand there pulsing with the high-grade luck of two different people, hearing couples argue and homeless people mutter, feeling heat release from the asphalt and car exhaust permeate my skin, smelling cheap perfume and stale urine.

Sometimes poaching luck isn't all it's cracked up to be, not when you can smell and hear and feel things you'd rather not experience.

I'm wishing I had someone I could talk to about this. Someone who would listen to me and nod in all the right places and offer me comfort and let me know that they understand. But even if you get married, unless it's to another poacher, your partner is never going to really know you or comprehend you or be able to help you make sense out of what and who you are. So inevitably, you're left with just yourself and your isolation and the knowledge that everything you do and experience is yours and yours alone.

You are a rock. You are an island.

Orson Welles once said that we're born alone, we live alone, and we die alone. And that only through love and friendship do we create the illusion that we're not alone.

I don't have any love or friendship in my life. I can't share this with anyone. No one who will understand what

I'm experiencing. And I'm thinking of another quote, this one by Mark Twain:

Grief can take care of itself. But to get the full value of joy, you must have somebody to divide it with.

I want someone to divide this with—the grief and the joy, the pain and the pleasure, the valleys and the peaks. Even if it *is* just an illusion. I'd rather have the illusion than the reality. But I'm stuck on this island of solitude, surrounded by this ocean of emptiness that stretches to the horizon in all directions, and I don't even have a volleyball to talk to.

As I'm standing there feeling marooned and morose, a homeless woman walks up to me singing "Rock-a-Bye Baby," which she stops singing long enough to ask me if I can spare any change for some food. Even though I know she'll probably just use it for booze, I give her one of the few hundreds left in my wallet, hoping in some way it will help with her own illusions.

"Thanks, Jack," she says with a smile in need of a toothbrush, then she walks away singing, "Jack and Jill went up the hill to fetch a pail of water . . ."

I watch her go, the nursery rhyme trailing behind her, and I find myself thinking about Jack and his ill-fated trip up that hill. True, even though he fell down and broke his crown, Jill came tumbling after, so he didn't have to suffer alone. Another Jack, Jack Sprat, he couldn't eat any fat but at least he had his wife to share his meals with and even things out. And Humpty Dumpty, the clumsy oaf, he had all the king's horses and all the king's men, even if, in the end, their efforts were futile.

But no one's tumbling after me. No one's helping me lick my platter clean. No one's coming to put me back together.

Mary had a little lamb, the dish ran away with the spoon, the farmer took a wife.

And I, like the cheese, stand alone.

32

I'm standing outside the front door of 636 O'Farrell with an old, dirty backpack over my shoulder, holding a large mocha from Peet's in one hand and the business card Barry Manilow gave me in the other. I'm hoping this won't take long. And that I don't end up drugged or tied up or kicked in the nuts.

It's the little things in life that make me happy.

How I got here is in a cab, which is waiting for me across the street, the meter running with the promise of an additional hundred bucks if he's still waiting for me when I come out. The last thing I want is to be walking around the Tenderloin at night, trying to flag down a cab while carrying two ounces of low-grade hard.

How I ended up with the backpack and the mocha from Peet's is a little more involved.

Knowing I'd need something to carry the bad luck with and not having a spare backpack in my office or the time to go shopping at North Face, I offered a hundred bucks to a homeless guy on Sutter Street, who would only part with his beat-up backpack for two hundred bucks and a large mocha from Peet's. While I didn't have a problem parting with the extra C-note, I tried to talk him into a venti mocha from Starbucks, which was right up the street on Kearny, less than a block away. But that only sent him into a schizophrenic rant on grandes and ventis and talls.

Since he refused to give me the backpack if I went to Starbucks and since I didn't have any other options available, I went to the Peet's on Montgomery and Bush. While I was there, I got a second mocha for me, along with a phone number from a cute little redhead with blue eyes and dimples. Then I grabbed the other thousand bucks out of my filing cabinet and flagged down a cab.

I drain the rest of my large mocha, then I put the empty cup in my backpack, glance once more at the address on the business card, and rap three times on the door.

When I knock, the sound echoes the way it does when an apartment is vacant, when there's no furniture or personal belongings to absorb the noise, when it's obvious that no one lives there, and I'm wondering if maybe I have the wrong place. I look at the card again and step back to double-check the address. Just as I'm about to knock again, the door opens and I'm looking up into the face of a tall albino man with dreadlocks and pale blue eyes.

"You have business?" he says, his voice thick with some kind of Eastern European accent. Maybe Czech. Maybe Romanian. Maybe Russian. I can't tell the difference.

I never was good with geography.

I hand him my card, which I hope answers his question, because I don't know the secret password.

He takes the card from me and gives it a glance, then flips it over and nods once before he steps back and stands to one side. "Come."

Obviously he's a man of few words, and with his dreads and his accent and his vampire-like complexion, he's a little intimidating, so I do what he says and I step through the door, which he closes and locks behind me.

"Follow me," he says, leading me toward the back of the apartment across scuffed hardwood floors and through empty rooms with bare walls, the paint cracked and peeling, the corners dark with shadows and mildew. The only decorations are window blinds, which are all dusty and drawn.

I wonder if the Albino and Tommy Wong use the same interior decorator.

I've never seen an albino before. Not in person. And definitely not in San Francisco. So presuming this guy doesn't have a brother or an uncle or a celebrity impersonator, I'm guessing this is the alleged luck poacher Bow Wow said he saw down on Market Street. Though it still doesn't make any sense why he would be poaching luck in the Tenderloin.

We end up in the kitchen, which is just as warm and charming as the rest of the apartment. No spice racks. No fruit bowls. No knife sets. Which I'm oddly thankful for.

No microwave. No toaster oven. No espresso machine. The only appliance other than the gas stove is a refrigerator that's about half the size of your standard Frigidaire. I figure the only things stored inside are body parts or dead cats. Then the Albino opens the refrigerator door.

Instead of condiments and juice and nonfat yogurt, the shelves of the refrigerator are empty except for several red, stainless steel drinking bottles on the top shelf, while the refrigerator door and the bottom shelf contain dozens of clear glass vials of varying sizes filled with a liquid as thick and as black as used motor oil.

My mouth suddenly turns dry and my heart starts to pound so fast I could be a plump, juicy rabbit pinned to the ground beneath the open jaws of a predator.

I'm staring at a refrigerator filled with bad luck.

And I understand why the Albino has been trolling around the Tenderloin.

I've never met a bad-luck poacher before. I've only heard stories about them from Grandpa. They're like Bigfoot. Urban legends of the poaching community. You're never really sure if you believe in them until you actually see one for yourself.

Like now.

I'm a little awestruck and, to be honest, a little freaked-out. After all, this is Bigfoot we're talking about, standing right next to me, all pasty-skinned and dreadlocked and sounding like the Terminator. Plus I know what happened to me when I poached bad luck just the one time. How it felt. Cold and desolate. A pernicious infection. A malevolent sludge flowing through me that I had to get out of my system as fast as possible. Just five minutes was enough to give me the shakes and the sweats and make me vomit until I had the dry heaves. I can't imagine what it's like to feel that all the time.

I watch as he removes one of the stainless steel bottles from the top shelf of the refrigerator.

"You're a Specter," I say.

"I poach bad luck, yes. But am not apparition."

I think he's making a joke, but I can't be sure since he sounds so serious.

"I've never met a Specter."

"Would you like autograph?" he asks, closing the refrigerator and taking the bottle of bad luck over to the counter.

"Maybe just a photo," I say, playing along. At least I hope I'm playing along. The last thing I want to do is get on the wrong side of a guy who poaches bad luck for a living.

He gives me a hint of a smile, so I figure I'm okay for the time being.

I watch him set the bottle on the counter, then he grabs a drinking glass from the cabinet.

"Are all Specters like you?" I ask.

"Like me how? Charming?"

"Well, no. Not that you aren't. Charming, I mean. I was thinking more along the lines of your appearance."

"Tall?"

"Not exactly."

"Good-looking?"

"Albino," I say, spitting it out. "I was just wondering because . . ."

"Because I look like ghost?"

"Yeah. Now that you mention it."

"I don't know any other Specters, as you call me," he says, filling the drinking glass with tap water. "So I do not know what others look like. I only know me."

He places the glass of water on the counter next to the stainless steel bottle.

"How long have you been poaching?" I ask.

"As long as I can remember."

I always wondered if Specters begat other Specters or if they were anomalies, born with some kind of a genetic poaching defect.

"Was one of your parents a Specter?" I ask. "Or were they just luck poachers?"

"I do not talk about my parents."

And that's the end of that conversation.

I watch him remove an empty two-ounce glass vial from one of the kitchen cabinets, then unscrew the lid and set it on the counter next to the glass of water. From one of the kitchen drawers, he pulls out a glass syringe, opens the stainless steel container, inserts the syringe, and draws the bad luck into the chamber.

"Is that low-grade hard?" I ask.

"Yes."

I take a step back and look around for something to hide behind.

"What about the vials in the refrigerator?" I say. "Can't you just give me one of those?"

"Those are all ordinary bad luck. I keep low-grade hard in bottles like this."

"Why? Is it more stable? Is it cooler? Is it safer?"

"No," he says. "Just happier."

I can only nod. There are some things I'd rather not try to understand.

Once the syringe is filled with low-grade hard, he inserts it into the two-ounce vial and depresses the plunger.

"Aren't you afraid you might spill some?" I ask, taking another step back and wishing I had something to put between us for protection. Like bulletproof glass. Or the Atlantic Ocean.

"I never spill," he says.

"Never?"

"No. But usually I do not have nosy poacher pestering me while I am working."

"Right. Sorry."

I shut up and watch him empty the syringe, filling the two-ounce vial, then he takes his finger, wipes the tip of the syringe, and puts his finger into his mouth.

While I cringe and nearly gag, there's no reaction from the Albino. No sense of pleasure or disgust or indication that he experienced any sensory input whatsoever. Then he takes the syringe, puts it in the glass of water, draws the water in, expels it back into the glass, and drinks the water down in four long swallows.

"What does it taste like?" I ask.

He wipes a single finger across his lips. "Tastes like me."

I'm not sure if that's enigmatic or disgusting, so I decide to let it go.

He places the syringe in the empty water glass, then caps the vial and holds it out to me in his open hand.

"What?"

"This is what you come for," he says. "This is what is on card."

"I know. But don't you have it in something a little less breakable? Like stainless steel or plastic or titanium?"

"It eats through plastic. So must be stored in metal or glass."

"Okay. I'll take metal."

"I don't have metal," he says, continuing to hold the two-ounce vial out to me in the palm of his hand. "I only have glass."

"But you said it's happier in stainless steel. I don't want it to be angry. I want it to be happy."

"Is happy enough," he says. "You take."

"But the bad luck Barry Manilow gave me earlier today was in a stainless steel vial. In a metal container. Encased in foam."

"I do not have foam or metal and am not Barry Manilow," he says, his face suddenly brightening with a smile. "But I am big fan. Do you think you could get me autograph?"

"It's just a joke. He isn't really Barry Manilow. He just looks like him."

"Oh." His hopeful expression falls from his face.

"Sorry. Look, do you have a small box and some Styrofoam peanuts or something? Maybe a—"

"I saw him once in concert. New York City. Madison Square Garden. I love the song 'Copacabana.' 'Her name was Lola, she was a showgirl . . .' "

He starts to move his head back and forth to the rhythm of the song, the vial still resting in his open palm, rolling back and forth from pinkie to thumb. He may not be concerned about spillage or breakage, but I don't exactly want to get splattered with thermonuclear bad luck.

"How about some Orville Redenbacher's gourmet popcorn?" I ask. "Or even some Jiffy Pop? Or a Ziploc bag and some uncooked rice? Anything? Anything at all?"

"Sorry. All I have is bag of coffee in freezer from Starbucks."

"Ground or whole bean?"

"Ground."

"Perfect," I say. "I'll take it."

While the Albino removes the one-pound bag of Starbucks from the freezer and packs the vial of bad luck inside, I decide to do some poacher bonding by telling him how much we have in common.

"I poached bad luck once," I say.

"Is that so?"

I nod, even though he's not looking at me. Which I appreciate. I'd rather he keep his attention focused on packing the bad luck.

"Three years ago in Tucson. I accepted a contract job for some low-grade hard. Half a million dollars. I'd never seen that kind of money. And you couldn't get that for ten orders of top-grade soft back then, so I couldn't turn it down."

I've never told this to anyone. Not even Mandy. She would have told me I was an idiot. Which I was.

"It made me sick," I say. "I had cramps and chills and couldn't stop throwing up for three days. I was paranoid that people were watching me, and I'd wake up from a dream thinking there were bugs crawling across me. It lasted more than a week. When I finally started feeling better, I went to grab some of the cash I'd stashed in the fireproof safe I kept in my apartment so I could buy some groceries and some new underwear, but the money wasn't there. I don't know what happened to it. It was just gone.

"I spent all day going through my place, from room to room, tearing everything apart, looking in clothes and furniture and artwork, anywhere I might have stashed the money. I even tore into the walls and the floors, thinking that maybe in my state of sick, paranoid delirium I might have tried to hide the money there, but all I managed to accomplish was to get myself evicted from my apartment.

"That's why I moved here," I say. "Eventually I managed to get back on my feet, but I still haven't managed to shake the effects. Worst decision I ever made."

The Albino doesn't respond, just continues to pack the coffee grounds around the vial of low-grade hard. I figure I've offended him with my story, with my attempt to show him how we have so much in common.

I'm about to apologize when he says, "Could be worse."

He doesn't elaborate or share the details of his existence. But I don't need him to tell me that this is his life, moving from city to city and from town to town, living in unfurnished apartments with mildew and peeling paint and empty cupboards, trolling the streets for the hopeless and the forlorn, the alienated and the alone.

No laughter or intimacy or joy. No family or lovers or friends.

No Jill. No spoon. No king's men.

And I realize he's not that much different from me.

"How do you poach bad luck?" I ask.

"Easy. I just touch."

"I know. What I mean is, how do you do it without it making you feel bad? Without it making you sick?"

He turns and looks at me with a blank expression and shrugs. "I just do."

I suppose he doesn't understand how or why he's able to do what he does any more than I understand how I do what I do. It's just the way we are. And it makes me wonder if we exist to balance each other out. The good luck and the bad luck. The yin and the yang. The light and the dark. Except I'm beginning to question which one I am.

The Albino relieves people of their bad fortune, frees them of their burdens, and makes their bad luck his, while I create hardships and improve my good fortune at the expense of others. I'm not exactly helping people find a better way of living.

I'm no Jesus or Mother Teresa.

I'm more like the kid who always gets his way and grows up to be the adult who believes he's earned the right to do whatever he wants.

The Albino finishes packing the bad luck and hands me the bag of coffee grounds, the Starbucks House Blend. I would have preferred French Roast, but at least it's not decaf.

"Thanks for the packing job," I say, putting the bag of coffee into the backpack next to the empty Peet's cup.

"Is no trouble. You go now."

And that's it. My cue to leave. Exit, stage left. The voice in *The Amityville Horror* telling the new homeowners to get out.

I look around at the empty kitchen, with no food and no charm, with nothing to give the place any sense of warmth, and I can't help but feel like I should do something to add some humanity to the Albino's existence before I go.

"Hey, you want to grab a drink?" I say. Not like I have the time, and he doesn't exactly seem like fun company, but I feel sorry for him.

"No. No drink."

"How about dinner? My treat."

He shakes his head. "I do not do well in public places."

Which crosses bowling and the Kabuki Springs & Spa off the list. But there must be something I can do.

"At least let me pay you for the bag of coffee."

"Is no charge."

"What was it?" I say, reaching for my wallet. "Ten bucks?"

"Please, is not necessary."

"No, I insist. It's the least I can do."

He stares at me with his pale blue eyes and I wonder if he's thinking about killing me. It's not like he'd be the first one to have that thought cross his mind today.

"Okay. Yes. Ten dollars is fine. Then you go."

I reach into my wallet and realize I don't have any small bills. "You got change for a hundred?"

33

When I step outside the door, my cab is gone.

You'd think with Donna's and Doug's good luck I wouldn't have these kinds of problems, but when you factor in the two ounces of low-grade hard I'm carrying in my backpack, nothing's guaranteed.

I wait a few minutes for another cab, but the only ones that pass are taken, so I glance up O'Farrell and see the sign for the Nite Cap bar at the corner of Hyde. Not that I'm expecting to find a ride there, but the two pints of Guinness I had at O'Reilly's and the mocha from Peet's are kicking around in my bladder like a second-trimester fetus, so I head that direction to make use of the facilities before my good luck starts running down my leg.

I could just walk down an alley and pull out my Peet's cup and relieve myself that way. After all, I am in the Tenderloin; no one would pay me much attention. But with my luck, I'd get busted for public urination and end up in a holding cell.

Plus, at least at the Nite Cap, I can mix my urine with some Coke and ice rather than drinking it straight.

Outside the Nite Cap a couple of drunks are hanging on each other and sharing a smoke. They could be homeless or patrons of the bar. Or both. One of them, who's wearing a beat-up red-and-white-striped stovepipe hat that looks like it was stolen from the Cat in the Hat, looks at me in my suit and says, "Hey, it's James fucking Bond," while the other one snorts out laughter as I walk past them into the bar.

I hate the Tenderloin.

Inside, the place is done up in contemporary seedy, with dark lighting and brown paneling and duct tape holding the carpet together. Two televisions at either end of the bar play silent sports highlights, while a Lucky Strike clock above the bathrooms keeps track of everyone's wasted time.

Hipsters and barflies hang out at the tables in the back or on stools at the bar. Two fraternity types are playing a game of eight-ball on the pool table, which is cramped against one wall beneath a hanging stained-glass Budweiser lamp, while an attractive Asian woman in stilettos and a micro-miniskirt is feeding money into the digital jukebox currently blasting something by Slayer.

She bends over to make her selection, and her spaghetti-strap top rides up, revealing a tattoo of a dragon across her lower back. I don't have time to stare, or to get caught staring, but I do it anyway because I can't help myself. Plus I love miniskirts.

When I look up from her ass, she's glancing at me over her shoulder with a smile, then she walks away from the jukebox and into the women's bathroom.

I walk up to the bar, slide in between a barfly and a hipster, and order a Coke.

"Just a Coke, dude?" says the hipster. "Why not add some Jack?"

"I'm on the wagon."

When you're packing two ounces of low-grade hard, it's prudent to avoid saying anything clever or sarcastic that might lead to a confrontation. Bad luck has a way of making people around it overreact. Like taking a comment personally. Or punching me in the face.

"My condolences," says the barfly, raising his drink to me. "Here's hoping you fall back off."

The bartender gives me my Coke, which I pay for and then drink half of before making my way toward the currently occupied men's room. While I wait, trying to keep my mind off the pressure building in my bladder, Slayer gives way to "Don't Stop Believin'" by Journey, which everyone in the bar starts singing. Moments later, the bathroom door opens and a middle-aged drunk stumbles out, zipping up his pants and belting out a horrible impersonation of Steve Perry.

I close the door and lock it, then unzip and release a

mixture of high-quality good luck into my half-finished Coke. I take no pleasure urinating into a Coke. If it were a Pepsi, then we'd be talking.

The draining of Donna's and Doug's good luck leaves me momentarily weakened and vulnerable, so as soon as I've shaken out the last drop, I steel myself and chug down the mixture of Coke and urine, which, in spite of the sugar, coca, lime, vanilla, and other flavorings, tastes more like urine than it does Coca-Cola. Once I'm done, I rinse the glass and ice with water and drink that down to get the last remnants of good luck, then I set the glass down on the sink and look at my reflection in the bathroom mirror.

I'm not a bad-looking guy. Easy on the eyes, or so I've been told. And although I'm on the plus side of thirty, I still get carded more often than not or asked what school I go to. One of the benefits of being a luck poacher. We maintain our youthful glow.

But staring at myself, I don't notice my smooth skin or my full head of hair or the color of my eyes. All I see is a thirty-three-year-old luck poacher who has no friends, no family, and who just drank a glass full of Coke and urine.

There's nothing like consuming your own bodily fluids to remind you that it might be a good idea to make some lifestyle changes.

When I come out of the bathroom, "Don't Stop Believin'" has given way to "The Man Comes Around" by Johnny Cash.

I think that's my cue to leave.

On my way out of the bar, the attractive Asian who was at the jukebox bumps into me, spilling her drink on herself.

"Hey!" she says, her voice high-pitched and loud. "What the fuck?!"

"Sorry about that," I say, even though it wasn't my fault. "How about I buy you another drink?"

"How about you watch where the fuck you're going?!"

"Yeah," says the hipster, who has turned around on his stool to watch the show and egg her on. "Watch where you're going, Jack."

Since she walked into me, she should be the one to apologize. But beginning a discourse on common courtesy and basic etiquette in this place probably isn't a good idea. I need to defuse the situation before it escalates. The last thing I want is to be the center of attention. And right now, everyone in the bar is looking at me.

"Here," I say, pulling a hundred-dollar bill out of my wallet and handing it to her. "That should cover your dry cleaning and your drinks for the rest of the night, plus a little something extra."

She looks at the Franklin in her hand, then wads it up and throws it at me. "What do I look like? A fucking prostitute?"

I look her up and down in her spaghetti-strap top and her micro-miniskirt and her stiletto heels. She's not wearing a bra and she has more eye shadow than Elizabeth Taylor in *Cleopatra*.

"Now that you mention it . . ."

The rest of her drink is suddenly in my face and dripping onto my suit and shirt. I lick my lips and taste rum and mint, so I'm guessing she was drinking a mojito.

"Asshole," she says.

I wipe the drink out of my eyes as Biff and Skip, the two fraternity types playing pool, walk over and join the party.

"What's your problem, dude?" says Biff, getting up in my face, while Skip stands behind him, posturing in a show of solidarity.

I should have just peed in an alley.

"No problem," I say. "It's just a misunderstanding."

"Then how about you start explaining," says Biff.

I bend down and pick up the crumpled hundred-dollar bill and hand it to Biff. "Maybe this will help to clear things up."

Biff looks at the C-note, then glances over his shoulder at Skip, who nods.

"Works for me," says Biff, who turns around and high-fives Skip. I walk out of the Nite Cap with the hot Asian prostitute following me out onto the sidewalk, yelling at me, causing a scene. The two drunks are still out there, but one of them is puking by the garbage can while the other one impersonating the Cat in the Hat pees against the wall.

No sooner am I outside when a car pulls up, a red Mercedes-Benz S-Class, out of which emerge Thug One and Thug Two in their matching suits. While they came out of a red Mercedes rather than a red wooden box, and while they're not wearing blue wigs or flying kites, I'm suddenly having a Dr. Seuss moment.

I'm trying to think of something to do that would help me to get rid of Thug One and Thug Two.

That's when I realize a little too late that the hot Asian prostitute works for Tommy, who she probably called on her cell phone when she went into the bathroom. The whole scene with the drink and the yelling was just to keep me occupied until Tommy's thugs showed up.

"That's him," she yells, pointing at me. "That's the one!"

"It's not polite to point, you know," I say.

Thug Two smiles at me and nods. "Nice to see you again, Mr. Monday."

I'm not thinking it's nice, as the Asian prostitute spits. No, it's not nice at all. Not one little bit.

Then Thug One grabs me by the arm and escorts me toward the back passenger door as Thug Two walks over to the hot Asian prostitute and hands her what looks like a wad of cash.

"You still look like a cheap whore," I say.

She flips me the bird, then turns and walks back into the Nite Cap.

I get into the backseat with Thug One while Thug Two gets behind the wheel and we drive off down O'Farrell toward Union Square.

How many times does this make that I've been kidnapped today? Three times? Four? Jesus, I've lost count. And I'm wondering if I should call Guinness.

"Hands on top of your head," says Thug One.

"You didn't say Simon says," I reply, but I do it anyway.

He searches my pockets, removing my Ray-Bans, phone, keys, and wallet, along with another roll of Mentos I picked up after going to Peet's. I'm worried he'll find the card from Barry Manilow with the address for 636 O'Farrell, but then I remember the Albino took it from me and didn't give it back.

After he finishes searching me, he returns the Ray-Bans, keys, and wallet, but he keeps the phone and the roll of Mentos.

What is it with these guys and taking my Mentos?

At least I left my poaching phone in my office desk. Not a good idea to carry it with me all the time, especially when I'm getting drugged and frisked and knocked unconscious by the Mafia and the Feds and vengeful sisters from Tucson.

"What's in the backpack?" he asks.

"A bag of coffee and an empty coffee cup. I think my self-respect is in there, too, but I can't seem to find it."

"I need to check the bag."

"Be my guest." I hand him the backpack. "If you come across my self-respect, there's a hundred-dollar reward if it's returned in its original condition."

I try to play nonchalant as he opens up the backpack and pulls out the empty coffee cup, opens it, then sets it aside and removes the bag of coffee. Pretending I don't care isn't easy, but I put on my best bored-husband-listening-to-his-wife-talk-about-her-friends face as he opens the bag of coffee and takes a whiff, then looks up at me with suspicion.

"What?" I say, trying not to look guilty.

He shakes his head with a look of disappointment, and I figure he somehow knows I've smuggled bad luck in the coffee. I don't know how he knows. Maybe he's psychic. Maybe I'm that transparent. Maybe he's like a drug-sniffing dog, only he's trained to sniff out bad luck. And he doesn't shed on the carpet.

He closes up the bag. "House Blend? No wonder you can't find your self-respect."

I almost laugh out loud. Instead I just shrug as he checks the rest of the compartments and pockets, then he puts the bag of coffee and the empty cup back into the backpack and hands it to me without another word.

I'm thinking maybe my luck has finally turned. No more bad news. No more unpleasant surprises. No more unexpected turns of events.

Then we're stopping and I'm getting out and walking into the Sir Francis Drake.

34

On September 26, 1803, Joseph Samuel, an Englishman convicted of killing a policeman in Sydney, Australia, was sentenced to be executed by hanging. Samuel maintained his innocence in the murder but to no avail. The noose was fastened securely around his neck and the cart upon which he stood was driven away.

On the first attempt, the rope broke and Samuel dropped to his feet. On the second attempt, the noose slipped off his neck and his feet safely touched the ground. On the third attempt, the rope snapped once again.

The governor was summoned to the scene and, after inspecting the ropes, which showed no evidence of having been tampered with, decreed it was a sign from God that Samuel's crime did not merit execution and granted him a full reprieve.

Right now, I'm hoping I'll be as fortunate as Joseph Samuel.

I'm in a hotel suite on the twentieth floor of the Sir Francis Drake, looking out a window at Union Square and the lights of San Francisco glowing beneath the dark August night.

I've been waiting here for half an hour, ever since Tommy's thugs dumped me off and told me their boss would be with me soon. Whatever that means. Apparently in Mafia-speak, *soon* means "whenever we get around to it."

Another of Tommy's thugs is guarding the door out in the hallway, and from my initial inspection there's no other way out, not unless I want to throw a chair through a window and play Superman. I tried the phone, but it went directly to the Mafia operator, so I wasn't able to get an outside line. Or talk to anyone who could get me some room service.

The last thing I had to eat was an apple fritter, and that was more than five hours ago.

At least the accommodations are an improvement over a windowless room in a condemned hovel or an alley next to a homeless guy who smells like urine. And I'm conscious, which is always a plus.

I don't know how long Tommy has lived here, but I have to admit he's added a lot of personal touches to the place. Paintings of birds and blossoms. Prints of goldfish and Chinese calligraphy. Potted bamboo and sculptures of double dragons and vases with white cranes. All symbols of wealth and good fortune.

Apparently, Tommy's not taking any chances.

Speaking of taking chances, I still have no idea how I'm going to get the bad luck into a deliverable form and infect Tommy, but I'm used to solving problems the same way Indiana Jones deals with Nazis and religious artifacts.

I'm making it up as I go.

Though my options are pretty limited. I don't have a needle and a syringe and, unlike good luck, bad luck can't be mixed into any kind of food or beverage without causing it to smell or curdle or burn. Besides, I doubt I'm going to get close enough to Tommy to spike his drink or stick a needle in his arm. Which leaves me with only one alternative.

While poached luck can be consumed by either eating it, drinking it, or injecting it, it can also be absorbed through the skin. Kind of like a salve or an ointment. Typically it's not as fast-acting as ingestion or injection, and it takes more product to get the same results, but it's still effective.

At least that's the way good luck works. I have no idea what happens when you get bad luck on your skin.

It's a long shot, but it's the only shot I have.

The problem is, to get the two ounces of low-grade hard out of the glass vial and onto Tommy, I'll still have to get close to him. And he's not the type to let me get buddy-buddy. Plus he always seems to have a thug or some hot double agent hovering nearby.

Unless I can transfer the bad luck into something larger that I can throw at Tommy.

I think about filling a glass with tap water and dumping in the bad luck, then tossing it in Tommy's face when he shows up, but the only container I have is an empty cup from Peet's. If bad luck can eat through plastic, then I don't think a postconsumer-recycled-paper coffee cup is going to do the trick.

I think about using the coffee grounds to absorb the bad luck, act as insulation, but I don't know how much time that would buy. Plus there's the chance I could get some of the bad luck on me. Even though I've got two strains of top-grade soft in my system, that's not enough to keep me from getting infected. If I were Tooter Turtle, I'd be calling for help right about now.

Drizzle, drazzle, druzzle, drome . . .

I'm still waiting for Mr. Wizard to get me out of here when the door to the suite opens behind me.

"Sorry to keep you waiting."

I turn around to find Tommy standing in the open doorway, wearing black pants, a red smoking jacket, and a smug expression—the kind you see on the faces of villains in James Bond films who have manipulated the situation to their advantage and think they've got you right where they want you.

Which he pretty much does.

In the hallway behind Tommy lurks a second thug, some generic goon with short hair and an expression like he has a pickle up his ass.

"What am I doing here?" I say, hoping I sound more self-assured than I feel.

"This is my home," says Tommy, spreading his arms wide like a magnanimous host. "You like it?"

"You live in a suite in the Drake? I guess I expected something a little more extravagant."

"Not just this suite. I have the entire floor. Every room. My own personal staff. No one has access to this floor unless I say so."

"Oh," I say.

"Extravagant enough?"

I hate it when I get put in my place. My father did that to me all the time. Which is another reason for me to resent Tommy.

"So why am I here?" I ask again.

"Let's just say I felt the situation called for a more comfortable working environment."

"And what situation is that?"

"Come with me and I'll show you."

Again with the mystery. Can't anyone just give me a straight answer?

Tommy stands just inside the doorway waiting for me. Since it doesn't look like I'm getting a shot at revenge anytime soon, I collect my backpack and follow Tommy out of the suite and into the hallway, which is decorated with paintings and sculptures like the ones in the suite. It makes me wonder how someone who knows that luck is a tangible commodity can continue to believe in symbols and tokens of good luck in the hopes of attracting it. That would be like someone who doesn't believe in Santa Claus continuing to write him letters. Or someone who doesn't believe in God going into church to pray.

It doesn't make any sense.

Or maybe I'm missing something.

"I see from the bottles you left in the safe-deposit box that you managed to get halfway through the list I gave you," says Tommy from in front of me while his goon plays caboose. "Though I noticed the deposit didn't include the luck you poached from Donna Baker."

At least he bought that I actually poached from the other marks on the list. Alex must have told him about Donna, the douche bag. I hope he chokes on a tofu dog.

"I decided to hold on to that for a while," I say, leaving out that Donna Baker's luck is currently flowing through me. "In case of an emergency."

"I respect a man who hedges his bets," says Tommy. "Though if you're betting against me, you should know that the house always wins."

The three of us walk down the hallway past doors to other rooms and more paintings of images meant to attract good luck. Tommy has done his best to surround himself with as many symbols of good fortune as he can find. But it's not enough. Tommy wants more. As much as he can get his hands on and at whatever cost.

"I have another job for you," says Tommy.

"What kind of a job?"

"The kind that will wipe your debt clean."

"Funny. I didn't realize I owed you anything."

"You owe me whatever I say you owe me," he says. "And you should know by now that I don't find you all that amusing."

"I guess I'll have to come up with some new material."

Tommy leads me to a door at the end of the hallway, which has yet another goon standing guard outside. That this is a dead end isn't lost on me.

"One last poaching job for you," says Tommy, stepping past the goon and swiping a card in the magnetic key lock.

The way he says it makes me wonder if I'll be leaving here in the back of a Mercedes or in the back of a garbage truck.

Tommy and his goon and I walk into the room, which is another suite decorated with lucky symbols, most of them of the Asian variety. One of them in particular, a large ceramic lucky cat with its left paw raised, sits in the center of the room on a glass coffee table next to another bamboo plant. If I didn't know any better, I'd swear the cat was winking at me.

Tommy walks to the closed door at the back of the suite and produces a key, which he inserts into the lock. I don't know what I expect to find in the room when he opens that door.

Tuesday Knight. Barry Manilow. A couple of Playboy Playmates, a jar of baby oil, and a giant Twister mat.

I'm hoping for option number three.

But when Tommy opens the door, I see a small boy in a windowless bedroom sitting on the floor at the foot of the bed wearing headphones and watching one of the Harry Potter films on a flat-screen television. A couple of empty cans of root beer and a bag of potato chips sit on the floor next to him. When he turns to look at us, his eyes go wide and the moment hits me like a car accident.

It's Jimmy Saltzman Jr.

35

"What's he doing here?" I ask, after we've stepped back out of the room and closed the door.

"I think the answer to that is fairly obvious," says Tommy.

"I mean, how did he get here? How did you know about him?"

"Let's just say your so-called *douche bag* driver was very helpful in recounting your exploits."

It didn't even occur to me to think that Alex would rat me out to Tommy. And I'm suddenly thinking about my visit to Mandy and hoping she's not in one of the other rooms on this floor.

"It was nice of his mother and father to go out to dinner and leave him home without a babysitter," says Tommy. "Today's parents are so responsible."

I don't even want to know how these guys lured Jimmy out of his house. You'd think a neighbor would have noticed something, but people don't pay attention to things like that. Especially when the person doing the kidnapping has accumulated a surplus of good luck.

"Any other surprises?" I ask.

"I don't really think of this as a surprise. You were obviously thinking about poaching his luck before. Now you get your chance."

I hadn't made up my mind what I was going to do about Jimmy. But even if I did decide to poach his luck, I definitely didn't want it to happen like this. It just doesn't seem sporting.

"Does that mean I get the reward?" I ask.

Tommy laughs. A big, throaty, head-thrown-back laugh that makes me feel like the kid in high school who gets his gym clothes stolen by the campus bully.

Once Tommy stops laughing, which comes to an abrupt end as if severed with a knife, he looks at me without any humor and says, "Your reward, Mr. Monday, is that you're still alive."

Yeah, and I'm wondering how much longer I have to spend my bounty.

"I like this better," says Tommy. "This way, I get what I want and I don't have to pay the five hundred thousand dollars."

"What if I refuse?"

"Then I'll just get someone else to do it. You. Her. Him. It's all the same to me."

"So it's that easy?" I say. "You'll let me leave? I can just walk out of here?"

"Not exactly."

He sits down on one of the couches and, from somewhere inside his smoking jacket, pulls out a gun. He doesn't aim it at me but just holds it on his lap to make his point. His goon lurks about while the other one presumably stands guard outside the front door.

I don't really need Tommy to elaborate on his intentions to know that my choices are limited, but I'm hoping I can stall until I come up with another option.

"I don't have my transference equipment," I say. "It's at my apartment."

"We have the proper equipment here. I'll have it delivered to your room."

"I need a cappuccino and an apple fritter in order to process the luck."

"There's a Starbucks downstairs on the corner," says Tommy. "But you'll have to make do with a cinnamon roll."

I could make a case for the apple fritter, but that wouldn't buy me much time. Besides, I have a feeling Tommy isn't in much of a giving mood.

"Any more excuses?" asks Tommy. "Or are you ready to settle your debt?"

I try to come up with something to keep stalling. Anything at all. But my reserve of excuses is as empty as a bulimic's stomach.

"What's going to happen to Jimmy after I poach his luck?"

"That's none of your concern. Besides, what does it matter to you what happens to him? He's just another mark."

"Call me curious."

Tommy looks at me and smiles. "The same thing that's going to happen to him whether you poach his luck or someone else does."

Knowing that Tommy's thought this out makes me feel like I'm two steps behind. I'm still trying to figure out my next move and he already has an exit strategy.

"So what's it going to be, Mr. Monday?" he asks, picking up the gun for emphasis. "Poach his luck and get on with your life? Or play the conflicted hero and get on with your death?"

I never was good with ultimatums.

"Make it a grande cappuccino," I say. "And if you can find a bear claw or something with raisins or fruit, that would be great."

"Good decision." Tommy stands up and puts the gun away and hands the key to Jimmy's room to his goon. "I'll have your coffee and pastry sent up. As soon as you've finished with your snack, you'll have five minutes to get me my luck. Any questions?"

"Yeah, are you a vegan?"

Tommy just laughs and heads toward the front door.

I'm thinking maybe I can somehow avoid poaching Jimmy's luck while finding a way to infect Tommy with the bad luck. Or let the police know that Tommy is holding a kidnapped kid hostage. Or discover a way to travel back in time so I can start this day all over.

"And in case you get any ideas about trying something clever," says Tommy, standing in the doorway, "I have your sister locked up in another room on this floor."

Then the door closes and he's gone, leaving one goon with a pickle up his ass and one poacher still looking for his self-respect.

36

I sit and wait for my coffee and doughnut like a cop who's been on the wagon for three months and can't wait to fall off. Except my anxiety has nothing to do with my addiction to Starbucks and deep-fried pastries and everything to do with how this day has, to use the words of Barry Manilow, turned into a complete clusterfuck.

I suppose Tommy could be lying about Mandy, but considering Alex told Tommy about Jimmy Saltzman, I don't really have any reason to doubt that he gave up my sister, too. And if Tommy could get a ten-year-old kid up to the twentieth floor of the Sir Francis Drake without raising any questions, I don't have any doubts that my sister is somewhere on this floor with me. And probably pissed off. Most likely at me.

So to take my mind off of my sister and Jimmy and the general mess this day has become, I strike up a conversation with Tommy's goon.

"So what's your name?" I ask.

He just stares at me and stands with his hands folded in front of him like a constipated statue.

"How long you been working for Tommy?"

More of the same.

"Has anyone ever mentioned that you have excellent social skills?"

Nothing. Not even a yawn or a dirty look.

So much for making small talk.

A few minutes later, my cappuccino and bear claw arrive from Starbucks. The goon from outside brings them in and sets them down on the coffee table next to the ceramic lucky cat, then he nods at the other goon in a show of goon solidarity before he resumes his post outside the door.

I break out the bear claw and start eating it, washing down each bite with some cappuccino, taking my time, trying to think of a way out of this.

If I can get the bad luck out of my backpack and into the cappuccino, I can douse the goon and get out of here, saving my ass and hopefully Jimmy's and Mandy's, too. But the goon is watching me like an obsessed stalker, making it difficult for me to scratch my ass without making him suspicious.

Had I thought about it earlier, I would have gone into the restroom and removed the vial of bad luck and palmed it or put it in my pocket so I'd be prepared to use it. But since I'm channeling my inner Indiana Jones, planning

ahead didn't occur to me. Plus the idea of having a fragile vial of bad luck cupped in my hand or stashed in my
pocket isn't exactly appealing. It's creepy enough carrying
it around in a bag of Starbucks House Blend.

That gets me to thinking again about using the coffee
grounds. Which gives me an idea. I don't know if it's any
good, but at least it's a plan, and right now it's the only
thing I have going for me.

I just hope I can pull this off in less than five minutes.

I pretend to finish my cappuccino, leaving the cup a
little less than half-full, then I stand up and grab my backpack off the table, accidentally knocking over the ceramic
lucky cat and causing the raised left paw to break off.

Good thing I'm not superstitious, otherwise I'm guessing I'd be pretty much screwed right about now.

I look up at the goon with a smile and shrug. "Oops."

He just shakes his head. But at least it was some kind
of a reaction.

"Ready when you are, Gabby," I say.

Gabby opens the front door and tells the other goon
what we're doing, then he leads me to the room where
Jimmy's being held.

"I've got five minutes, right?" I say.

He nods once, then unlocks the door.

"I like a man of few words," I say, stepping inside.
"Makes it easier to win an argument."

Then the door closes and locks behind me, leaving me
standing there holding my backpack and my half-empty

Starbucks cup. Some might look at the situation and think of the cup as half-full, but I'm not exactly brimming with optimism.

Jimmy is no longer watching *Harry Potter* but is standing in the middle of the bedroom, watching me with suspicion as the movie plays silently on the flat-screen behind him.

"What are you doing here?" he asks.

The attitude and sense of bravado are gone. Now he just looks like a scared little kid. I guess getting kidnapped and locked inside a hotel bedroom will do that to you.

Aware that Gabby might be listening outside the door, I unplug the headphones from the flat-screen so the sound of the movie helps to drown out any conversation.

"I'm here to help you," I whisper.

"Why? I thought you were one of the bad guys."

"It depends on your definition of *bad*."

From the expression on his face, I can tell this doesn't provide Jimmy with any sense of relief.

"It's complicated," I say. "For the sake of argument and time, let's just pretend I'm one of the good guys. Okay?"

"But I saw you with him."

"You mean the old Asian guy?"

Jimmy nods.

"Trust me," I say. "It wasn't by choice."

Jimmy seems to mull this over. I wish he'd hurry up because we're down to four minutes.

"So you're really here to help me?"

"Theoretically," I say, as I set the half-empty Starbucks cup on the desk, then remove the bag of Starbucks House Blend and the empty Peet's cup from my backpack.

"What's that for?"

"It's all part of the plan. Do you have to go to the bathroom?"

"No," he says, looking embarrassed.

"Not even a little bit?"

He just shakes his head.

"Are you sure?"

"Yes," he says, his voice barely above a whisper. "I'm sure."

That's when I notice that the crotch and one leg of his pants are wet.

Well, that's just perfect. Without additional liquid, my idea isn't going to work. And the last thing I want to do is release all of my own good luck and end up defenseless.

"Okay," I say. "There's only one way we're going to get out of this, and even that's a long shot. So if this is going to work, then you're going to have to trust me. Do you trust me?"

Jimmy shakes his head.

"Wrong answer," I say. "Honest, but wrong."

I open the bag of coffee and pour some grounds into my unfinished cappuccino until the mixture is thick and goopy, then I fill the empty Peet's cup about half-full with coffee grounds. With my back to Jimmy I unzip my pants and empty my bladder into the cup, my eyes tearing up as

Donna's and Doug's top-grade soft leaves me. Although I do get a certain pleasure out of peeing on Starbucks coffee grounds inside a Peet's coffee cup.

After I've filled the cup about two-thirds of the way with my urine and Starbucks House Blend, I set the cup down on the desk, zip up, and remove the two-ounce vial of low-grade hard from the bag of coffee. Just touching the vial causes my skin to break out in gooseflesh and sends a tiny earthquake shuddering through my bones, so I try to tell myself that it's only used motor oil.

I also tell myself that this is going to work, that the coffee grounds will act like a sponge to soak up the bad luck and keep it from eating through the postconsumer-recycled-paper cup. At least right away. But right now, I'm about as confident as a Chicago Cubs fan in September.

"What's that?" asks Jimmy, pointing toward the vial.

"You don't want to know," I say, starting to unscrew the cap.

"Why?"

"Just make sure to stay clear and don't make any sudden movements or sounds."

"Why?"

"Because I'm nervous."

"Why?"

"Because it's dangerous."

"Why?"

"Because I said so."

"Why?"

My hands are shaking and my nerves are screaming. I'm not sure if it's because of the vial of bad luck or the incessant questions from Jimmy or that I'm doing this without any protection, but I realize I can't do this. I can't risk spilling any of this bad luck and getting it on me. If I do, neither of us is going to get out of here.

I screw the cap on tight and set the vial down next to the cup, walk over to Jimmy, and crouch down in front of him. "Put out your hands."

"Why?" he asks, putting his hands behind him.

I don't have time to make up a story that he'll believe enough to trust me, so I'm just going to have to go against type and tell him the truth.

"Because I need to borrow something from you that will help us to get out of here."

"What do you need to borrow?"

"Your luck."

"My luck? How can you borrow my luck?"

"I'm special," I say. "It's the way I was born. It's just a talent that comes naturally."

"Like magic tricks?"

"Yeah. Kind of like that."

He stares at me, his hands still hidden. "I know a magic trick."

"That's great," I say. "But we don't have time for games."

He stares at me and makes a poopie face.

"Look," I say. "I know we got off to a bad start, but if

we're going to get out of here, we're going to have to work together. You're going to have to trust me."

Nothing. Just the same poopie face. I'm beginning to think I might have to choke down the concoction of Starbucks and urine to give myself some measure of protection. Except with only one cup of bad luck, I don't think my plan has a chance of working.

"You promise when you're done with it, you'll give it back?" says Jimmy.

"Cross my heart and hope to die," I say, which is probably a mistake, considering that I'm about to break my promise and then pick up a vial of thermonuclear bad luck. But at this point, I'm willing to promise anything.

With a nod, Jimmy draws his hands out from behind his back and holds them out in front of him, palms up, vulnerable and innocent and trusting.

I take a deep breath and reach out to take his hands in mine, images of my grandfather and my mother and my sister swirling through my head. I see my mother dead and bleeding in the car. I see my sister, angry and pointing for me to leave. I see my grandfather, his eyes filled with a combination of longing and disgust.

And I can't do it.

"Good job," I say, standing up and walking away. "You passed the test. Now we can get out of here."

"Really?"

"Really. Just do as I say and stay behind me."

Though to be honest, I should stay behind him. If he

gets splattered with bad luck, he'll be fine. Me? That's a different story with a not-so-happy ending. But really, how much worse could things get?

I take another deep breath, then I pick up the vial and unscrew the cap. I want to save most of the bad luck for Tommy, plus I don't know for sure if this will work, so I pour a quarter of the vial's contents into the Peet's cup filled with the goopy concoction of coffee and urine. I manage to do it without spilling any on me or passing out, which is always a good sign, then I cap the vial and slip it into my left pants pocket and hope no one kicks me in the nuts.

"So can you really borrow someone's good luck?" asks Jimmy.

"No. That was just part of the test."

"That's too bad. It would be pretty cool if you could."

"Yeah," I say. "That it would."

I put the bag of coffee into my backpack and sling it over my shoulders, then I pick up the harmless, half-empty cup of cappuccino and coffee grounds and hand it to Jimmy.

"I'm going to have to leave you here for a few minutes," I say, "but I'll be back with the key. Your job is to hold on to this and not let it spill. Okay?"

"You promise you'll come back to get me?"

"I promise."

I grab the Peet's cup with the urine and the bad-luck-soaked coffee grounds and knock on the door. "All done."

The door opens and Gabby is standing right in front of me. I don't expect him to notice that I went in with a

Starbucks cup and came out with a Peet's cup without the sippy top, and he doesn't. So far so good.

"Take me to your leader," I say.

I can feel the cup growing warm in my hands. This isn't a cuddle-by-the-fireplace type of warm. This is more like a door-waiting-to-be-opened-to-feed-the-angry-fire-growing-behind-it kind of warm.

Gabby closes and locks the bedroom door, putting the key in his left pants pocket. With him this close and with my nerve starting to break, I almost throw the contents of the cup in his face. But I need both goons within range for my plan to work.

He points me to the front door and I obey. The cup is growing warmer in my hand. I can feel it starting to melt, to conform to the shape of my fingers and palm, and I'm thinking, if bad luck can eat its way through plastic, what will it do to my hand?

I open the front door and step out into the hallway past the other goon. As soon as Gabby steps out into the hallway, I sling my cup of bad-luck-urine-coffee-sludge into both of their faces.

Sludge and liquid splatters across their cheeks and foreheads, across their necks and shirts. A glob hits Gabby in the left eye, while another glob lands on the second goon's lips. For a moment neither of them reacts other than to wipe away the mess, and I think this was another major judgment in error. Then Gabby staggers back into the doorway and they both start to scream. That's when I notice that the splatters of goop are spreading out, growing something that looks like tendrils, and absorbing into their flesh.

I guess it works.

Before I have a chance to lose my nerve or worry about getting any of the bad luck on me, I step forward into the doorway and kick Gabby in the nuts. Not very sporting, but then I'm a luck poacher. When he falls down, I shove him over with my foot, then fish inside his pants pocket and retrieve the key to Jimmy's bedroom, leaving the two goons writhing on the floor and screaming.

Grandpa always told me that all luck, good and bad, was a living organism that maintained a symbiotic relationship with its original host. But taken out of that relationship and introduced to a new host, there was no telling how the luck was going to behave. Chances are good luck wouldn't have much of an adverse reaction, since good luck is more benign; a friendly stray just looking for a home. But bad luck, he told me, is more like a virus or a cancer, attacking its new host and spreading from cell to cell; a rabid animal with an insatiable hunger.

And when bad luck gets hungry, it wants to feed.

I never believed him until now. I'd be lying if I said I wasn't thinking about grabbing Jimmy's hands as soon as I had the chance so I wouldn't end up on the menu. But the look on Jimmy's face when I open the door, one of pure relief and trust, makes me realize that I'm going to have to get out of this situation on my charm and good looks.

Which have worked wonders for me, so far.

"Come on," I say.

Out in the hall, the two goons have fallen silent. I stop at the corner and look toward the front door, where they're both on the floor, unconscious. Or at least that's what I'm guessing. With the way this day has gone, I wouldn't be surprised if they'd turned into zombies.

"Remember to stay behind me," I say, turning back to Jimmy. "But stay close. Okay?"

Jimmy nods, then he takes one of his hands off the Starbucks cup and points at me. "What happened to your hand?"

I look down and realize I'm no longer holding the Peet's cup. I don't remember dropping it. At some point I must have. Or flung it aside. Or maybe it just disintegrated. But now my right hand, my poaching hand, is coated with melted postconsumer-recycled, wax-lined paper that looks like it's fused with my flesh.

"It's nothing to worry about," I say, even though I'm more than a little concerned. Freaked-out would probably cover my emotional state, but right now, there's not a whole lot I can do about it. Except learn how to poach left-handed.

I take the Starbucks cup from Jimmy and pat my pocket to make sure the vial is still there, safe and secure, though I can feel its warmth against my thigh and I wonder if having it this close to my testicles is a good idea.

"You ready?" I say.

Jimmy nods. Being with him like this, without the attitude and looking at me with complete trust, almost makes me understand why parents would go through the trouble of dealing with all of the bullshit of having kids.

Then I remember how he told me I smelled like cat pee, and the moment passes.

"Okay then," I say. "Let's go."

37

We make it past the unconscious goons and down the hallway to the elevator without running into any trouble. Which makes me uneasy. I don't know how many other people Tommy has working for him, but I figure the screams from the goons would have drawn some attention.

Or maybe anyone who works for Tommy is just used to the sounds of people screaming.

I press the button to call the elevator and stand with my back to the door, scanning the hallway in each direction, the Starbucks cup in my damaged right hand. I consider arming myself, but after seeing how fast a quarter of the vial ate through the other cup, I'm reluctant to dump the remaining bad luck into this one. The last thing I want is a handful of bad luck and wet Starbucks coffee grounds. Plus, I want to make sure I have Tommy in my sights before I do anything.

We stand there, waiting for the elevator. Or rather, I

stand there. Jimmy keeps moving back and forth on his feet.

"What are you doing?" I whisper.

"I have to pee."

I just stare at him. "You really need to work on your timing."

I listen for the sound of approaching footsteps and then glance back at the elevator, willing it to hurry.

"But I really have to go," says Jimmy.

"Then go."

"Here?"

"It's not like it'll be the first time."

The hallways remain silent, the elevator still hasn't arrived, my heart pounds inside my chest, and Jimmy takes a leak against the wall.

Well, at least one of us is relieved.

Finally the elevator arrives with a *ding*. The moment the doors open, we step inside the cab. Before I can push the button for the lobby, Tommy appears in the hallway.

"Going somewhere?"

He's not alone. He has Mandy with him, wearing a red satin dress and no shoes. Tommy must have a thing for red. But right now, he has one hand holding Mandy's hair, her head pulled back, and the other hand holding a glass syringe with the needle already partially inserted at the base of Mandy's neck. The syringe is filled with a black liquid. I'm guessing it's the same low-grade hard Tommy stole from me the first time we met.

I never was good with irony.

"Step out of the elevator," he says.

Jimmy lets out a little sniffle behind me, and I turn to see that he's crying and pressed into the corner of the elevator. If he hadn't already peed, he'd be standing in a puddle of urine.

"Now," says Tommy.

Instead, I press the button to hold the door open and stand there with my left hand on the button and the other holding a useless cup of Starbucks cappuccino and coffee grounds. Chalk up another one to poor decision-making.

I look at my sister, held hostage by Tommy, the needle of bad luck pressed into her neck.

"Hey, Mandy," I say.

"I can't believe you got me mixed up in this, Aaron."

"Aaron?" says Tommy. "I think I like Nick Monday better. More panache."

"At least we can agree on something," I say. "Now let her go."

"I don't think you're in any position to tell me what to do," he says, pushing the needle in a little farther for emphasis, causing some blood to trickle out. "All I have to do is depress this plunger and your sister's troubles will just be starting."

"And all I have to do is throw the contents of this cup on you and so will yours."

Tommy's gaze flicks down to the Starbucks cup in my right hand, then returns to my face. "You're bluffing."

"Am I? How do you think I took care of your two goons?"

Tommy stands there holding on to my sister's hair, his thumb remaining on the plunger.

"But if you throw it on me, it'll get on your sister, too," he says. "You wouldn't want to do that."

"I'll take my chances," I say. "What do I have to lose?"

I'm impressed. I even sound convincing to myself.

"Stop screwing around, Aaron," says Mandy. "This isn't a game."

"I'm not screwing around," I say.

My finger is growing tired holding down the button, and I can feel my shoulders tightening up. Behind me, Jimmy lets out a sniffle. I don't know what I'm doing or if this is going to work. All I know is that I can't let Tommy get his hands on Jimmy. If he does, Jimmy's as good as dead.

"It's your call, Tommy," I say.

Before Tommy can respond, an alarm goes off in the elevator, a sudden loud buzzing apparently set off by the doors being held open for too long. With both Tommy and I on edge, we react at the same time. Tommy depresses the plunger and I fling the contents of the Starbucks cup at Tommy and Mandy. As soon as the clumps of wet coffee grounds hit them, Tommy lets go of Mandy and starts yelling and wiping at himself, trying to get the coffee grounds off as Mandy pulls out the syringe then runs off down the hall in her bare feet.

"Mandy!" I yell as the elevator doors close, leaving

Jimmy and me standing there listening to an instrumental version of "Looks Like We Made It" by Barry Manilow. Then the elevator starts to move. But instead of going down, we're going up, and a few seconds later, the elevator doors open up to Harry Denton's Starlight Room.

"Come on," I say to Jimmy.

We step out of the elevator and into the club. My first thought is to get Jimmy someplace safe so I can try to find Mandy, but I don't know who to trust. And taking the elevator back down is a good way to run right back into Tommy. Plus I've decided it's probably not the best idea to take a ride in an elevator twenty-one flights above ground level while carrying a vial of bad luck.

The Starlight Room is pretty empty for a Tuesday night. Or a Wednesday night. Whatever today is, not a lot of people are at Harry Denton's. The remains of a buffet table are in the main room, with hot food pans and chafing dishes and a carving station. A few stragglers are still picking at what's left. It's a younger crowd and everyone's dressed up in jackets and ties and dresses, so I manage to blend right in. Except for the ten-year-old kid in front of me who smells like urine.

And don't think I can't appreciate the irony in *that*.

I head toward the bar, looking around for a familiar face, anyone who might be able to help, but the handful of drunks at the bar are all strangers. I can think of only one person I might be able to trust, and even that's a question mark since I barely know her.

"Is Tuesday Knight here?" I ask at the bar.

"No, sir," says the bartender, who's so good-looking he makes a Ken doll look like the Elephant Man. "Is there something I can help you with?"

"Not unless you can turn back time or tell me how to deal with an angry sister infected with bad luck."

"Sir?" he says.

"Glass of water."

I need to get this bad luck out of my pocket and into something I can use as a weapon against Tommy. Although I've been told more than once that I carry a concealed weapon in my pants, somehow I don't think that euphemism is going to help me in this situation.

"I need to use the bathroom," says Jimmy, speaking of concealed weapons.

"Again?"

"It's different this time."

I point toward the bathrooms past the far end of the bar and away he goes. For a second I wonder if I should go with him, but I can see the restroom doors from where I'm standing, so no one can get in or out without my noticing.

I glance toward the elevator and watch to see if the doors open, but so far no sign of Tommy. I don't know if that's a good thing or a bad thing, but I figure it's only a matter of time before he makes an appearance.

I turn back toward the bartender as he arrives with my water, grab the glass, and prepare to follow Jimmy into the bathroom to mix up my bad-luck cocktail. Then, out of the corner of my eye, I see an explosion of color duck out of sight into one of the booths. I walk over to see if it's who I think it is, and I find Doug slouched down in one of the booths, wearing a guilty smile.

"What are you doing here, Bow Wow?"

"Just enjoying the view, Holmes," he says, sitting up.

He must have followed me to the Drake and come upstairs to look for me.

"I thought I told you to go home."

"I won't get in the way. Word."

"The word is home. That's where you should be."

"Come on, Holmes," he says, whining and giving me his puppy-dog face. "I'm part of your posse. Let me help."

The truth is, as much as I want to send him on his way, I do need his help. I know this is probably a bad idea, but I seem to be so full of them today I can't help myself.

"Do you have your cell phone?"

"Right here, Holmes." He pulls it out, his expression serious and eager.

"Good. What I want you to do is call 911 to report a kidnapping."

"A kidnapping? Foshizzle?"

Whatever that means.

"Tell them that the kid's name is James Saltzman, Jr. and he lives at 1331 Greenwich," I say. "And that Tommy Wong, who lives on the twentieth floor of the Sir Francis Drake, is the one who kidnapped him."

"Oh, snap!"

This would be so much easier if I could understand what Doug was saying.

"Then wait for the police downstairs. You got it?"

"Got it," he says, sliding out of the booth and glancing down at his foot. "Sweet!"

"What?"

"My shoelace came untied." He bends down to retie it. "That means I'm about to receive some good news."

Or it means he should tie his shoelaces tighter.

"Great," I say. "Just don't forget what I told you."

"I won't forget," he says, standing up. "You can count on me."

"And whatever you do, don't mention my name."

"Sure thing, Holmes," he says, dialing 911. "Bow Wow is on the case!"

I watch him walk toward the elevator, talking to the emergency operator, using words like *gaffle* and *peeps*. I'm wondering if I should have just made the call myself when I notice the elevator doors closing and I realize I've missed seeing whoever came out. When I look back toward the bathrooms, I see the door to the men's room swinging shut.

Shit.

Behind me, Doug is telling the operator that Tommy Wong is kickin' it at the Drake as I run to the bathroom. When I bang open the bathroom door, I stumble inside and find no one at the sink, no one at the urinals, and no one in the stalls. Just sticky tile and an unflushed toilet.

Men really are disgusting pigs.

When I come out of the bathroom, I don't see any sign of Tommy or Jimmy in Harry Denton's, either in the bar or in the lounge area.

"Did you see a ten-year-old kid come through here?" I ask the bartender. "Or an old Asian guy in a red smoking jacket?"

"I didn't see any kid," says an old-timer sitting at the bar, more drunk than sober, "but some Asian Hugh Hefner just went that way." He points to a door beneath a stairway exit sign.

I run to the exit and push into the stairwell and am racing down the stairs as I hear the sound of a door shut below me. When I reach the entrance to the twentieth floor, it's locked. I need a key card to access the floor. I run down another flight to see if I can get in that way, but the door is locked, as is the stairwell door on the floor below that.

And I'm thinking I just got played.

I race back up the stairs, wishing I'd adhered to a more consistent exercise program, relieved to find that I don't need a key card to get back into Harry Denton's. But my relief is short-lived as an alarm sounds, followed by half a dozen people who come bursting through the stairwell door, followed by the smell of smoke and burning fabric. When I walk inside, I find the lounge area filled with smoke, the tablecloths covering the buffet tables on fire, and the nearby silk drapes in flames. The ceiling sprinklers have gone off, but the fire is spreading and a couple of people are trying to put out the fire with extinguishers. The more-drunk-than-sober guy who told me he saw Tommy go down the stairs decides to help by picking up a chair and throwing it through one of the windows.

I guess he wanted some fresh air.

The sprinklers soak my suit as the fire spreads from the drapes to the booths, the sound of approaching sirens coming through the broken window from the streets below. I'm about to see if the elevators are still working when I see Doug trying to stamp out some flames with his Nikes.

"Doug, what are you doing?"

"Fighting a fire, Holmes," he says, his untied shoelaces in imminent danger of catching on fire. "And it's Bow Wow."

"Right. Sorry. But aren't you supposed to be down in the lobby, waiting for the police?"

"I know," he says. "But this gizzled ho in a red dress came out of the elevator, and next thing I know, she's knocking over the buffet table and starting a fire and everything went off the hook."

Mandy.

I look around but don't see any sign of her.

"Where did she go?" I say.

"Last I saw, her dress was on fire and she was heading for the elevators."

Shit. I run to the elevators and press the button, but nothing's happening. Probably shut down due to the fire. I turn around looking for where Mandy could have gone and see the bathrooms and the EXIT sign for the stairs and another door that says NO EXIT—ALARM WILL SOUND. I'm about to head for that one when someone grabs hold of my hand.

I turn to find Jimmy staring up at me, his hair and face and clothes soaked. It takes me a moment to realize that he's holding on to my right hand. His luck should be pouring into me. But there's nothing. Not even a hint of the euphoria I would expect to feel. Apparently, the wax and paper that melted into my skin is acting as some kind of an insulator or barrier. Whatever it is, Jimmy's luck is still inside him.

"What happened to you?" I say.

"I thought I saw the old Asian guy, just as I was coming out of the bathroom, but he didn't see me, so I ran into the women's bathroom to hide."

"Did you see a woman in there? The one in the red dress we saw before?"

Jimmy shakes his head.

"Shit," I say, then turn around and look at Doug, his Nikes starting to melt and his shoelaces smoking. I wonder if *that's* good luck. "Doug, come on! We have to get out of here!"

"It's Bow Wow, Holmes." Then he realizes his feet are about to go up in flames and he gives up his valiant but futile attempts at being a firefighter.

I lead Jimmy and Doug through the exit door, planning to run down all twenty-one flights if we have to and hope we can get out of the building without running into Tommy. But that hope vanishes when we see Tommy coming up the stairs below us, followed by two of his goons. And they've got guns.

With Harry Denton's on fire and the elevators shut down, we don't have any other option. So we run back into Harry Denton's and through the other exit door and up another flight of stairs to the roof.

38

The door to the roof has another warning sign: NO ROOF ACCESS—ALARM WILL SOUND.

Not much of a deterrent when the floor below you is on fire and you're being chased by three Mafia types with guns. So I push the door open and step out onto the roof with Jimmy and Doug behind me, ignoring the alarm as we look for a way to barricade the door. But they don't design hotel roofs the way they used to.

"Wow," says Jimmy, looking around. Above us, a blue, neon star rotates slowly around, bathing the roof in pale light. "I've never been on the roof of a hotel before."

"Me either," says Doug. "This is the shizzle."

"Glad I could add to your life experiences," I say. "Now help me find the way down."

We find the fire escape on the Sutter Street side of the hotel, on the opposite end of the roof from the fire, so at least we won't have to worry about dodging flames coming out of shattered windows.

Along the way, Doug finds a penny, heads up, and pockets it. "It's good luck, Holmes."

At this point, I'm not going to argue with Doug. We can use all of the help we can get.

On the street below us, two fire engines have pulled up in front of the building and a crowd has started to gather on the sidewalks. The circus is starting.

"Okay," I say. "Doug, you first."

"It's Bow—"

"Yeah, yeah, whatever. Just go."

As Doug climbs down the ladder onto the first landing, Jimmy looks over the edge and says, "I'm not going down there."

"You don't have a choice," I say.

"But I'm scared."

"I know you are. But you'll be fine. I won't let you get hurt."

"Promise?"

"Promise," I say, though I wonder if I've just agreed to more than I can deliver.

Jimmy looks once more over the edge, then starts to climb down the ladder.

"I'll be right behind you," I say. "And it might help if you don't focus so much on the height."

Before I can follow Jimmy, the roof door bangs open and I hear Tommy shout out behind me, "Enough."

I turn around to see Tommy flanked by Thug One and

Thug Two, both of them pointing guns at me. And I can't think of a single triple meter rhyme.

"Back on the roof," says Tommy. "And Mr. Monday, step away from the boy."

I look down at Doug, who has made it to the next landing and is looking up at me, starting to climb. I shake my head once, then I turn back to Tommy.

"What makes you think I haven't already poached his luck?" I say.

"Let's call it a hunch," says Tommy. "Now step away."

Jimmy is halfway down the ladder, watching me. I don't step away, but instead nod to Jimmy and say, "Come on."

Thug One walks toward us, his gun trained on me. I know this can only have a happy ending if I pretend to do what it is that I know how to do so well. I just hope Jimmy's good luck is strong enough to keep him safe.

As Thug One closes the distance, I extend my right hand toward Jimmy. "Trust me."

"Stop," says Tommy.

I doubt he or his thugs will risk shooting me at this point, but that thought doesn't exactly leave me overflowing with confidence as I grasp Jimmy's right hand in mine. Then Thug One grabs me and pulls me away.

I've never had to fake a poaching before. I suppose it's like faking an orgasm, but I've never faked one of those, either. And as far as I know, neither has any woman I've ever slept with. But to make this work, I have to give a good performance, so I open my mouth in a single, gasping intake of breath and force tears out of my eyes, which isn't too much of a stretch considering I've just been clubbed on the back of the head with a gun.

I drop to my hands and knees, pretending to be overwhelmed with the power of Jimmy's Pure luck. I even offer up a couple of full body twitches and hope I'm not overdoing it.

Then Thug One points his gun into the base of my spine. "Get up."

I stand up, gasping, wiping the tears from my eyes, and offer up one last shudder for my performance.

I'd like to thank the Academy . . .

"That wasn't a smart move," says Tommy.

"Funny," I say, taking a deep breath, "that's the last thing my father ever said to me."

"Lucky for you they won't be the last words you hear," says Tommy.

I look over at Jimmy, standing by the fire-escape ladder, his eyes wide as he looks back and forth from me to Tommy and his thugs. Behind him, Doug's head peeks up over the edge of the roof, then disappears.

"What happens now?" I ask, trying to keep Tommy's attention on me and away from the fire escape.

"The inevitable," says Tommy, who motions to his thugs.

Jimmy looks at me, his expression filled with panic. "Don't let them take me."

"It'll be okay," I say, hoping I sound more confident than I am. Hoping Jimmy's good luck protects him and the police are on their way up and things play out according to my plan. Though who am I kidding? There isn't any plan. There's just chaos and chance and luck.

Thug Two walks over and opens the door, which seems to be his forte, while Thug One takes Jimmy by the arm and leads him toward the door.

"Don't let them take me," says Jimmy, looking back at me, his eyes wide and pleading. "Please!"

Then the door closes and the three of them are gone, leaving me on the roof with Tommy and a double serving of doubt and guilt.

"Where are they taking him?" I ask, moving away from the edge of the roof and, more important, away from the fire escape.

"That's none of your concern," says Tommy. "He's worthless to me now. You, on the other hand, have managed to increase your value. At least for the short term."

As I continue to circle around Tommy, he turns and follows me, still pointing his gun. I know he's not going to shoot me and risk losing the luck he thinks I poached, but it's still unnerving to be held at gunpoint by a sociopathic Mafia kingpin.

"How short is short?" I say.

"That depends," says Tommy, his back to the fire escape.

"On what?" I ask, as Doug's head appears above the roofline.

"On how much you're willing to sacrifice."

I shake my head, hoping Doug gets the message, but the only one who gets it is Tommy.

"You haven't even heard my terms," says Tommy.

"Why don't we discuss them in your suite. I've had enough of the roof."

"Good idea," says Tommy, walking toward the door, his eyes locked on me.

Behind Tommy, Doug climbs up the ladder and steps down onto the roof.

I follow Tommy to the door, hoping I can get him out of here before Doug does something stupid. But then I'm reminded that this is Doug we're talking about, who believes he's protected by a brass ring on a cord around his neck rather than by the luck I stole from him.

"After you," says Tommy. He reaches the door and puts his free hand out to open it.

Before I can get to the door, Doug's cell phone goes off, playing "Who Let the Dogs Out?" Tommy turns around, his reflexes faster than I would have imagined for an old guy, and shoots once. Before I have a chance to blink, Doug crumples to the roof.

"No," I say, the word coming out in a gasp.

Just after Tommy's gun goes off, the roof door slams open, smacking Tommy in the face, sending him stumbling back several steps before he falls down, his head hitting the roof, the gun falling from his hand and bouncing away, his eyes shut and his mouth open. Out cold.

Before I can grab the gun or head over to check on Doug, Mandy steps out onto the roof, naked and holding a carving knife in her hand.

"Mandy," I say, taking a step toward her. "Are you okay?"

"Do I look okay?" she says, limping toward me, the carving knife held out in front of her with both hands, her chest rising and falling in deep breaths. I back away, alternately glancing from Tommy to Doug to Mandy, trying to figure out what to do, though I keep my eyes above the horizon because it's a little weird seeing Mandy naked. Not that I'm attracted to her or anything. This isn't a *Flowers in the Attic* moment. But discovering that my sister is a full bald eagle is something I could have lived without.

And here we are, right back where we started.

"LET'S JUST RELAX," I say. "Why don't you put that thing away?"

From the glint in Mandy's eye and the way her upper lip is twitching, I can tell she's not completely reasonable, so I back up toward the edge of the roof, casting another glance at Doug, who remains motionless.

"This is all your fault," she says, pointing at me with the knife for emphasis. "All of it. Everything. Your fault!"

In addition to her being naked and limping and holding a knife, I notice that her hair is singed and smoldering and that she has burn marks on her shoulders and waist.

Above us, a helicopter comes into view. At first I think it's the police, until I see the CBS logo on the side.

I try to think of something I can say to calm Mandy down. To defuse the situation. But I'm afraid anything I say will be misconstrued. So I just give her a smile in the hopes that it will ease the tension.

"Do you think this is funny?" she says, stabbing at the air to punctuate the last three words.

"No," I say, backing up until I'm less than three feet from the edge of the roof. "It's not funny at all."

A crowd has gathered on the street twenty-two stories below, their faces indistinct in the glow of the streetlamps, but I can see all of the news vans, reporters, and cameras trained at the top of the hotel. The CBS helicopter circles around us again, the cameraman hanging out the open door with a video camera.

Mandy suddenly realizes she's on television and tries to cover up. But when all you have to hide behind is a carving knife, modesty tends to run up a white flag.

Right about now, Mandy's daughters are probably home watching the news and wondering what their mom is doing on the roof of the Sir Francis Drake with a butcher knife. Her husband is probably wondering why his wife isn't wearing any clothes.

I'm kind of wondering that myself.

"What happened?" I ask.

"What happened?" she says, letting out a single, bitter laugh. "I'll tell you what happened. First I fell halfway down a flight of stairs and twisted my ankle. Then I got into an elevator that took me up instead of down and the next thing I know, I'm stumbling into Harry Denton's and knocking over a buffet table and setting myself on fire. *That's* what happened."

Well, that explains the knife and why she's naked and singed. It doesn't explain the waxing, but there are some things I'd rather not know.

"I'm sorry I dragged you into this," I say. "I never intended for this to happen, but—"

"Fuck your intentions, Aaron. I'm infected with bad luck. I can feel it moving through me. It's like I'm being raped from the inside out. Do you have any idea how that feels?"

I do, but I don't think now is the time to get into a game of one-upmanship.

"I put this life behind me," she says, brandishing the knife again for emphasis, just in case I'd forgotten about it. "And then you showed up and ruined everything."

"Mandy, I understand you're angry—"

She lets out another short, bitter laugh.

"—but we're not the only ones involved here." I point behind her with both hands to the supine figures of Tommy and Doug.

Doug's phone goes off again, the Baha Men asking their timeless, repetitive question. Then it goes to voice mail.

When Mandy turns around, I run over and grab Tommy's gun. I don't know if it's the realization that two bodies are up here with us and one or both of them might be dead or that I'm now holding a gun, but Mandy drops her knife and starts to cry. I take off my suit coat and put it around her, buttoning it to keep her warm. Plus I'm getting a little skeeved out by the whole naked-sister, Brazilian-wax thing.

"Get away from me," she says, pushing my hands away and turning around.

"Mandy—"

"Whatever you have to say, I don't want to hear it."

"You don't understand. I was—"

"I don't want to hear your excuses, Aaron." She turns back around to face me, her cheeks wet with tears. "I just want you to leave me alone."

We stare at each other, me trying to think of something to say to make everything all right, and Mandy looking like it wouldn't matter what I said.

"Don't ever come near me or my family again," she says.

"But—"

"Ever." She turns and limps across the roof. Before I can come up with any other excuses, the door shuts behind her and she's gone.

I consider going after her, not because I think I can get her to change her mind but because I don't want to leave Mandy on her own, infected with bad luck. I'm afraid she won't make it out of the hotel alive. But then Tommy lets out a little moan and I realize I have to take care of him before I do anything else.

I walk over to him, the gun held out in front of me, just in case he wakes up. But the moan appears to have been a onetime thing. He's still unconscious, his eyes closed and his mouth hanging open. I walk around until I'm standing at his head, then I remove the vial of bad luck from my pocket.

I kneel down and set the gun next to me, then I uncap the vial and dump the contents into Tommy's open mouth. He gags once and coughs. Before he can spray any drops of the bad luck in my face, I grab the gun and stand up and move around him, holding the gun on him just in case.

Tommy coughs again. His body spasms and twitches. Then his eyes open and he sits up, grabbing at his throat, his hands going to his chest and then to his stomach. He looks up at me, his eyes wide.

"You . . ."

I nod. "Me."

He gets to his feet like the old man he is and stands there gasping and wheezing, his eyes locked on mine, his face seeming to grow older by the second. It's as if all the good luck he's been consuming was like some fountain of youth that kept the years away, and now they're all coming back at once.

"By the way," I say, "the police are on their way. You should have a lot of fun in prison. I hear kidnappers are real popular."

Tommy reaches up and touches his face, his hands shaking, and he lets out a strangled sob. Then his eyes grow wide again and for a moment I think he's going to rush me. Instead he turns around and stumbles past the door toward the back of the hotel. At first I'm thinking he's trying to pull some kind of trick, but then he just steps off the edge of the roof, like he didn't know it was there, and he's gone, without so much as a scream or a *good-bye*.

I run over to the edge of the roof and look down. In the wash of light from the hotel room windows about twenty stories down, I see Tommy's body sprawled out on an adjacent roof of the Drake. And he's not moving.

I've never killed anyone before. Not on purpose, anyway. But if the bad luck I poached three years ago was responsible for one death in Tucson, then Tommy is number two. Four, if you count the two goons downstairs.

I'm a busy guy.

Still, I'm not sure how I feel about Tommy's death. *Relieved* is probably a good place to start. And I guess you could say it's taking me a moment to adjust to the reality of what just happened. Remorse doesn't really factor into the situation, though I'm not planning to make a career out of this. Being a professional hit man isn't my thing. Let's just say I'm not shedding any tears.

At least this should get Barry Manilow off my back.

I give Tommy one last look to make sure he's still dead, then I go to check on Doug.

He's flat on his back, his eyes closed, his arms out to the side and his legs splayed out as if in some ritual sacrifice. The only thing missing is blood. I don't see any. Not on his chest, not on the roof, not anywhere. So I bend down and check his pulse and realize he's still alive.

I'm thinking maybe he didn't get shot at all. Maybe Tommy missed or Doug just fainted out of fear. Then I notice the half-inch-thick gold medallion emblazoned with *BW* hanging around his neck, and I see the hole right in the center of it.

"Doug," I say, shaking him gently. "Doug, wake up. Doug."

His eyes flutter open and he takes a deep breath, then he blinks his eyes a couple of times, smiles, and looks up at me and says, "It's Bow Wow, Holmes."

I help him sit up and he lets out another deep breath, followed by an "Ouch." He runs his hands over his torso, then he looks up at me.

"Was I shot?"

I nod. "I think your bling saved you."

He looks down and holds up the medallion and pokes his finger through the hole, then he looks down at his New York Jets jersey and does the same to the hole there before he lifts up his shirt. A big bruise is in the center of his chest. In the middle of the bruise is the bullet, partially embedded in his flesh, a small trickle of blood running down to his navel. On either side of the bullet, now in two pieces, hangs the brass ring Doug's father gave him.

Doug looks up at me. "I told you it was a good-luck charm, Holmes."

I have to admit, I don't have any explanation as to how this happened. After I poached Doug's luck, he shouldn't have been able to survive a car accident, let alone getting shot. Good-luck charm or not, he should have been dead. But like I said, there's no such thing as coincidence.

I think about Doug's superstitions and how he holds them so close. How he believes in them. How he attributes all of his good fortune to his good-luck charms and the actions he takes to avoid or counteract bad luck. Maybe there's more to good-luck charms than I've always believed. Maybe they do offer some kind of protection or draw in good luck. Maybe when someone who was born with good luck carries around a charm or a talisman, it gets imbued with that same quality of luck.

Kind of like a sponge.

Or maybe it's not the charm at all. Maybe it's the person carrying the charm. Maybe it's the quality of the individual rather than the quality of the luck.

After all, if a luck poacher can spend his life dealing in good luck and still end up addicted or broke or friendless, maybe someone who isn't born with good luck or someone who has had his luck poached can still have good things happen to him because of the quality of person he is and the positive actions he takes.

Maybe it's not just who you are or the way that you're born, but also the things you do that determine your luck.

Nothing like an unexplained occurrence of good luck to challenge your entire belief system.

Doug puts his fingers to the bullet and removes it, holds it up, and checks it out for a few moments, then he puts the bullet in his pocket before removing the two halves of the brass ring and slipping them in after it.

"Looks like Bow Wow's got a new lucky charm," he says.

Who am I to disagree?

"I'm glad you're okay, Bow Wow."

He smiles at me. "Thanks, Holmes."

I help him to his feet, and as we start to walk toward the door, Bow Wow looks around and says, "What happened to the dude who capped me?"

"He had to go."

"What about the kid?"

"I don't know," I say. "Let's see if we can find out."

We leave the roof and walk down the stairs and out of the Starlight Room, which is still on fire but apparently everyone's okay. I hope the same can be said for Jimmy and Mandy. And that I have the opportunity to fix things before it's too late.

As we continue down the stairs to the lobby, I can't help but feel like I'm the reluctant hero in a Hollywood movie, trying to remember my lines or what I'm supposed to do next. Problem is, there's no one to give me a cue. I have to improvise. Make up my own script.

I just hope it has a happy ending.

39

When we get downstairs, the lobby and reception area are swarming with emergency personnel and police. I walk up to one of the police officers and ask him about Jimmy Saltzman.

"Who are you?" he asks.

"We're the ones who called in the kidnapping," I say, gesturing to Doug and me.

Doug nods and says, "Word."

"Hold on," says the cop.

I look around and notice a dozen or more people being tended to by paramedics for injuries and smoke inhalation, including the drunk guy who threw the chair through the window. I don't see any sign of Thug One or Thug Two, but I catch sight of Mandy sitting in a chair in my coat and a pair of pajama bottoms that I'm guessing she got from the female hotel employee who is sitting with her, holding her hand.

In spite of Mandy's proclamation, I start to head over to her, but then her husband, Ted, shows up and they embrace. Mandy starts sobbing so I decide it would probably be a bad idea to see how she's doing. Instead, I watch her and Ted as they walk toward the hotel exit, holding each other. Then the uniformed police officer steps in front of me and all I can see is his face.

"Come with me," he says.

As Doug and I start to follow, the officer points to Doug and says, "Not you. Just him."

"But I'm the one who made the call," says Doug.

"Just wait here, Bow Wow," I say. "It'll be all right."

"Okay, Holmes."

I leave him pouting and follow the police officer out the front entrance, where a guy in a suit says, "I'll take it from here."

It's Elwood.

"You still have my Mentos?" I say.

He reaches inside his coat pocket, brings out the roll, and hands it to me. I peel back the wrapping and take one, then hand the roll back to him.

"Thanks," I say.

We walk across Powell, where a black sedan is parked in front of Sears Fine Food. Elwood opens up the back door and I climb inside and sit down across from Barry while Elwood closes the door and waits outside.

"Well, if it isn't my favorite luck poacher," says Barry.

"I can't say the feeling's mutual. What do you want?"

"Apparently Tommy Wong's luck ran out on him when he fell eighteen stories to his death, so I wanted to thank you for a job well done. Though I don't know what you were thinking getting a kid involved."

"Jimmy?" I say. "Do you know where he is?"

"Relax, he's fine. The police grabbed Tommy's men as they were trying to leave the hotel. The kid's on his way home safe and sound with his mom and dad."

"Did his parents ask what happened?"

"Couldn't tell you," says Barry. "But I'm guessing you'll come up in the conversation at some point."

I'm not exactly thrilled about being the topic of conversation in the Saltzman household, but at least I know Jimmy's okay. And he still has his good luck. And Doug's still alive. Which should count for something.

"So we're square, then," I say.

"Not quite," says Barry.

"What now?"

He pulls out another business card and writes something down on the back of it, then hands the card to me. It's an address, a place in Japantown, with a date and time, tomorrow at noon.

"Meet me there," he says, "so we can discuss the arrangements of your employment."

"My employment?"

"You'll be working for us now. Poaching luck. Just like you promised."

Note to self: Never make promises to federal agents when you're under the influence of top-grade soft. It's like postcoital honesty. You can't be held accountable for what you say.

"Any questions you have will be answered tomorrow," he says, and leans back in his seat, looking smug and satisfied. I want to punch him or steal his luck, but I meant what I said about trying to change my ways. Plus I'm more of a pacifist.

The door opens, I get out and Elwood gets in, like musical chairs only without the sound track, and I'm the one left standing.

Barry leans forward in his seat and says, "Don't be late."

The door closes and the sedan drives off. I watch it turn the corner on Post before I walk back to the Drake to find Doug, who's still standing by himself looking forlorn and lost.

"Come on," I say. "Let's get out of here."

"I think they want us to answer some questions."

"I've answered enough. Are you coming?"

He looks around like he's trying to ditch a bad date, then he nods and follows me out the entrance. No one yells at us. No one stops us. Either Doug's good-luck charm is working overtime or the SFPD is just incompetent.

We walk down Sutter toward my office, coming to Doug's car on the way. I don't know if it's the bright-yellow paint job or the thought that if I wanted to borrow his car all I'd have to do is ask, but for the first time in a while, I actually have a plan.

"Why don't you go home, Bow Wow."

"You need a ride, Holmes?"

I shake my head. "Thanks, but I'm going to take care of a few things at the office, first."

"Anything I can do?"

"Just paperwork," I say. "Boring stuff. No guns or roofs or fires."

He nods several times, like he's listening to a song with a really good beat. After a few more beats, he says, "Thanks, Holmes."

"For what?"

"For letting me help."

"Sure thing, Bow Wow. I'll see you tomorrow."

He gets into his car and drives off as I walk to my office, where I climb the stairs and open the door and sit down in the glow of the desk lamp and fire up my laptop.

The first thing I do is a search for deaths in Tucson, Arizona, three years ago, looking for anything spectacular or unusual that took place shortly after I poached that bad luck. Eventually I come across a story about a man by the name of Garland King, who died in a freak acetylene torch accident less than a week after I left town.

I'm remembering how Tuesday told me that drowning wouldn't be as bad as an acetylene torch.

The story doesn't mention anything about family or children, but I do a search for Garland King and find an obituary that mentions how Garland was survived by two daughters named Tracy and Deanne. Tracy and Dee.

I write down all of the information, then I grab a flathead screwdriver out of my desk, go over to my filing cabinet, slide it to one side, and crouch down. With the screwdriver, I loosen a piece of floor molding, behind which a chunk of wall has been removed. From inside the wall, I pull out a small metal box, which contains ten grand in hundreds. I pocket the money, then put everything back the way it was, lock up the office, and make my way back through Union Square and down to O'Farrell.

When I knock on the door at 636, the same empty silence echoes within. I wait for nearly a minute and am about to knock again when the door swings open and the Albino is standing there in the doorway.

"You forget something?" he says. "Or you still looking for date?"

"Neither. I'm here on business."

He looks at me a moment, then stands aside. "Come."

He closes the door behind me and we walk back to the kitchen, where he opens up the refrigerator and says, "What grade you like?"

"I wasn't actually looking to buy product. I was more interested in your services."

He closes the door and turns to look at me with his pale blue eyes. There's not a hint of emotion on his face. His expression is as blank as a corpse.

"You want me poach from someone?"

I nod and pull out the ten thousand dollars and set it down on the kitchen counter. He gives the money a single glance, then returns his gaze to me.

"Who?"

I pull out my wallet and dig through it until I find the photo of Mandy and me, which I hand to him. "From her. Her name is Amanda Hennings. She goes by Mandy."

He studies the photo with that same, unnerving intensity, then looks up at me. "Who is Amanda Hennings?"

"She's my sister."

I then proceed to tell him how she got infected, how it was my fault, and how I'm trying to do what I can to make things right. I leave out the part about how she told me she never wanted to see me again.

He looks back down at the photo and continues to stare at it for nearly a minute as I stand there in the silence of his cold, empty kitchen, waiting for him to respond.

He hands the photo back to me. "Is no charge. Will do for free."

"What? Why? I mean, not that I'm complaining but . . ."

"Because is your sister."

A luck poacher doing a job for free? He's going to give the rest of us a bad name.

"Thanks," I say. "But let me help with something. Office supplies, travel expenses, meals and entertainment . . ."

"No money. Just address, please."

So I give him Mandy's address and thank him again for his generosity, then I pick up the ten grand and am about to put it away when another thought occurs to me. I reach into my wallet and pull out the business card Barry Manilow gave me with the address and tomorrow's meeting time and I hand it to the Albino. Then I show him the cash again.

"Any chance you'd be willing to make a delivery?"

40

The next morning I wake up early and give Doug a call and ask him to meet me at my office at ten o'clock. Then I pack up a suitcase of personal items, a duffel bag full of clothes, several fake IDs with old aliases, an ice chest with some food, and any money I have hidden. It doesn't come to much. Just a little more than twenty-five grand. But it's enough to settle things up.

On my way out, I see the old homeless guy again with the cat wearing a clean sweatshirt and a new pair of Reeboks. The homeless guy, not the cat. The cat's sleeping and content while the homeless guy digs into a to-go container of Thai food.

"You were right," he says, through a mouthful of pad thai. "Tequila made that lemonade go down real smooth. And then I found this sweatshirt and shoes in a bag by the bus stop."

"Try some rum with this one," I say, handing him my last bottle of lemonade, which he takes without any complaints this time. "It'll taste like a mojito."

"A mojito? Nice!"

I reach the Drake just after nine o'clock and find Gigantor stationed out in front, watching me approach like he's expecting me.

"Miss Knight doesn't like to be kept waiting," he says, opening the front door.

"Did we have an appointment?"

"No, but she wants to see you."

At least it's good to know my instincts haven't completely abandoned me.

We ride up in the elevator to the twenty-first floor in silence for most of the way, until I finally turn to him after the sixteenth floor and say, "Come on. Say, 'It is your destiny,' just once."

He takes a deep breath and stares straight ahead.

"I know you went home and practiced it in front of the bathroom mirror," I say. "Admit it."

Nothing. Not even a twitch or the hint of a smile.

"Party pooper," I say, as the elevator doors open and I step out into the blackened and smoke-stained interior of Harry Denton's.

Firemen and guys in suits whom I presume to be either insurance agents or hotel brass are walking around, pointing and gesturing and shaking their heads or nodding. I find Tuesday Knight in the bar, which managed to escape relatively free from fire damage.

Tuesday has traded in the skintight, leopard-print skirt and matching high heels for a more conservative pair of Lucky Brand jeans and Doc Martens. Unfortunately, she's also wearing a long-sleeve T-shirt and a bra.

"Mr. Monday," she says, putting out a hand to shake mine.

Any other time, this would be an awkward moment with me trying to come up with an excuse for not shaking her hand or just poaching her luck for shits and giggles. But I'm wearing gloves, which allows me to reciprocate without any concerns. Plus they help to cut down on any questions about why my right hand is covered with a film of wax and postconsumer-recycled paper.

"What happened here?" I say, playing innocent, hoping some of it sticks.

"Apparently some woman stumbled into the remains of a buffet line late last night and ended up setting the place on fire." She leads me away from the others to a more private spot at the other end of the bar.

"Anyone get hurt?"

"Nothing serious," she says. "Except for an old Asian man who panicked and apparently jumped out of one of the windows."

It's nice to see the spin doctors already handing out prescriptions.

"So I heard you were expecting me," I say.

"I was. According to some witnesses, the woman who set the club on fire was a brunette in a red dress, and I thought it might have been our mutual friend."

"Doubtful. I'm pretty sure she checked out last night."

"Of her hotel?"

"Sure," I say. Honesty might be the best policy, but manipulating the truth requires a lot more skill.

"Did you find out anything about her?"

I hand Tuesday the information I wrote down. "Her name is Tracy King. She's from Tucson, Arizona."

Tuesday reads over my notes, then looks up. "Why was she impersonating me?"

"I don't know," I lie. "Her own father died, so maybe she was trying to pretend to have your father for a while. Or maybe she just wanted to get some free hotel rooms and club passes."

Again, the whole honesty-is-the-best-policy thing? Sometimes it's really more of a theory.

Tuesday looks over my notes again, then folds them up and puts them in her purse. "Thank you for the information, Mr. Monday. Quite frankly, I'm surprised you found it so quickly."

"It's nice to know I exceeded your expectations."

"Well, I appreciate your efforts." She reaches back into her purse. "And I make good on my promises." She removes her billfold and flips it open to her checkbook and starts to write out a check to me for twenty thousand dollars.

"If you wouldn't mind, could I get that in cash?"

41

On my way out of the Drake, I stop off in Starbucks and order a grande cappuccino from a twentysomething barista with fuchsia-colored hair and the glasses of a high school librarian. I don't ask for her phone number and she doesn't offer up anything other than a polite smile and a "Have a nice day."

I'm not sure if that's a good or bad thing, but it's definitely different.

Half an hour later, I'm sitting in my office and draining the last of my coffee when Doug shows up.

"Yo, Holmes," he says, walking in the door. "How's it hangin'?"

"Big and low," I say, enjoying the smile on his face, fighting to keep the smile on mine, knowing it's the last time I'll ever say that to him.

This growing attached to people really sucks.

Doug sits down in the chair with his hands in his pockets and immediately slides down into a slump that's a perfected art form. "So what's on tap for today?"

I consider telling Doug the truth, but that would just disappoint him, so instead I opt for telling him an edited version. "I'm leaving town for a while, Bow Wow."

"Like a vacation?"

"Yeah. Something like that."

"Swizzle," he says. "You must have had itchy feet. So where you gonna be chillin'?"

"I'm playing it by ear. Making it up as I go."

"That's cool," he says, nodding in approval. "When you comin' back?"

"It's open-ended. That's what I wanted to talk to you about."

Doug remains slouched but takes his hands out of his pockets and clasps them behind his head. "Lay it on me, Holmes."

"How would you like to run the business while I'm gone?"

"No shit?" He sits up and drops his hands. "Forizzle?"

"Forizzle," I say, though I'm still not really sure what that means. But Bow Wow does and apparently I've spoken well.

His face breaks open into the Grand Canyon of smiles and his eyes tear up. For a minute I think he's going to run around the desk and give me a hug, but then he blinks back the tears and sucks it up. "I'd be honored, Holmes."

At first I wasn't sure it was such a good idea to make the offer to Doug, considering that I'd poached his good luck. But after watching him survive getting shot in the chest, I have a feeling he's going to be just fine.

Sure, it goes against everything I've always believed in, but I'm beginning to think that maybe there's more to good luck than just being born with it.

While waiting for Doug to show up, I arranged to have the rent on the office covered for the next two months, and I did the same with the phone Thug One took from me. I don't know where the phone is and I don't really care. After two months the service will be deactivated and Nick Monday will cease to exist. But for the next eight weeks, any phone calls for Nick Monday, private investigator, will continue to be received.

"I've set it up to have all of my calls forwarded to you," I say. "Just let them know you're handling things while I'm gone and give them your phone number so they can call you directly."

"But what if I don't know what to do, Holmes?"

"I'll check in every now and then to see how things are going. But don't worry about it, Bow Wow. You'll do great."

Although the first part is a lie, I have no doubts that Doug can probably run his investigations better than I did. Though he might want to cut down on the gangsta vernacular.

I show him the files in the cabinet and on the laptop,

which has all of the information about any legitimate jobs I've taken over the past couple of years. I took any personal files out of the cabinet and dumped all of my non-business-related information off the laptop and onto a flash drive this morning before Doug showed up.

"I think that's about it," I say. "Any questions?"

"When are you leaving, Holmes?"

"Today. In an hour. Which is something else I need to talk to you about."

"You need a ride to the airport?"

"Not exactly."

Fifteen minutes later, Doug has forty thousand in cash and the keys to my office and I have the keys to one screaming-lemon-colored Prius.

With the forty grand I figure Doug can get another car and either pay the rent for another six months or open up his own business in a new location. I know he'll be upset once he realizes I'm not coming back, but I hope he'll forgive me.

I drive to my apartment, pack up my duffel bag and suitcase and ice chest, and head out of San Francisco a little more than an hour before my scheduled meeting with Barry Manilow. With any luck, the Albino has already made his delivery and Barry won't be bothering me anytime soon.

I plug in my smartphone, the one I use for poaching, and check the navigation, which tells me I should reach my destination in just over four hours. I'm not expecting to get any business calls, and wouldn't answer them if I did, but I need a phone and it's billed to an alias that no one can trace back to me.

I drive north on 101 across the Golden Gate Bridge, then I cut across Highway 37 to Interstate 80 and head east until I reach a Motel 6 on the outskirts of Reno just past three in the afternoon, where I book a room and then grab some fast food before I head to the casinos to improve my financial situation.

I come back a few hours later with an additional eight thousand dollars.

I spend the next day bouncing from casino to casino, winning a few hundred on the slots and a thousand at blackjack before moving on to another game or another casino. I haven't had this kind of luck since Tucson, and I wonder if I somehow managed to poach some of Jimmy's good luck. Maybe the wax and paper coating on my right hand didn't prevent the transfer of luck. Maybe it just acted as a filter, allowing something to trickle through.

Or maybe it's just that for the first time in three years, I'm free of the bad luck I've been carrying around.

Except I don't believe that's the only reason. But the only other explanation for my change of good fortune goes against everything I've ever known about good luck, everything I've ever learned. It challenges me to believe that good luck can be manufactured by actions and conduct in addition to existing in someone's genetic code. It challenges me to believe that there's an additional answer for how good luck works. And right now, the only challenge I'm interested in is making as much money as possible in a short time.

With more than a dozen casinos and saloons in downtown Reno, plus another two dozen casinos in the outskirts and in Sparks, I can walk away with more than thirty grand a day without arousing anyone's suspicion. But it's just a short-term solution. A quick payday to help build up some cash flow. I can't stick around for much longer than a few days. Places like Reno and Vegas are ripe for luck poachers, so it's only a matter of time before someone decides to come looking for me here.

But that's not the only problem with sticking around. I can't keep winning and expect to get away with it. Success makes people suspicious, especially when your success means walking away with something that belongs to them. You can spread your winnings out among the casinos, but you can only leave with the house's money so often before someone takes notice.

Plus, with an ability like mine, it's hard to forget what you're capable of doing. It's like breathing or sleeping or getting an erection. It just happens. It's a natural part of who I am. I don't know how Mandy manages to avoid the temptation. Though it would probably be easier if I weren't in a town that attracts luck the way a singles bar attracts desperation.

Every day I see people hitting progressive jackpots and having winning streaks at the craps table or roulette, dozens of marks with medium-grade good luck and top-grade soft, and I struggle with my desire to poach their luck. It's like being in Disneyland and not being able to go on any of the rides.

So three days after stopping in Reno and with just over a hundred grand in my pockets, I pack up everything and head east on Interstate 80 toward Utah. I'm not sure where I'm going. Maybe Colorado Springs or Santa Fe or Austin. Or maybe New Orleans. I've always wanted to live there. Chances are it's already claimed by another poacher, but I'm thinking I can start up my private investigator services again, try to go straight.

I know it's a long shot, but after everything I helped to ruin in San Francisco, I'd like to think I could manage to create something good somewhere else. Balance out the cosmos. The karma. Whatever. I owe it to Mandy and Jimmy and Doug to give it a try. Hell, I owe it to myself.

All poachers are adept at changing who we are. At adapting and letting go. Every new identity is just a suit you wear, a persona to exist in for a couple of years, maybe five if you're lucky, until it's time to move on to the next one.

Abandon your life. Become someone else. Repeat.

I'm hoping this time I can put on a new suit that fits the new me. Stop living from city to city and identity to identity and find something that matters. Find *someone* who matters. Build a life that actually has some meaning beyond what's-in-it-for-me? Shed the skin of my former self and discover that there's more to life than just being a luck poacher.

My father would probably laugh in my face. Go all Popeye on me and tell me that I am what I am and that's all that I am. That I'll never be anything more than a waste of carbon. A disappointment. Maybe not so common, but still a thief.

If nothing else, I want to prove my father wrong. Show that I can change. That I can live up to my potential without the benefit of my genetic disposition. But when you're a luck poacher, your old life has a way of finding you and tempting you and reminding you that starting over isn't as simple as it sounds.

The truth is, you can't give up who you are that easily.

The tires hum on the asphalt, the past falls away in the rearview mirror, I speed down the highway toward a new future, and my phone starts to ring.

ACKNOWLEDGMENTS

Over the past several years I've been fortunate to cross paths with numerous people to whom I owe a tremendous amount of gratitude.

Writers and editors. Reviewers and booksellers. Community relations managers and event coordinators and owners at dozens of bookstores. And last, but certainly not least, all of my readers. You're the reason I'm able to keep doing this.

While it would be impossible to list everyone here who has influenced and inspired and supported me, just know that my life is richer for having you in it. I hope you know who you are.

Now, on to the usual suspects . . .

Michelle Brower, who likes what I write and helps me to navigate the waters and who gave this book the second half of its title. I'm lucky to have you in my world.

Kara Cesare and Ed Schlesinger, who believed in me

and who helped to fine-tune the manuscript and brought out the best in it. Drinks are on me.

Everyone at Gallery Books and Simon & Schuster who provided their creativity and their talents and who let me share my thoughts. Thank you for listening.

Cliff Brooks, Ian Dudley, Heather Liston, Shannon Page, and Keith White, who beat me up over the first drafts and never pulled any punches. I still have the bruises.

And finally to my friends and my family, who have always been my biggest fans and have been there for me whenever I needed you. Thanks for the love.